Embracing Her

HEART

The Bradens &

(Pleasant Hil...

Love in Bloom Series

Melissa Foster

ISBN-10: 1941480373
ISBN-13: 978-1941480373

EMBRACING HER HEART

Cover Design: Elizabeth Mackey Designs

WORLD LITERARY PRESS
PRINTED IN THE UNITED STATES OF AMERICA

A Note to Readers

I am thrilled to bring you the Montgomerys, another fun, close-knit family and group of friends to fall in love with. If this is your first Melissa Foster book, all of my books are written to stand alone, so dive right in and enjoy the fun, sexy ride!

The best way to keep up to date with new releases, sales, and exclusive content is to **sign up for my newsletter** or **download my free app**.

www.MelissaFoster.com/News

www.MelissaFoster.com/app

Two Love in Bloom Worlds Become One!

Meet the Bradens & Montgomerys (Pleasant Hill – Oak Falls)

I am excited to share some fantastic news with you! The Bradens at Pleasant Hill and the Montgomerys have become one magnificent series! In book three, *Trails of Love*, the Montgomerys and the Bradens are going to be deeply inter-twined. For that reason, I am combining the series to make it easier for readers to keep track of characters, weddings, babies, etc. What this means is that after the first two books (*Embracing Her Heart* and *Anything for Love*) you will see both worlds in most of the books. Some stories might weigh more heavily in one location than the other, but they are all going to cross over. In book one, *Embracing Her Heart* you will met the Montgom-erys, and in book two, *Anything for Love*, you will meet the Bradens. I hope you love them all as much as I do!

About the Love in Bloom Big-Family Romance Collection

The Bradens & Montgomerys is just one of the series in the Love in Bloom big-family romance collection. Each Love in Bloom book is written to be enjoyed as a stand-alone novel or as part of the larger series. There are no cliffhangers and no unresolved issues. Characters from each series make appearances in future books, so you never miss an engagement, wedding, or birth. A complete list of all series titles is included at the end of this book, along with previews of upcoming publications.

Visit Melissa's Reader Goodies page for free ebooks, checklists, family trees, and more! www.MelissaFoster.com/RG

A Special Surprise for Fans!

I am part of a fantastic group of romance authors called the Ladies Who Write (LWW), and we have created a fun, sexy world just for you! In *EMBRACING HER HEART* you will hear about LWW and meet member Amber Montgomery. In the next book in the Bradens & Montgomerys series, *ANYTHING FOR LOVE,* you will meet several other fictional members of LWW in a much bigger way, each of whom, along with Amber, will have their own book written by me and the other LWW authors. For more information on our group, and to stay up to date on the release of LWW books, visit www.LadiesWhoWrite.com and sign up for our newsletter.

Chapter One

"OUCH!"

Brindle? Grace blinked awake at the sound of whispers in the dark room. It took her a moment to remember she was in her childhood bedroom at her parents' home in Oak Falls, Virginia, and not in her Manhattan loft. She narrowed her eyes, trying to decipher which of her five sisters were intent on waking her up at...She glanced at the clock. *Four thirty in the morning?*

"Shh. You're such a klutz."

Sable. Of course. Who else would think it was okay to wake her up at this hour besides Brindle, her youngest and most rebellious sister, and Sable, the night owl?

"I tripped over a suitcase," Brindle whispered. Something *thunked.* "Oh shit!" She tumbled onto the bed in a fit of laughter, bringing Sable down with her—right on top of Grace, who let out an "*Oomph!*" as her parents' cat, Clayton, leapt off the bed and tore out of the room.

"Shh! You'll wake Mom and Dad, or the dogs," Sable whispered between giggles.

"What are you doing?" Grace tried to sound stern, but her sisters' laughter was contagious. The last thing she needed was to be awake at this hour after a grueling week and a painfully long drive, but her sisters were excited about Grace coming home, and if Grace were honest with herself, despite the mounds of scripts she had to get through during her visit, she was excited to see them, too. Other than a quick trip for her friend Sophie's wedding, she hadn't been home since Christmas, and it was already May.

"Get up." Brindle tugged her off the bed and felt around on the floor. "We're going out, just like old times." She threw the slacks and blouse Grace had worn home the night before in Grace's face. "Get dressed."

"I'm not going—"

"Shut up and take this off." Sable pulled Grace's silk nighty over her head despite Grace's struggles to stop her. She knew it was a futile effort. What Sable wanted, Sable got. Even though she and her twin sister, Pepper, were a year younger than Grace, Sable had always been the pushiest of them all.

Grace reluctantly stepped into her slacks. "Where are we going?" She reached for her hairbrush as Brindle grabbed her hand and dragged her out the bedroom door. "Wait! My shoes!'"

"We'll grab Mom's boots from by the door," Sable said, flanking her other side as they hurried down the hall tripping over each other.

"I'm *not* wearing cowgirl boots." Grace had worked hard to shake the country-bumpkin habits that were as deeply ingrained as her love for her six siblings. Habits like hair twirling, saying *y'all*, and wearing cutoffs and cowgirl boots, the hallmarks of her youth. She stood on the sprawling front porch with her hands on her hips, staring at her sisters, who were waiting for her to put on her mother's boots.

"Step into them or I swear I'll make you climb that hill barefoot, and you know that's not fun," Sable said.

"God! You two are royal pains in the ass." Grace shoved her feet into the boots. *They're only boots. They don't erase all of my hard work.* Oak Falls might be where her roots had sprouted, but they'd since spread far and wide, and she was never—*ever*—going to be that small-town girl again.

The moon illuminated the path before them. The pungent scent of horses and hay lingered in the air as they crossed the grass toward the familiar hill. *Great.* They were taking her to *Hottie Hill.* Grace groaned, wondering why she hadn't tossed them out of her bedroom and locked the door instead of going along with their crazy like-old-times plan. Three weeks at home would be both a blessing and a curse. Grace loved her sisters, but she imagined three weeks of Sable playing her guitar until all hours of the night and her other younger sisters popping in and out with their dogs and their drama, all while their mother carefully threw out queries about their dating lives and their father tried not to growl at their responses.

Brindle strutted up the steep hill in her boots and barely there sundress, expertly avoiding the dips and ruts in the grass, while Grace hurried behind her, stumbling over each one as she tried to keep up.

Sable reached the peak of the hill first. She turned on her booted heels, placed her hands on her hips, and grinned like a fool. "Hurry up! You'll miss it!"

It was one thing to deal with family drama from afar, when all it took was a quick excuse to get off the phone, but *three weeks?* Grace couldn't even blame her decision on being drunk, since she had been stone-cold sober when her sister Amber had asked her to help bolster her bookstore's presence by hosting a playwriting course. *You made it, Gracie! You're such an inspiration to everyone here,* Amber had pleaded. *Besides, Brindle is leaving soon for Paris, and it's the last time we'll all be together for months. It'll be like old times.* Grace was living her dream, writing and producing off-Broadway plays, although lately, that's all the *living* she was doing, and the diva attitudes of the industry were grating on her last nerve. Besides, how could she say no to Amber, the sweetest sister of them all?

Grace slipped on the hill and caught herself seconds before face-planting in the grass. "Damn it! This is the last thing I want to be doing right now."

"Shh," Brindle chided as she reached for Grace's hand.

Sable ran down the hill annoyingly fast. Holding her black cowgirl hat in place atop her long dark hair with one hand, she reached for Grace with the other and said, "Get up, you big baby."

"I can't believe you dragged my ass out of bed for this. What are we? Twelve?" Grace asked in her own harsh whisper.

"Twelve-year-olds don't sneak out to watch the hottest men in Oak Falls break in horses," Brindle said as they reached the top of the hill.

"Liar. We've been doing it since you were twelve," Sable reminded her.

"I can't believe *they're* still doing this at this ungodly hour." *They* were the Jericho brothers, and they'd been breaking in horses before dawn since they were teenagers. They claimed it was the only time they had before the heat of the day hit, but Grace thought it had more to do with it feeling more exciting doing it in the dark.

The Jericho brothers were the hottest guys around. Well, at least since Reed Cross left town after high school graduation.

Grace tried to tamp down thoughts of the guy who had taken her—and given her *his*—virginity, and turned her heart inside out. The man she'd turned away in pursuit of her production career, and the person she'd compared every single man to ever since. She refused to let herself go down memory lane.

"I'm exhausted," Grace complained as they reached the peak of the hill overlooking the Jericho ranch. The Jerichos owned several hundred acres and were very active in the community, opening one of their barns once a month to the community for *jam sessions*, where anyone that played an instrument could take part. People of all ages came to enjoy the music, dance, and take part in various games like potato sack races, ring toss, and touch football. It was just another of the small-town events that Grace hadn't regretted leaving behind.

"It's not like I haven't seen these guys a million times," she pleaded. "Besides, Brindle, you've slept with Trace more times than you can probably count. It's not like you haven't seen him shirtless. Why are we even—"

"Shh!" Brindle and Sable said in unison as they pulled Grace down to her knees.

She followed their gazes to the illuminated riding ring below, where the four Jericho brothers, Trace, Justus, aka "JJ," Shane, and Jeb, and a handful of other shirtless, jeans-clad guys were milling about. They were *always* shirtless, because what men weren't when they were proving they were the manliest of the group?

"Trace and I are over," Brindle whispered. "For real this time." She and Trace had been in an on-again-off-again relationship forever. They were a hopeless case of rebellious guy and rebellious girl, up for anything risky. Two people who didn't have a chance in hell of ever settling down but seemed to fill a need in each other's lives—or at least in their beds.

"That's not what Morgyn said." Sable smirked. Morgyn was a year older than Brindle and just as outgoing.

"Why didn't you drag her out instead of me?" Grace complained.

"I would have, but she wasn't home," Brindle explained.

Grace and her sisters had spent many hours as teenagers lying on this same hill when they should have been sleeping, watching the Jericho brothers and other guys ride wild horses or rope cattle. Pepper and Amber had come with them only twice. Pepper had complained the whole time about it being a waste of brain power, and Amber had been more embarrassed than turned on by the shirtless cock-and-bull show. *If only I'd been born shy.*

She laughed to herself. *Shy? Right.* She'd blazed a path in a man's world. There was no room for *shy* in her repertoire. And there was no room for this nonsense anymore, either. She pushed up onto her knees. "Brindle, maybe at twenty-four this is still fun, but I'm twenty-eight. I've got work to do in the morning, and I'm so far past this it's not even funny."

"*God*, Grace! You've turned into a workaholic ice queen," Sable whispered as she yanked Grace back down to her stomach. "And I, your very loving sister who feels the need to keep you young, aim to fix that. Starting *now*."

Grace rolled her eyes. "Ice queen? Just because I've grown up and don't find this type of thing fun anymore?" As she said the words the men below walked out of the ring and stood on the outside of the fence, their muscular arms hanging over the top rail.

"*Ice queen* because you think you're too good for—" Sable swallowed her words as Trace and JJ pushed open the enormous wooden barn doors and a wild horse blasted into the ring with a shirtless man on its back.

Their gazes snapped to the show below. It wasn't a Jericho on the back of this horse for its first ride, and despite her protests, Grace squinted into the night to get a better look at the virility before her.

"Damn," Brindle said in a husky voice.

"Holy shit, that's hot," Sable whispered. "See, Gracie? Totally worth it."

Grace took in the arch of the rider's shoulders as the horse bucked him forward and back, his thick arms holding tightly to the reins. His wavy brown hair and the square set of his chin sent a shudder of recognition through her.

"Ouch! Grace! You're digging your nails into me." Sable pried Grace's fingers off her forearm.

"Is that…?" Grace choked on the anger *and* arousal warring inside her. She'd recognize Reed Cross anywhere, even at a distance, after all these years of seeing him only in her dreams. She pushed to her feet, unable to make sense of seeing the forbidden lover she'd risked everything to have—and then cast aside—in Oak Falls, with the guys who'd once hated the sight of him. What the hell was he doing here? The last she'd heard, he'd moved to somewhere in the Midwest after high school.

"Reed…?" His name rolled off her tongue too easily, and she stumbled backward. Memories of being in his arms slammed into her, his gruff voice telling her he wanted her, he loved her. She didn't want to remember what they'd had, and as her sisters reached for her, trying to pull her back down to the grass, she took off running the way they'd come.

"Gracie, wait!" Sable shouted in a harsh whisper as she and Brindle ran after her.

Grace ran fast and hard, trying to outrun the memories, and knew it was a futile effort, which only pissed her off even more. She spun on her heels, anger and hurt burning through her. "You didn't think to *warn* me?"

"I knew you wouldn't come," Sable said.

"Damn right I wouldn't." She started down the hill again.

"Wait, Grace!" Brindle grabbed her hand and tried to slow her down, but Grace kept going, dragging her sister with her. "*What* is going on?" Brindle pleaded. "Why are you so mad?"

Grace slowed, realizing in that moment that Sable had kept her secret for the past decade. That was something she hadn't expected. Then again, she hadn't expected to have a visceral, titillating reaction to seeing Reed again, either. Hell, she hadn't expected to ever see him again. *Period.* He had been the quarterback at their rival high school. Small-town rivalries weren't taken lightly back then, and she and Reed had been careful never to be seen together for fear of Grace, a cheerleader, being ostracized by her friends. As graduation neared, they both knew Grace wanted to follow her dreams and write and produce plays in the Big Apple. They might have stayed together if Reed had told her that he would be willing to move away from the small town one day, but he'd been adamant about never leaving his family.

At least he had been until she'd ended their relationship to pursue her dreams.

Then he'd left town for good.

Or so she'd thought.

That still stung, even now, as his deep voice carried in the air, bringing with it memories of the secrets they'd shared and the stolen sensual nights they'd enjoyed.

"I thought you were over him," Sable accused.

"I am!" Grace huffed. She absently touched her lips, remembering the taste of spearmint and teenage lust mixed into one delicious kiss after another. Kisses that had never failed to leave her body humming with desire. *Great.* Now she couldn't *stop* thinking of him. This was bad. Very, very bad. She never should have allowed her sisters to drag her out and unearth memories she'd rather forget.

"Over *who?*" Brindle demanded as she traipsed through the grass beside Grace.

Grace ignored her question, unwilling to reveal her decade-old secret.

"Then what's the problem?" Sable snapped, also ignoring Brindle's question. She grabbed Grace's arm, stopping her in her tracks.

Unlike Grace, Sable had no qualms about one-night stands or taking what she wanted from a man. *Any* man, it seemed to Grace, as long as he struck her fancy for the moment. Even though Sable hid nothing when it came to her sexuality, she and Grace had a deep bond, and she was the only one of Grace's five sisters Grace had ever trusted with her sexual secrets. Sable *knew* how hard it had been for her to break up with Reed all those years ago. Grace's heart slammed against her chest as they stared each other down. She'd thought she was over Reed Cross. She *was* over him. She'd put him out of her mind. *Mostly.*

Sure, it was Reed's face she conjured up on lonely nights, and it was his lopsided grin and easy laugh she recalled to pull her through the toughest of productions. But that was *her* secret, not one she'd shared with Sable.

She should have stuck to weekend visits home, as she had for the past several years. Weekend visits were safe. *Fast.* Brindle never would have dragged her out if she'd be facing a long drive home in twenty-four hours. She couldn't stay for three weeks, especially now that she knew Reed was back in town. Tomorrow she'd tell Amber she couldn't teach the class after all, and she'd drive back to the city, where there was no chance of running into Reed Cross.

Brindle threw her arms up toward the sky. "Will someone *please* tell me what the problem is? Why are you storming off? And why are you mad at Sable? It was *me* who wanted to come out and see Trace tonight. Not her! I thought it would be fun, like old times. We'd laugh and joke and talk about how sexy he was."

"Grace." Sable's tone softened, her eyes imploring her for forgiveness Grace couldn't give.

"There's no problem, Brin," Grace managed, holding Sable's gaze. "I just…" *I'm confused and angry by my body's stupid reaction to a man I don't need in my life.* "I'm just exhausted." As unreasonable as it was, since she'd caused their breakup, she still felt the sting of his betrayal after they'd broken up, when he'd left his beloved family—and *her*—behind.

Chapter Two

THE MORNING SUN beat down on Reed Cross's back as he climbed the porch steps of the Montgomerys' old Victorian home and began removing the ceiling, trying to ignore the memories that assaulted him every time he stepped foot on the property. He used to leave orchids on this very porch every month for Grace, his first love. It was bittersweet, coming back to Oak Falls and taking over renovation projects for his uncle Roy, who had suffered a heart attack and needed help completing the jobs to which he'd already committed. He'd been back for four months, and still he felt Grace's presence everywhere, just like he had after they'd broken up all those years ago.

Pushing thoughts of the past aside seemed a constant battle, and once again he tried to do just that and focus on the job at hand. He'd already removed a good bit of the decking to check out the joists and get a handle on the extent of the damage and was knee-deep in debris when he heard the sliding doors open. He wiped his brow, expecting to see Cade or Marilynn, the owners of the house. His eyes caught on a pair of gorgeous long legs and traveled north, over silky pajamas skimming a scorching-hot curvaceous figure. His gaze slowed at full breasts peeking out from beneath tumbles of thick dark hair, awakening every nerve in his body. Nerves that had been unexcitable for months.

The woman cleared her throat, startling him from his reverie, and his gaze darted up to her face. His heart nearly stopped at the familiar mossy-green eyes staring back at him. His body turned cold with shock, and just as quickly his teeth ground together as his mind spiraled back to their senior year in high school, when Grace Montgomery had been *his*. Memories of sneaking out after dark, sharing secrets, holding hands, and loving each other fiercely rushed forth—followed by the hurt of her choosing New York over him.

His eyes narrowed despite the unexpected arousal simmering beneath his skin.

"Grace…" Even after a decade her name tasted sinfully good rolling off his tongue.

Her hand slid from the doorknob, hanging limply by her side. She opened her mouth to speak, but no words came. A long moment later, "Reed," slipped from her lips like the secret he'd once been.

His gut clenched with longing. He couldn't help but study her—and that pissed him off as much as it eased the worries about his ability to *feel* that had plagued him for years. He hadn't been all in with a woman since Grace, and he'd begun to think he'd exaggerated what he'd felt when they were together. But there was no misreading the heat thrumming through him. She looked incredible, and confused, and as her hand settled on her hip—the hand he remembered all too well digging into his back when they'd made love all those years ago—he realized she also looked angry. Definitely *angry*.

But still incredible.

In the space of a breath he was fighting the urge to figure

out how to spend time with her and recapture the fire between them despite everything she'd put him through.

"Are you done gawking?" she snapped.

"I...Sorry. You caught me off guard. I was expecting to see your parents." He held her gaze, forcing a smile even though he suddenly felt stuck somewhere between a teenager caught peering through a window, a jealous ex-boyfriend, and a lust-filled man.

She folded her arms over her chest, forcing a barrier between them, and smirked.

Ouch—

At least he hoped it was a smirk rather than a scowl. After the clues he'd missed with his ex-girlfriend, Alina, who had been sleeping with his now *ex*-business partner, he no longer trusted his instincts where women were concerned. And when it came to Grace Montgomery, he'd never been able to think past the emotions she stirred within him and the future he'd hoped they'd have. She was the tsunami that had obliterated every-thing else in his world, and as he struggled to find his voice, he fought the urge to tangle his hands in her thick, lustrous hair and remind her of what she'd walked away from.

"I hope you don't look at my mother like that," she snapped.

"What? No. Jesus, Grace." In her eyes he was probably a quintessential asshole, checking her out without any thought to their past. In reality, he'd been taken just as off guard by his leering as she was. "I don't usually—"

"Don't usually let your eyes wander?" She scoffed. "Right."

"Believe it or not, yes," he said angrily. "Who the hell do you think I've become? I didn't expect you to walk out here at all, much less wearing nearly nothing and..." He tried to figure out what to say next, what to *feel*…

"Why are you here, Reed?"

He didn't need this. Not when he had just begun rebuilding his life. After being screwed over by Alina, he'd vowed to stay away from anything that made his head spin, and Grace *definitely* made his head spin.

He studied her, while trying not to at the same time. The chip on her shoulder was bigger now, overshadowing the sexy smirk on her lips. She'd always exuded confidence, but somehow that, too, seemed more intense. His heart thumped harder with the memory of the first time he'd spotted her standing on the sidelines in her cute cheerleading uniform as he headed out to the football field. She'd challenged him with her glare, as if she were playing on the rival team rather than cheering for them. She'd hated that cheerleading outfit, but damn, he'd loved it. And that challenge she'd emitted? He'd taken her up on that in a hot second.

But she'd kicked him to the curb once, he reminded himself. Why was he giving her any consideration at all? He had a job to do, and sure, he'd momentarily lost his footing and checked her out, but it wasn't like that was a crime. She was hot, and they had history. *That's as far as it goes.*

"I asked you why you're here," she repeated, her green eyes shooting spears he didn't deserve.

He stepped closer, curious about how she'd react, and yeah, he just fucking wanted to be near her. "I'm fixing your parents' porch. Obviously."

"Not *here*, Reed. Why are you back in Virginia?"

"That's not really any of your concern," he said, stepping deeper into her personal space despite his brain telling him to back off. "You're so frustrating, demanding answers. How about a hello?"

"Me? I'm the frustrating one? You…" she stammered, and he grinned, pleased he was having the same effect on her that she had on him. "Damn it. Why do you smell so good when you're sweaty?" She pushed at his chest. "Back up. Get away from me."

He grabbed her wrist, unwilling to let her get away, despite knowing he should. But how could he? He couldn't believe after all these years she was right there in front of him. His first love, the first and *only* person he'd ever truly given his heart to. He couldn't just pretend his heart wasn't going crazy or that he wasn't suddenly flooded with emotions he hadn't felt in forever. He stepped even closer, testing himself, expecting the spell to break, but it only got stronger.

Oh yeah, baby, you still feel it, too.

He had no idea why he was pursuing her when she had the power to destroy him, but as was the case in high school, he was powerless to resist her. Alina had never affected him half as intensely as even *thoughts* of Grace always had. Maybe that's why he'd lost no sleep over ending his relationship with Alina. She'd been convenient, and maybe on some level he'd loved her the only way he'd been able to, but nothing—*nothing*—compared to the immensity of his feelings for the woman before him. The one he now realized he'd never moved on from.

"Back up," she repeated, her voice thinner now, a little shaky.

"Why should I? You're the one who came out here." He raked his gaze down her body. "Dressed like *that*."

They'd been surrounded by rivalries from the get-go. Opposite teams all the way—until a day just like this, when she'd challenged and he'd pushed.

She pressed her lips together, holding his stare. Her eyes still tore straight to his heart. Another challenge he wasn't about to back away from. He closed the minuscule distance between them. Her breasts grazed his chest.

She sucked in a sharp breath and stepped back. He followed her onto the threshold of the door.

"You might as well get used to seeing me," he said in a low voice, pausing to let his words sink in. It took all his willpower not to ask if she'd thought of him as often as he'd thought of her. But this was a dangerous game he was playing, and he knew the answer could make it even more so. She'd walked away once, and he'd been forced to leave town. He was never going to leave his family again. Not for her or anyone else.

"I'm not leaving again, Grace." He released her wrist and took a step back as all that lust morphed to anger, and a rush of cold air filled the space between them.

"It doesn't matter anyway," she said with too much venom, "because I am."

They stared at each other, challenging, sizing up, remembering—*wishing?* He shifted his gaze away in an effort to reclaim his sanity and squinted up at the sun, pushing aside the fact that she was making him a hell of a lot hotter than the sun ever could. She was a big-city girl now, he reminded himself, just like Alina. He'd followed Grace's career over the years despite himself and knew she had achieved what she'd always wanted.

At their expense.

Hadn't he learned his lesson?

With that uncomfortable thought, he turned his back and reached for his tools, needing the distraction. But he felt her presence, hot and alluring, behind him and *had* to take one more look. She stood with her hands on her hips and didn't seem concerned over her lack of clothing. There was some type of disconnect between Reed's brain and his body, and it took all his effort to keep his eyes locked on hers when they were begging for another quick sweep of the womanly curves his first love had developed.

Fuck. Get a grip. There was only one way to do that. He needed to convince himself she wasn't worth the risk.

"You always were good at leaving things behind," he said coldly.

Her jaw fell open and a sound of disbelief escaped, sending a pang of regret to his gut. She stormed into the house, giving him an eyeful of her barely covered, and even-more-beautiful-than-before, ass—pushing that spear of regret in deeper.

GRACE PULLED THE door and the curtains closed and paced her bedroom, crossing and uncrossing her arms, trying to suck air into her lungs. What the hell was Reed doing back in town, and why was he working at her parents' house? She hadn't even realized her parents *knew* him. She stared at the swinging curtains, and much to her dismay, her body was still trembling and *hot*. She hated him for making her feel that way. But it wasn't only Reed she was mad at. She had a bone to pick with Sable.

She threw open the bedroom door, heard Clayton jump from the bed and land gently on the floor with a soft *meow*, and headed down the hall toward the scent of freshly brewed coffee. Sable was staying at their parents' house while her apartment over her auto shop was undergoing renovations. With the exception of their rock-star brother, Axsel, who traveled endlessly with his band, and Pepper, who worked as a research and development scientist outside of Oak Falls, her siblings stopped by often for meals at their parents' house.

She found Sable and Amber standing by the kitchen sink, staring out the window at Reed. They were so busy gawking, they didn't even notice she was there. Sable was dressed in cutoffs, cowgirl boots, and her favorite Stetson, while Amber wore a short flowery dress with her boots—typical Oak Falls attire. For some reason that annoyed Grace even more. Why did *small town* look so right and comfortable on her sisters, when it felt ill fitted on Grace? A streak of jealousy floated through her, and she tucked it away, reminding herself of how hard she'd worked to break out of that small-town mode.

"Take the damn shirt off already," Sable said as she twisted the ends of her long dark hair. The three of them, along with Axsel, were brunette, like their mother, while Brindle and Morgyn were fair-haired, like their father, and Pepper was a beautiful mixture of both.

Her sister's comment did nothing to calm Grace's racing heart from the brief—and abrupt—encounter with the full-on torturous beast outside. His toffee-brown hair was thicker now. His kissable lips were fuller. Add in sun-kissed skin, honest eyes, a strong, square jaw, and a dusting of scruff, and *holy cow*. Reed Cross was still hotter than any man she knew, and Grace had met some seriously *fine* men.

"Grace knocked him off his game with her I'm-just-standoffish-enough-to-make-you-want-me act," Amber said as she reached a hand down to pet the head of Reno, her golden retriever. Amber was epileptic, and Reno was her service dog. "But Gracie could knock anyone off his game."

Grace softened at her sister's words. She missed their un-conditional love and friendships. It seemed to her that other than her childhood best friend, Sophie, who now also lived in New York, true friendships were hard to come by in the city. But she knew there was nothing like the love of younger siblings. Even when they were growing up and bickering over everything under the sun, her younger siblings still looked up to her like she held all the world's answers. Little did they know that she looked up to them, too. Not that any of them, including her, ever had all the right answers. Decisions around the Montgomery home were often made late at night, with the seven of them huddled together and plenty of hot chocolate and laughter on hand. Sometimes there were tears, too, but no matter how sad one of them was over a breakup, bad grades, career woes, or anything else, they'd always had one another's backs. Part of having one another's backs was helping them find a bright spot in a dark moment.

And Sable was about to have a very dark moment for keep-ing news of Reed working on the house to herself.

Grace crossed her arms against her resurfacing anger. "Knock him off his game?" she said in response to Amber's comment. "More like I annoyed the hell out of him."

Sable and Amber both spun around.

"You're here!" Amber, completely oblivious to the tension sparking between Grace and Sable, threw her arms around Grace, hugging her tight. Her seizure-alert necklace lay familiar and present between them. Pepper had developed the necklace when she was in graduate school and had since patented and sold it all over the country. It featured a button that Reno could push with his nose if Amber had a seizure and included an internal GPS system to alert family members and emergency services to Amber's location. Their mother trained service dogs, and she trained each of the seizure-alert dogs she worked with to use the necklaces. Thankfully, the alert system had been needed only once, since Amber's seizures were controlled well with medications.

Sable must have noticed Grace's scowl, because she mouthed, *Don't be mad.*

"When did you get in?" Amber asked.

"Late last night," Grace said, surprised Sable and Brindle hadn't already outed her for running off in a huff.

"I'm super excited about your class." Amber's hazel eyes sparked with excitement. "I've cleared out the office and brought in more seating for the lounge area in case you want to teach there. Thank you so much for agreeing to do this! It means the world to me."

How could she burst Amber's bubble by telling her she was going home? And really, *why* was she running away from Reed? She was a big girl. She could deal with being in the same town as him for a few weeks.

"I'm looking forward to it," she said honestly. It wasn't the class that made her stomach flutter. "How many people have signed up?"

"Only four so far, but that's a start."

"It'll be a nice change. I'm used to working with big casts and crews. Where is everyone this morning?" Grace glanced out the window, catching sight of Reed's broad back as he tore wooden planks from their tethers and tossed them aside like toothpicks. Gone was the lean teen she'd fallen in love with. She'd noticed the breadth of his shoulders, his muscular chest, and his thick thighs when he'd been breathing down her neck. When he'd grabbed her wrist, there had been a moment, a *connection*, so startling she'd been unable to breathe. No wonder her sisters were gawking. The man was built like a solid, intoxicatingly beautiful red oak.

"Mom's at the store," Sable explained. "Dad took Dolly and Reba to the park." Dolly and Reba were ten-month-old golden retrievers their mother was raising to train as service dogs. "Brindle's working on something for her drama class's upcoming play, and Morgyn had to meet a supplier at her shop." Brindle was a full-time teacher at the high school, and she also ran the drama club for the elementary school. Morgyn owned Life Reimagined, an eclectic store where she created her own fashions and accessories, as well as repurposed gently used items. "Brindle and Morgyn are going to the county fair later, and they're coming by tonight to hear my band play. You're coming tonight, too, girlie, so don't even think about trying to back out."

Sable tapped Grace's shoulder, jolting her brain back into gear and reminding her that she was irritated with her secret-holding sister. But before she could get a word out, Reed reached over his shoulder, nimbly gathering his T-shirt, and tugged it over his head, unveiling planes of hard, tanned flesh. A collective gasp rose between them as he tossed the shirt aside. All his delicious muscles flexed as he picked up another plank and rested it on his shoulder. Grace's fingers curled with the desire to touch him—confirming once again that it had been way too long since she'd been around a *real* man—*and* that she had to get the hell out of Oak Falls.

She opened her mouth to try to capture all the energy coming to life inside her and aim it at Sable for keeping Reed's presence from her *again*, but her mouth had gone bone-dry.

"Girls! Give that poor man a break."

Their mother's voice cut through her Reed-induced trance. They spun around as their mother set two bags of groceries on the counter. Marilynn Montgomery was a strong woman. Some said it was from years of gardening, horseback riding, and training service dogs, but Grace thought it had more to do with raising seven complicated and often wild children.

"You'd think you were a bunch of horny teenagers the way you drool over that man." Their mother pulled Grace into a warm hug, squeezing her longer than usual, giving her the extra love Grace hadn't realized she'd needed until just then. "How's my sweet girl?"

Hot, bothered, and frustrated. "Good, Mom," she said, because she was pretty sure her mother wouldn't appreciate the truth.

"We're not drooling. We're just making sure he's working and not goofing off," Sable said, turning to watch Reed again. "It was Grace who was trying to get him into bed, not us."

Obviously Sable wasn't going to make this easy. Maybe Grace would have to leave after all.

"Ugh, Sabe, you're so raunchy," Amber said, her cheeks flushing.

"Grace is the one who went out there half naked to flirt with him," Sable pointed out.

"Grace?" Her mother's brows knitted as she looked over Grace's silk cami and pajama shorts. "You didn't go out there like that, did you?" She poured a cup of coffee and shook her head. "Poor Reed probably didn't know what hit him."

Grace rolled her eyes. If her mother had known that Grace and Reed had once secretly dated, she'd never have hired him.

"I didn't go out there to flirt with him. I went out to find out why the heck someone was making noise this early. I had no idea you were renovating. I thought Dad was tinkering again. Why didn't anyone tell me?" Her father taught engineering at the community college and had summers off, during which he often took care of odd jobs around the house.

"Oh, honey." Her mother's gaze softened. "You have so much going on with your plays. Right after one gets going, you dive into the next, and you finally got some time off. I didn't think it was a big deal."

Sable suppressed a smile, and Grace knew her sister was thinking the same thing she was. *Reed Cross is a very big deal.* Sable dug through the grocery bag, trying to dodge the weight of Grace's stare.

"Anyway, where'd you find that guy?" Grace tried to act nonchalant, busying herself filling bowls with food and water for Clayton, who was currently winding himself around Reno's feet. Reno buried his nose in the cat's fur, while Sable gave Grace a nice-try look.

"It's the saddest thing," their mother said. "I hired his uncle, Roy Cross, who came highly recommended and lives in Meadowside, but Roy had a massive heart attack a few months ago. Reed dropped everything and came back to town to help him complete all the projects he'd taken on. Apparently, Reed followed in Roy's footsteps and he's some type of big historical preservationist in Michigan."

Michigan. So that's where he took off to.

Their mother began putting groceries away and said, "All I know is that any man who would drop everything to help his family is a man worth his weight in gold."

"Pepper would say that a man needs to treat a woman like a diamond before he's treated like he's worth a penny," Amber said.

"Yes, well…" Her mother smiled warmly. "Our girl Pepper might find herself eighty years old and alone in a house full of computers, books, and electronic gadgets one day if she's not careful. I love your sister, but she's pickier than a cotton gin."

They all laughed.

Sable opened a box of cinnamon buns and held one out toward Grace. "Here, Gracie. You can take Reed a cinnamon bun and apologize for your bitch attack this morning."

"Sable. *Language*, please," their mother chided, causing Sable to roll her eyes and Amber and Grace to smile. "Although, there is that *look* you give men, Grace. I wouldn't call it bitchy, but I've noticed that you're not quite as soft as you once were."

Grace set the bowls on the floor for Clayton. Reno ambled over and tried to stick his nose in, but Clayton hissed.

"Leave it," Amber said, and Reno backed obediently away.

"Not quite as soft? Was I ever *soft*, Mom?" She'd certainly tried to change, but had she become hardened or *bitchy*?

Her mother lovingly touched her hand. "You weren't really soft, Grace, just softer than you are now."

"Maybe so, but I don't have a *look*. If anything, I'm just tired and maybe a little cranky from being woken up at four thirty in the morning by the Pop 'n' Fresh girls." Grace arched a brow at Sable. "And then again at God-knows-what-time by *him*."

"Mm-hm," their mother said, exchanging a look with Amber that Grace couldn't read. The two of them were putting away groceries shoulder to shoulder, and Grace swore she heard them whispering, too.

"Right," Sable said sarcastically. "And I don't have a *look* either." She snorted a laugh and popped a piece of a cinnamon bun into her mouth.

"Oh my," their mother said. "I can only imagine what Morgyn would say to that. She thinks you have a look, a laugh, a line, and anything else a woman might need to snag a man."

"You don't need a *look*, Sabe. You're not exactly shy about letting guys know what you want, or who you want it with," Grace said. "I, on the other hand, am a little less obvious and much pickier. Although not nearly as picky as Pepper, so don't even go there."

"Oh, please! Picky?" Sable narrowed her eyes, pointed at Grace, and said in a singsong voice, "*Ice queen.*"

The sound of a man clearing his throat sent them all spinning in the direction of the doorway, where Reed stood looking mildly embarrassed and wickedly hot. He'd put his shirt back on, but it clung to his athletic frame. His hair was tousled, and his skin glistened with perspiration, which for some reason made him look even sexier. Grace tried to ignore her quickening pulse, but it was hopeless with the sensual heat rolling off the man she'd once known so intimately.

Reno bounded toward him.

"Settle!" Amber said.

Reno skidded to a stop in front of Reed, a bundle of fluffy energy, his tongue hanging from his mouth as his eyes begged for attention. The dog's reaction told Grace how well Reno already knew their visitor. She silently repeated the command to her own libido—*Settle. Settle. Settle*—but unlike the well-behaved dog, it didn't listen, and lust simmered deep in her belly. From the look Sable was giving her, and the devilish grin spreading across Reed's lips, everyone in the room could see it.

Chapter Three

REED TRIED NOT to let the way Grace was staring have an effect on him, but he knew the fiery passion she was capable of, and the ravenous look of desire in her gorgeous green eyes was impossible to ignore. The chip on her shoulder she'd flaunted earlier gave her an edge that made her even more appealing. Surely if she knew her defensive attitude only made her hotter, she'd do what she could to temper it, and for that reason alone, he'd never clue her in.

He cocked a smile and hiked a thumb over his shoulder, trying to remember why he'd come into the house in the first place. "I knocked, but you probably didn't hear me."

"Reed, come on in, honey." Marilynn lifted a coffee mug. "Would you like a cup of coffee?"

"No, thank you," he said as Amber crouched to love up Reno.

Sable leaned her hip against the counter, her eyes dancing between him and Grace. As if Grace had just realized she was staring, she shifted her gaze away. Reed wasn't sure if he was relieved or disappointed.

"I wanted to show you what I've found outside. Do you have a moment? And is your husband around? I'd like to show him, too."

Sable pushed away from the counter. "What'd you find?"

"Something bad?" Amber took a curious step closer.

It didn't escape him that Grace had not made a move to get closer. If anything, she'd retreated a step or two.

"Cade is out, but you can show me." Marilynn set her coffee cup on the counter and headed out the door. Amber, Sable, and Reno followed her.

Seeing Grace's close-knit family magnified how much Reed had missed his own family while he'd been in Michigan. And just seeing Grace made him realize how much he'd missed *her*. He hesitated at the door, unwilling to let this morning's encounter be the last thing said between them. Grace crossed her arms, the lust in her eyes cooler now but still there. *Has it remained for all these years, or is this new?*

She lifted her chin and drew her shoulders back.

He took a step closer and said, "I'm sorry I woke you this morning."

"It's fine," she said. "I have work to do anyway."

Even when she was trying to keep her distance he was drawn to her. He knew that beneath that steely facade, she had a soft, feminine side that needed to be loved and taken care of. Grace had always been a walking dichotomy of tenderness and strength. A true beauty inside and out that Reed knew had nothing to do with skimpy pajamas. Her very essence was sweet and loving. Breaking through the iron gates she'd erected around it hadn't been easy all those years ago, and he could see that hadn't changed. But something had, and it wasn't Grace.

It was *him*.

He wasn't going to let her get away that easy.

"Would you like to join us?" He nodded toward the door.

For a moment she just looked at him, expressionless. She wore no makeup, and her creamy skin was void of a tan. Clearly her life in New York didn't allow for much time outside, which saddened him. He knew how much she had enjoyed the outdoors. Had that changed? What else might have changed?

"Apparently house renovations are a family affair around here," he added, going for levity.

She laughed under her breath, and a few dark tendrils fell in front of her eyes. A genuine smile spread across her lips, illuminating the flecks of gold in her eyes. She blinked up at him from beneath her hair, looking sexy and youthful, pulling more memories from the recesses of his mind.

"No, thank you," she said, sending a strange sense of disappointment through him.

Sunlight cut a path between them, creating a line he wanted to cross to the woman he'd never been able to forget. But he knew better, damn it. Why was this so hard? Her life was hundreds of miles away, and he was just beginning to rebuild his life here with his family. It was hard to turn away with so much left unsaid, but really, what could he say? *Was it worth it? Did you find the exciting life you were seeking? Are you happy?* Or the question he really wanted to ask but knew he never would— *Do you regret not giving us a try for the long haul?* It wasn't even a fair question. They'd been nothing more than lovesick kids.

Following his gut rather than his heart, he nodded curtly and went outside to join the others.

Reno lumbered toward him. "Hey, buddy," he said, reaching out to pet him as he approached the others.

"Is it worse than we anticipated?" Marilynn stood with her hands on her hips and a serious look in her eyes, reminding him of Grace.

"It's not bad. Pretty much what I expected to find." The dog went to Amber's side. Reed loved animals, but he was glad for the space. His mind was still on Grace, and he needed to focus on the job, not the hungry look in her eyes he'd seen when he'd first walked into the kitchen.

It wasn't easy to switch into work mode, but he did his best. He caught himself glancing at the house several times, hoping Grace might be unable to resist joining them. But those sparks of hope were doused by reality.

As he walked them through his findings, Marilynn and Grace's sisters listened to every word. Sable added her two cents along the way, which consisted mostly of, "We *have* to fix that," while Amber and Marilynn agreed.

They came around the corner of the house, returning to the place they'd started, and Reed noticed that Grace's bedroom curtains were open. His gaze swept over the neatly made bed and the cat curled up in the center, and he felt another wave of disappointment when he realized Grace wasn't anywhere in sight.

GRACE SAT IN the gazebo on the hill reading through the scripts she was considering for an upcoming performance. She had taken these three weeks off, but her job as an independent producer never stopped. There was always another production to get underway. She'd been at it all day, and she was no closer to making a selection than she'd been when she'd started. It didn't help that she pictured Reed as the lead role in each story, imagining him reciting the lines, acting out the scenarios—in nothing but a pair of jeans, boots, and that wickedly naughty smile of his. She needed to stop this silly daydreaming. It's not like she'd follow through with her desires, and she didn't need to play with either of their emotions in that way.

Wouldn't Sable just love that? Her vixenish sister would encourage her to take him and leave him, and probably give her a detailed lesson on how to do it well. While Grace had never *taken* Reed, she'd loved him, and she'd already done the leaving him part, and *that* had been treacherous. She hadn't even allowed herself to admit how badly she'd hurt both of them until years later, when she was still missing him and trying to convince herself she didn't.

She tipped her face up to the sky, listening to the leaves rustling in the trees and letting the gentle breeze wash away her memories.

Her phone buzzed with a text message, pulling her from her thoughts. She opened Brindle's text and smiled at the selfie, all smoky eyes and blond hair. Her youngest sister had the darkest lashes and brows she'd ever seen on a natural blonde, giving her a sultry appearance that matched her rascally personality. Another text bubble popped up and Grace read it. *Hey, sis! You coming tonight? I need to talk to you about stuff.*

Grace's writer's mind immediately homed in on the word *stuff.* If Brindle were a playwright, she'd correct her, tell her to be more specific, to give the viewers something to latch on to. *Stuff* was just another small-town idiosyncrasy that usually grated on Grace's nerves. When it came to her sisters, however, she was never affected in the same way as she was with strangers. Use of the word *stuff* fit Brindle's personality perfectly. Brindle was always moving a million miles an hour, going from one thing to the next, wanting to experience everything life had to offer, which was why she'd planned a solo trip to Paris for the summer. Grace would never be that brave.

She sent a quick reply. *Missed you at breakfast. I'll be there and can't wait to see you and Morgyn. Bringing Trace or flying solo tonight?*

She threw in Trace Jericho's name just to get a reaction from Brindle, because what fun was it to have younger sisters if she couldn't taunt them every once in a while? Brindle's response came immediately. *Solo. I told you we're done! We'll talk tonight. Xox.*

She and Trace had been *done* at least a dozen times in the last year alone. Grace set her phone aside. She was excited to spend time with her sisters, even if she'd rather it was at her parents' house, where they wouldn't have the noise of Sable's band to contend with. Amber wouldn't be at the party. Like Pepper, Amber had never enjoyed rowdy crowds. Grace had always thought her parents were crazy to have seven children so close together, but her mother claimed that it wasn't children that made life difficult; it was the parents' inability to give up certain aspects of their own lives in order to care for them.

She glanced across the property to the barn, where she'd spent her youth mucking stalls and helping care for the dogs her mother trained. She'd never regretted escaping those chores for life in the city, even if she loved the animals.

She watched her mother working with one of the dogs she was training in the field by the barn, and just beyond, their horses, Sonny and Cher, grazing in the pasture. She thought about what her mother had said about her not being as *soft* as she used to be and wondered again if she'd become too harsh. She was definitely different than she used to be. More refined, she liked to think, not the workaholic ice queen Sable claimed she'd become.

She caught sight of Reed walking toward his truck, his T-shirt tucked into his back pocket. When she'd seen him last night, she'd been so conflicted that she was tempted to run home to New York and jump into the arms of her very hot, very interested neighbor, Jasper Lennox, just to prove to herself that she didn't want Reed Cross. She'd gone out with Jasper twice, and he'd been a gentleman from the moment he'd opened the cab door to the second he'd kissed her good night with too much tongue and not enough...*something*. She never could put her finger on exactly what was missing from any of the men she'd dated over the years, but something was *always* missing. She had yet to find a man who held her intellectual *and* her sexual interests. But she knew that being with Jasper wouldn't prove that the rampant heart thumping and the lust searing through her veins was all a farce.

There was no denying that Reed Cross was sex on legs, with magnificent muscles and a perfect dusting of dark chest hair, the exact opposite of the waxed and manicured actors and metrosexuals she was used to. Reed was handsome, but even if he had gained weight or come back marred in some way, she knew she'd feel the same way she did right now, because he wasn't just good-looking. He still owned a piece of her heart.

Surely those frenzied emotions were just the remnants of love that every woman felt when they saw the first guy they'd ever given their heart to. Right? As desperately as she wanted someone to take her into the O-Zone, she was pretty sure Reed shouldn't be that person.

She watched him place his tools in the back of his truck and grab a water bottle from the cab. He tipped his head back and drank it down. She couldn't help imagining his warm lips on hers. What would it be like to tangle with all that masculinity? Maybe Sable was right and she had acted a little bitchy, but wouldn't any ex-girlfriend after a guy told her he'd never—*ever*—leave his hometown, and because of that, she'd been forced to end the relationship, only to find out less than a month later that he'd taken off for what looked like forever?

She looked down at the stack of papers beside her and realized she'd been working for nearly eight hours. Wasn't she supposed to be visiting with her family and fitting in work here and there? A shiver ran down her spine with the realization that she just might be the workaholic Sable accused her of being. Did that mean she'd become an ice queen, too?

The way her insides thrummed at the sight of Reed, she didn't think there was anything *icy* about herself. But she'd be damned if she'd do anything more to solidify that image in her sister's mind.

Or in anyone else's.

Grace needed to prove to herself that she wasn't an ice queen. She could flirt with the best of them. She was a *pro* at flirting. *A goddess of flirtation.*

She gathered her scripts, determined to prove Sable wrong, and traipsed across the yard. Who better to practice flirting with than Reed? She knew he would give her the positive reinforcement she needed, and after the way he'd leered at her, there was no chance of being rebuffed.

Or was there?

The closer she came to him, the faster her heart raced and the more she wasn't buying her own lie. What if he turned her away? A man like Reed probably had half of the townies after him. Younger, prettier women dressed in stupid Daisy Dukes and cowgirl boots, with perfect little bodies and sweet dispositions.

She slowed her pace, trying not to think about Reed with other women. *Of course he's been with other women.* He'd probably already made his way through at least a dozen of the women in town. Girls she'd grown up with. Why wouldn't he? All men really wanted was a quick lay.

That thought made her a little nauseous—and jealous. Mostly because Reed had never been that way, but also…the idea of him in another woman's arms bothered her far more than she liked.

She stopped walking when she was close enough to see every dip and groove in his six-pack abs. When he lowered the water bottle, their eyes met—and held. His blue eyes were as dark as the night sky, and the intensity in them held her captive, making her feel naked and strangely feminine at once. She was a cutthroat producer, able to work in a man's world without feeling intimidated. She was strong and professional and hadn't thought of herself as anything remotely close to feminine since…*we were together in high school.*

She looked down at her summer dress, suddenly wondering why she'd chosen it. Was it because Reed had always insisted she was feminine? Did she look too *country bumpkin?* Oh, shit. Now what craziness had infiltrated her brain? She was worried about what she was wearing for the benefit of Reed?

Intimidation trampled through her, unfamiliar and uncomfortable, as Reed's stare continued to burn a path between them. Maybe she was an ice queen, because she was melting beneath the heat of his smoldering gaze. He took a step toward her, and her nerves took over, shattering her determination.

This isn't failure, she told herself. She knew how to flirt. She just didn't want to flirt with *him* after all.

At least that's what she told herself as she spun on her heel and hurried away.

Chapter Four

REED SAT ACROSS the dinner table from his aunt Ella and uncle Roy, in the house where they'd raised him. It was a simple three-bedroom rambler, far from extraordinary in any way, but it felt much larger and full of love in ways no other home ever had. Reed's mother, Lily, was Ella's sister and had died in childbirth. His father, Frank Gilbert, had abandoned him to Roy and Ella as a baby. Although Reed had lived with Roy and Ella since he was two days old, his aunt and uncle had always hoped Frank would return, and for that reason he'd always called them Aunt Ella and Uncle Roy rather than Mom and Dad. Reed had only seen his real father once. He was four years old at the time, and the only thing he remembered from the visit was the scars on the back of one of Frank's hands and forearm. When Reed was nine years old, after years of hoping his father would claim him, he desperately wanted to *belong* to Roy and Ella. To be a Cross, not a Gilbert. To shed the sadness of his past. Unable to have children of their own, they had been thrilled to adopt him, though by then the endearments of aunt and uncle were already ingrained. But that didn't mean Reed thought of them as anything less than his mother and father.

Reed was glad he was there for them now, as Roy recovered

from his heart attack. But being there came with a heavy dose of guilt for leaving all those years ago and not visiting often enough. Some might say catching his girlfriend and business partner in bed together was the worst thing a man could endure. Reed knew otherwise. It had been a blessing in disguise, the catalyst to sell his business and return home to rebuild his relationships with his relatives. He'd thought it was odd that he'd felt worse about selling his business than he had about losing his girlfriend, but after seeing Grace, he knew he'd never been in love with Alina.

He was done making any more half-assed attempts at filling the emptiness in his heart.

"How's the Montgomery job going?" Roy asked. He was getting stronger every day, but Reed knew it was killing him not to be healthy enough to handle the renovations himself. For as long as Reed could remember, Roy had worked from sunup until well past sundown, and he had never failed to take his wife out every Saturday night. He'd also made time to teach Reed about building, renovations, historical preservation, and everything in between, while doling out important life lessons. They'd tossed footballs, reviewed school projects, and talked about everything from dating to his father—a sore subject for both of them.

"She's a beauty of a house." Reed speared a piece of steak with his fork, thinking about the headstrong look in Grace's eyes as she'd pranced across the grass in that pretty little dress. He'd been sure she was going to give him hell, until she'd turned tail and scurried away.

His uncle arched a gray brow. "And?"

And he'd wished like hell she had given him grief or said something. *Anything.* Reed shrugged. "Nothing. It's not that big of a job, although I did find some sheathing that needs replacing. It's a gorgeous porch."

"Is that why you look like your insides are trying to climb out?" Roy asked. "You've dealt with these situations before."

Reed ground his teeth together, annoyed with his own transparency. While he and Grace had kept their relationship a secret from Grace's family for fear of one of her younger siblings accidentally exposing them, he'd never kept it from his aunt and uncle. He'd been so head over heels with her he'd wanted to share his happiness with the people he loved most, and he'd finally invited her for dinner. They were careful not to spend too much time at his house, as his classmates lived on the same street and he didn't want to cause trouble for Grace. Unfortunately, his aunt and uncle had also borne witness to the longing that had eventually driven him away from the memories, and away from them.

There was no sense trying to hide his discomfort. "Grace is in town visiting her parents."

Roy and Ella exchanged a curious, and concerned, glance.

"Don't worry," Reed reassured them. "It won't interfere with my doing the job."

Roy set his normally jovial, and now serious, gray-blue eyes on Reed and said, "The job's the last of my concerns."

"Your hearts were once one, honey," Ella said with an empathetic gaze. Her dark hair was flecked with white around her temples, and crow's-feet lined her warm brown eyes. Ella was a petite woman with narrow shoulders, pin-straight posture, and a kind word always at the ready. She'd been the best mother Reed could ever hope for, and although she'd always been as dainty as Roy was rugged, Reed had noticed an unfamiliar strength in Ella since Roy's incident. Where Roy had always been an overprotective husband, now it seemed Ella had taken on the same role toward him.

"It's been a long time. I'm fine." Reed shoveled food in his mouth to try to bury the lie.

Ella and Roy had always sat beside each other at meals, and until now Reed hadn't thought much about it. But now he understood that urge to be as close as possible to the person they loved. And hell if he wasn't feeling the same way about Grace.

Ella set her hand on Roy's, and with a warm gaze locked on her husband, she said, "The heart never forgets a first love."

Reed looked around the cozy dining room. The walls were littered with family photographs. There was one of him and Roy standing in front of a church that Roy had renovated and another of Reed standing by the river holding up a fishing pole with a perch proudly displayed. A photo hanging across the room showed his gap-toothed smile beaming out from behind one of Ella's homemade birthday cakes, six candles brightly lit. There was a lifetime of memories within these walls.

"*Anyway,*" Reed said, needing to change the subject. "I was glad not to find too much decay in the foundation of the porch. Marilynn had been prepared to reduce the size of the porch rather than replace it because of cost." Thinking of Grace and the flowers he used to sneak up to her porch, he said, "Who knows what memories we would have been casting aside."

"You're just as nostalgic as your uncle," Ella said warmly. "But, honey, memories live in our hearts. Whether the physical place or person changes or remains the same makes no difference. Someday you'll find a woman who will fall in love with that old-school charm of yours."

If his track record was any measure of his relationship abilities, he wouldn't bet on that.

Reed rose to clear the table, and Ella reached for his hand. "Honey, leave the dishes. It's Saturday night. Why don't you go out, relax, and have fun for a while? You could go to the county fair."

He remembered wanting to take Grace to the fair when they were in high school, but the goddamn rivalry bullshit had gotten in the way.

No, thank you. He'd stay as far away from that fair as he could.

"I have painting to do at my place. Besides, I saw the guys this morning." His ass was still sore from taking the first ride on that wild horse. But man, had it been exhilarating. He'd become reacquainted with Shane Jericho when he'd first arrived back in town and was working on a barn renovation. They'd been the ultimate rivals in high school, but they'd instantly hit it off. Shane and a couple of his siblings ran their parents' cattle business and horse ranch. Funny how a few years could change people.

He wondered just how much Grace had changed.

"Yes, but working with horses at dawn is not exactly relaxing," Ella said.

"I'm not here to relax, Aunt Ella. I'm here to help." Although he had to admit that after working in the hot sun all day and thinking about why the hell Grace had practically run away from him, he could use a drink—or three.

"Reed, honey, we appreciate how attentive you've been, and Lord knows that it's wonderful to have you back home for good," Ella said. "But you're a young, good-looking guy, and there are plenty of pretty women in our town. Go out. Have some fun."

He was tempted to do just that, if only to take his mind off

Grace. Some of the guys were going to a creek party tonight. A few laughs might do him some good.

"Go on, boy," Roy urged. "Get the hell out of here, and give me and my woman a little privacy."

"Well, if you put it that way." Reed laughed.

Forty minutes later, he parked his truck alongside a few dozen others at Jericho Ridge and followed the sounds of laughter and live music toward the creek. The air smelled of burning wood, pine, and sweet perfume. His boots sank into the dirt as he came to a clearing at the bottom of the hill. The night was alive with couples bumping and grinding to the music along the creek bank. Between ending his partnership, moving, and taking over his uncle's business, he hadn't really taken any time to relax. He made his way through the crowd, scanning the familiar faces he'd come to know over the past few months. It was still weird, seeing them as friends rather than rivals, but the air buzzed with positive energy, and he felt the stress of the day falling away.

"Hey, Reed!" Shayla, the redhead who worked at the Stardust Café where he often stopped for coffee before work, waved from down by the water.

He smiled, waved, and headed for his buddy Chet Hudson, a firefighter, who was standing near the band with Trace and JJ. He made his way toward them and spotted Sable playing the guitar. His mind immediately went to Grace, and he scanned the crowd again, looking for the tall brunette whom he seemed to piss off at every turn.

"Reed." Chet slapped him on the back. "How's it going, dude? I wondered if you'd make it tonight."

"I wasn't sure I would, but I'm glad I did." *Especially knowing Grace might be here.* "How's it going?"

41

"Hot women, cold beer, good music. Life is good," Trace said, clinking his beer with JJ's. He reached into a cooler at his feet and handed a cold bottle to Reed. "Here you go, brother."

"Thanks." He cracked it open and took a long swallow. "I forgot Sable played in a band. I thought she just owned that garage in town."

"Surge," Chet reminded him. "Her band has been together since high school."

"I remember," Reed said. "They played at halftime our senior year. Seems like a lifetime ago."

"Cougars!" Trace hollered.

"Mustangs all the way," Reed retorted.

Chet nodded in agreement. He was from Meadowside, too.

"Don't start that high school bullshit," JJ said. "The last thing I want to see is you two tumbling in the dirt over whose team is better. It sure seemed like everything back then, didn't it?"

Trace bumped shoulders with Reed. "Anyway. Sable's hot, right? She's single, too. You should take a crack at her."

Reed laughed under his breath and took another swig of his beer, noticing the way Chet's eyes narrowed at Trace's remark. "Thanks, but uh…" *I'd rather find Grace.* "I'm cool."

"If I had a dollar for every time I heard that lie," Beckett Wheeler said from behind him. Beckett was a bigwig investor and another of Reed's former rivals—but then again, weren't they all?

At six foot two, Reed and Beckett stood eye to eye. "Hey, Beck. How's it hanging?"

"Long and straight. You?" He flashed an arrogant grin.

Reed laughed. It was hard to believe these were the same guys he'd stared down across the football field.

"Well, Reed Cross," Beckett said in a hushed tone. "Don't turn around, because there's a whole lot of pretty women checking out the *cool* guy."

Reed turned, and a group of twentysomethings he didn't recognize smiled flirtatiously, whispering to one another as they eyed him up. Reed smiled, but his eyes fell beyond the group to Grace, wearing the same summery dress she'd had on earlier in the day. She stood by the bonfire with her sisters Morgyn and Brindle, who were chatting, their gazes gliding over the crowd, while Grace fidgeted with her beer bottle. He recalled that nervous habit from when they were kids. It was a soda bottle back then, but the way she tapped her index finger on the glass told him she wasn't comfortable.

He watched her for a few minutes, drinking in the way her hair kept falling in front of her eyes and the little shake of her head she used to brush it away, only for it to fall right back again. Another familiar mannerism. She used to do the same thing when she was younger. *At least some things haven't changed.*

"Dude!" Trace hollered.

Reed turned just in time to see JJ shove Trace into the creek, then double over laughing. Trace reached up and hauled JJ into the water. Then all hell broke loose. Women screamed and shouts filled the air as people began kicking off their boots and shoes. Guys tore off their shirts, and girls egged them on, running barefoot into the water.

"Let's go!" Brindle grabbed Morgyn's hand, dragging her off the bank. "Come on, Grace!"

Reed's attention homed in on Grace as she backed toward the woods. He remembered skinny-dipping with her in this very creek when they were alone at night, and it saddened him to see her trying to escape the fun.

"Woo-hoo!" A guy sprinted past and into the water. A group of women shrieked as he splashed them.

Seconds later the creek was full, leaving only a few stragglers on the banks. Reed tugged off his boots and socks, then closed the distance between him and Grace.

"Reed?" Her eyes widened as he reached for her arm. "No!"

"You're not in the city anymore, Grace." He hoisted her into his arms and she pushed at his chest. "It's time to have some fun."

"Put me down! What the hell do you think you're doing?" She fought and kicked as he neared the edge of the creek. "My shoes! My dress!"

He flipped her sandals off and they tumbled to the dirt. "I can take your dress off, too, if you'd like." He laughed, lost in the feel of having her back in his arms.

"Put. Me. Down!" she demanded.

He ignored her pleas. She flailed and struggled to no avail as everyone around them laughed and splashed. "Stop fighting me, Gracie. You won't win."

She screamed and pleaded, and as he waded into deeper water, her arms and legs wrapped around him. Damn, she felt incredible, bringing back more sinful memories. Memories he'd like to relive.

"No! *Please!* Stop!" Her hair blew around her face, and she had a wild, sexy look in her eyes.

"With you hanging on to me like this? Not a chance in hell." Cold water inched up his waist and over her hips. He gripped her thighs, feeling their warmth against his palms.

"Reed!"

She began climbing him like a tree to keep from getting wet, which only made him laugh and hold on tighter. Her lips were a whisper away. He was sure he'd died and gone to heaven. The hell with what happened all those years go. The heat in her eyes held him captive as she crushed her sweet softness against him, her body contradicting the anger in her voice. The rest of the party faded away, until there was nothing but the warmth of Grace's breath on his cheeks, the look of longing in her eyes, and the feel of her hands pressing into the back of his neck as he lowered his lips to hers, taking the kiss he'd spent years missing.

GRACE WAS LOST in a sea of steamy sensations. Reed's mouth was as possessive and demanding as she'd remembered. He tasted of beer and potent male, an intoxicating combination underscored by the hard press of his chest against hers. One rough hand moved along her thigh, then cupped her ass so firmly, her entire body clenched with desire. His other arm circled her body like a seat belt, keeping her close as his fingers threaded into her hair and then fisted *tight*. She'd forgotten the sting of that grip, but her body hadn't. Ripples of lust slithered through her, and her hips rocked forward. His scruff abraded her cheeks as he angled her face to the exact place he wanted and took the kiss deeper. Even through their clothes and the cold water splashing her skin, heat blazed between them.

Grace buried her hands in his hair, meeting every luscious stroke of his tongue with an eagerness of her own. Reed didn't just kiss. He *took* and *consumed*. Every move brought a tightening of his arms, making it hard to breathe—and oh, that was glorious! *This* was the element that was missing from every single kiss she'd ever had after leaving Oak Falls. This intensity, the way his biceps pulsed against her and his body anchored her.

"Grace…"

His gravelly voice trailed off, but that didn't keep it from winding through her like liquid fire. "Reed—" His name slipped from her lips, hungry and needy. Her eyes flew open. "*Reed!* Oh shit! No, no, no." She struggled to free herself, but his grip was too tight.

"Calm down," he said.

"Don't tell me to calm down! We *kissed!*" *Oh God!* What was she thinking?

"Several times in fact," he said all too smugly, and flashed that boyish, lopsided smile that made her heart flip-flop. "We haven't lost it, Gracie. Our kisses could start a firestorm."

"Don't talk about it!" *Firestorm? They could cause an earthquake!* She pushed on his shoulders, trying not to get sidetracked by the endearment he'd used, which made her heart tumble. She had to get away from him before any other organs became reckless. All around them people laughed and splashed. She was glad to see Brindle and Morgyn too preoccupied with Trace and his friends to have noticed her momentary indiscretion.

"Admit it. Our kisses are fucking hot, Grace." Reed tightened his grip on her, a challenge simmering in his eyes.

"*Fine.* Our kisses are still hot." *More like toe-curling.* "Now will you let me down?"

"You sure you want me to?" He waggled his brows.

No—and that's a problem. "Yes, please. *Now.*"

He slowly lowered her until her thighs skimmed the frigid water. She squealed and scrambled back up his body, clinging to him like her life depended on it.

A deep laugh rumbled up Reed's chest, and he held on tight, his hands splayed across her soaking-wet panties. Like one of Pavlov's dogs, her sex clenched with anticipation, and she groaned.

"Reed, please!" She pointed to the grass and saw Sable standing on the banks, watching them with an amused expression. *Damn it.* She'd never hear the end of this.

He carried her out of the water and set her feet on the grass. Grace wrapped her arms around herself to ward off the cold as she scanned the ground for her sandals. Her heart was beating so hard she was sure he could hear it.

"Gracie." He reached for her hand. His gaze was softer now, and his smile less challenging, tempered even.

"It's *Grace*," she said, shivering.

"You'll always be Gracie to me."

Was he purposely trying to turn her insides into pretzels? She never should have come out tonight. "That was part of our problem," she said before she could stop herself. "I'm not small-town *Gracie* anymore, Reed."

His eyes turned serious. "I know. You're an award-winning playwright and producer, and I'm happy for you."

She lowered her gaze, feeling stupid for making such a point about her name, and when she looked up again, she was bowled over by how much she wanted to say to him. But she had no idea how, or where, to start. How could she ask him why he'd told her he'd never even consider leaving his family and then done so only a few weeks later? She couldn't, that's how.

Instead she said, "Thank you, but it sounds more glamorous than it is."

"Can we talk? Sit by the fire, dry off for a bit?"

"Talk? Or are you going to try to put those weapons on me

again?"

"Weapons?" He arched a brow.

She had to laugh at his confused expression. "Your lips. They're like crack. *No,* worse than crack. They're like a sip of beer to an alcoholic. One sip leads to a shot, which leads to a glass, then a bottle, and the next thing you know, I'm passed out in your bed—"

He stepped closer, the heat in his eyes stealing her voice. His wet jeans grazed her thighs, wreaking havoc with more than her voice. She took a step back, but his hand swept around her waist, keeping her close. "I'll keep my lips to myself. We've got a decade of bad feelings between us, Gracie, and a few kisses sent me right back to where we were all those years ago. I'm pretty sure you were right there with me."

She opened her mouth to deny it but realized it would be an outright lie.

"I'm going to be working at your parents' house for a while. All I'm asking is to clear the air."

"It's a bad idea," she said too quickly. "I mean…It's a good idea to clear the air, but no more kisses."

"No more kisses," he agreed, though his arrogant smile told her he didn't believe she wanted that rule.

"No touching, either." She peeled his hand from around her waist.

He held both hands up, his amused smile making him even more handsome. "No touching. Anything else?"

"It would be great if you could stop breathing. It hinders my ability to think rationally."

That earned another sexy laugh. "No can do, Gracie. Fair warning, I might use that to my advantage."

"I'd expect nothing less," she said with a smile. She'd wondered over the years if she'd exaggerated or romanticized his personality, but she hadn't. He was still as honest and affable as ever.

"Do I get to make rules, too?" he asked.

Save for his demanding kisses, Reed had never been one to ask anything from her. They'd seen each other only when they could steal away undetected. Sable had covered for her after she'd caught Grace sneaking out one night and learned of their secret relationship, but still, it had never been enough time. She'd always wanted more, but she'd been afraid of the grief she'd get from her friends if they knew she was dating the rival quarterback. Grace had complained more about their lack of time together than Reed had. Now it all seemed so silly, but back then the rivalry between schools had felt like a black cloud hanging over them.

She figured she owed him a rule or two and said, "Go for it."

"No hiding from the truth." He held her steady gaze. "That's all I ask. We did so much hiding when we were kids. I just want to lay it all out in the open."

Could she do that? Tell him how hurt she'd been when he'd left town, when she knew she'd already made her choice and had no right to be hurt?

"What do you say, Grace? The ball is in your court."

The last time she'd held the ball she'd walked *off* the court and had regretted it ever since—despite knowing she'd done the right thing for herself at the time. She was older now, and she knew better than to start something that would end in heartache. Surely they could handle being friends.

"Okay," she said, earning another panty-melting smile. *Down, girl.*

Reed retrieved her sandals and his boots, and as they made their way toward the bonfire, she was glad she was soaking wet, because she was playing with fire. She needed all the help she could get to douse the flames.

Chapter Five

THE HEAT OF the fire warmed Grace, but she was still shivering, and she knew it had more to do with nerves than cold as she stood in the wet grass beside Reed. Even the heavy musk of burning wood wasn't enough to erase Reed's alluring scent. If confidence and loyalty had a scent, it would smell like Reed. The thought was odd, given how badly he'd hurt her by leaving town, but it was there in her head, as real as the man standing beside her. He looked like a million bucks in drenched denim and soaked cotton, while her sisters had made fun of her *city dress*—a simple princess-waisted summer dress with diamond patterns and an A-line skirt—amplifying her insecurities about not fitting in with the country setting.

"Sorry I startled you this morning," Reed said as he stepped closer, his arm brushing hers.

Had he always insisted on standing so close? It wasn't exactly awkward standing there with him, but it wasn't completely comfortable, either. She didn't know how to react to the tingling his touch sparked, or where to start in the whole coming-clean process. But she didn't like anyone knowing she wasn't in complete control and said, "It's okay. Sorry if I was bitchy, but nobody warned me you were here."

"Who could have warned you? Nobody knew about us back then except my aunt and uncle." He glanced at the people climbing out of the creek. "It's like we were some kind of dirty little secret."

She swallowed hard against the truth. "We were a secret, but not dirty. Just young and stupid. Sable and Sophie knew. They both covered for me sometimes, remember? But I think Sable gets a kick out of shocking me."

He laughed softly, eyeing her rebellious sister, who was playing the guitar across the lawn. "I had forgotten about Sable knowing. I guess we don't owe her one anymore." His gaze swept down Grace's body, and an appreciative smile lifted his lips. "You look incredible tonight."

"Thanks, but according to Brindle and Morgyn, my dress looks *matronly*." She tugged at the wet material clinging to her legs. "It's perfect for a summer party in the city, but I sort of stick out like a sore thumb here."

"That was always part of our problem." His expression turned solemn. "You were never supposed to fit in or look like everyone else, but you thought you were. You thought being different was a bad thing, when really, you were meant to stand out. You outshone everyone back then, Grace. And you did the right thing, breaking things off with me and leaving town to follow your dreams. I was just too young and blinded by my feelings to see it."

The sincerity in his voice cut through her like a knife, but the old hurt rolled in again and came out without warning. "I didn't want to end things with you, but you said you'd never leave Meadowside." *And then you did.* She swallowed those words, but holding them in made her feel like a bomb ready to explode, and she started breathing harder. "I can't do this here."

"No hiding from the truth, remember?"

She lowered her voice to a harsh whisper as partygoers began gathering around the fire. "I'm not *hiding*, but I'm not going to air our dirty laundry around all these gossip mongers."

He put a hand on her lower back, guiding her away from the bonfire. "Then let's do it in private."

Unsure if she wanted to lay her heart on the line after all, she glanced up the hill toward the parking area and considered leaving, but how could she? She'd ridden over with Sable, and her sister would need her truck to get herself and all her gear home.

"Come on," he said, urging her toward the hill with his hand on her back again. "I've got a jacket in my truck you can use to keep warm, and we'll find someplace private to talk."

Her pulse quickened at the idea of being alone with him, even though she knew once they started talking, her hurt wouldn't allow for any line crossing. "You're soaked. Maybe we should do this another time."

"I'm fine, and we're doing this now," he said sternly.

"When did you get so pushy?"

His eyes narrowed. "Since kissing the woman who still sets my world on fire after a freaking decade."

There was no mistaking the authority in his tone, and Lord help her, because all her loneliest parts were waving surrender flags. "I have to tell Sable I'm getting a ride home."

She headed for Sable, and he moved with her. "Reed. I can do this alone."

"Right. Sorry." He shook his head as if he hadn't realized he'd been following her and crossed his arms, watching as she slipped her feet into her sandals and headed for Sable.

She felt the heat of his gaze blazing a trail behind her and

Sable's hawklike focus on her up ahead. By the time she reached Sable, she was annoyed about being caught in a web of inspection.

Sable stopped playing her guitar and called out, "You leaving with Reed?" so loud that everyone around her looked over.

Great. Grace would probably be the talk of the town at Gossip Central, aka Stardust Café, tomorrow. She made a point of answering loud enough for everyone to hear. "He's just driving me home. I'll see you there."

Or maybe she was really trying to deliver that message to herself. As she made her way back to Reed, every step brought a thrum of anticipation followed by a pang of anxiety.

Reed fell into step beside her.

"It's like you're ready to step into the shoes we filled all those years ago," she said, even though she didn't know if that was true. She needed boundaries, more rules, or *something.* Feeling out his intentions gave her a modicum of control. "I outgrew those shoes. I'm sure you did, too."

"I don't want to fill those old shoes, Grace," he said as she slowed her pace. "I'm just not afraid to admit that I still feel something for you, and I don't want to pretend otherwise."

She stopped walking and studied his face for a moment. He was dead serious.

"Ready?" he asked.

"I honestly have no idea, but I have a feeling we need to find out."

He cocked a grin and returned his hand to her lower back as they ascended the hill, as if he already knew the answer, sending her stomach into knots again.

"That's what you said the first time I convinced you to meet me after school," he reminded her. "Remember?"

Yeah, she remembered all right. They'd seen each other at football games, and she'd ended up searching for him when their teams went head-to-head. Then she'd seen him in town at the public library, where she used to hang out with Sophie. He'd asked her to meet him there after school one day, and that had been the start of it all.

"I'm going to take that smile as a yes," he said as he opened the door to his truck and retrieved the jacket he'd promised. He held it up, and then his expression became pinched and he tossed it behind the front seat. "Hold on."

"What's wrong with that jacket?"

He ignored her question and dug around back there, pulling out a navy hooded sweatshirt. He helped her put it on, and the smile that crept across his lips as the soft cotton tumbled down her hips was one of sheer pleasure.

"That's better, Gracie. Just like the old days."

"In the old days my clothes wouldn't be wet."

He helped her into the truck and said, "At least not the clothes anyone else saw."

He closed the door and sauntered around the truck to the driver's side as if he hadn't nearly made her swallow her tongue.

REED WAS FUCKED. Royally screwed. He put on the heat in the cab of the truck for Grace, but he was sweating like a bulldog. She'd always heated him up from the inside out, but now that they'd kissed, he couldn't stop thinking about doing it again. They had things to work out, but man...

He tried to focus on the road, but he couldn't think past

Grace being beside him again. Had she always been there, even in her absence? Was that why he'd never fallen for anyone else?

As if guided by echoes of their past, he drove to the Majestic Theater at the edge of town. The stone theater had more character than any other property for miles around. He parked at the front entrance, which was curved, bowing outward in a semicircle, with a black-and-white painted marquee above a set of weathered maroon and glass double doors that read MA EST C (the "c" was missing the curve at the top). The side entrance was taller, with two grand, and horrifically marred, stone pillars with ionic capitals on either side of the arched doorway, and above, the frieze, or the horizontal portion above the columns, had alternating patterns of triglyphs and metopes usually found in Greek architecture. Reed imagined the building in pristine condition, with its low sloped roofs of varying heights, which made it look as if it were layered. The front doors were flanked by boarded-up spaces where windows had once been, giving the building the appearance of a sleeping, aged monster.

Reed wanted to get his hands on the beast and bring it back to its original beauty. It had been abandoned since they were kids, which had made the field behind the building the perfect make-out spot. His pulse kicked up, remembering the night they'd both lost their virginity in that field.

Good times.

He felt Grace glaring at him.

"Seriously? Here?" She laughed under her breath.

"I thought we weren't hiding from our past." He stepped from the truck and grabbed his extra pair of jeans from behind his seat, aware of Grace watching him as he stripped off his drenched jeans.

"What are you doing?" she asked.

"Taking off my wet clothes."

"Oh my God." She turned and looked out the passenger window.

"It's not like you haven't seen me naked before."

"Still! That was years ago!" she snapped, shielding her eyes with her hand. "You keep clothes in your truck?"

"Pants and a shirt. I'll have to go commando." He finished putting on his dry pants and then came around to help her out.

She scowled as she climbed from the truck. "Did you say that just so I'd think about you being naked under those jeans?"

"No, but now that you said that, it's a nice benefit." He chuckled as she rolled her eyes.

"I just can't believe you brought me here."

"Where did you want me to take you? It's not like the house I bought came furnished, and besides, I'm still renovating, and you're staying with your parents. Come on, it'll be like old times."

"No, it will *not*. You promised to keep your lips to yourself."

"Yeah, but *you* didn't." He grabbed hold of her hand with the tease and led her around the theater, to the very spot where they'd spent dozens of nights lost in each other's arms. She tried to pull her hand free, but he held on tight. He knew his Gracie, and she would storm off and walk home before she'd admit to wanting to kiss him. He wasn't about to let that happen. They needed to talk.

She finally stopped trying to yank free and said, "Wait. I just realized what you said. I thought you were just here helping your uncle. You bought a *house?*"

"I told you I'm not going anywhere. I've been here for four

months, and your parents' porch is the last of my uncle's company's commitments. I've made solid investments. I can afford to be picky and only take on projects that I'm excited about. I've got some irons in the fire. I'm joining forces with my uncle so he'll never be in this position again. It's about time Cross and Son made our debut."

They stopped walking and both looked out over the abandoned railroad tracks, the boundary line between Meadowside and Oak Falls. They'd always sat on the Oak Falls side of the tracks, though as far as Reed remembered, it hadn't been a conscious decision. Now he wondered if it really had. He'd have done anything to make sure Grace was comfortable.

"Cross and *Son*." Her expression warmed. "That's great, Reed. That's what you had hoped to do when we were kids. But does that mean your father never came around?"

He gazed into the darkness, trying to mask the anger toward his absentee father that never failed to simmer just beneath his skin. "Nope, but I'm over it. The last thing I need in my life is someone who doesn't want to be there."

"That's a shame. I'm so sorry. I'd hoped you two might one day have a relationship."

She looked sweetly sexy with his sweatshirt hiding her gorgeous figure, and genuinely hurt for him, with an unsure look in her eyes. Her hair was wild from their struggles in the creek, and her long legs were like roads to a treasure trove of smarts, sassiness, and sultry seduction. As gorgeous as she was, it had always been Grace's heart that he'd been most attracted to. She'd worried endlessly over him, her siblings, and mostly Sable, who acted like the last thing she wanted was an overprotective sister. He'd secretly wondered if that big heart of hers might become her downfall, causing her to decide not to leave home for college, or when she did, to come running back, giving up her dreams to make sure they were all okay.

But Grace had proven to be even stronger than he'd imagined. Not that he'd hoped she'd give up her dreams for him, but he'd worried she might. He'd been so conflicted by then, he'd supported her dreams instead of confessing how much he'd wanted her to stay.

Trying once again not to get mired down in their past, he waved to the grass, still holding her hand. "Want to sit or take a walk?"

"Walk," she said quickly, giving away her nervousness.

They followed the railroad tracks, as they'd done so many times before, along the open fields that ran behind the buildings at the entrance to town.

"Nothing's changed," she said. "It's hard to believe they never fixed up the theater."

She glanced up at him through long, dark lashes, and electricity arced between them. It wasn't just the sparks of sexual tension heating up the air; it felt complicated and layered, and it vibrated with as much hurtful history as it did hopeful sensuality. She shifted her eyes away, and he felt her hold his hand a little tighter. *Good.* He wasn't alone in his confusion.

"Some things have changed," he said, "but until they're willing to sell the theater to someone who wants to pour blood, sweat, and tears into it, it'll remain empty."

"Good luck with that. People around here have had the same jobs, the same *lives*, forever." She winced. "Sorry. That probably sounded snotty."

"No, it's true. But it's one of the things I like about it here. I like that the place we came together is still the same as it always was and that the library still has our initials carved in a tree out back. And that the diner where my aunt and uncle took me to celebrate every birthday is still here and run by the same couple." He stopped walking and turned toward her. "And I like that you're here, and that we ran into each other. I never stopped thinking about you, Grace."

Her lips parted as if she was going to say something, but just as quickly, she pressed them together.

"Why is this so hard for you, when everything between us used to be so easy?"

She fidgeted with the hem of his sweatshirt, and he grasped for something to get her talking.

"I put an offer in on the theater."

Shock registered in her eyes. "You...? What are you trying to do? Re-create the past?"

"Hardly. Do you think I want to relive losing you all over again?" He let that sink in for a minute. The property was a smart investment. The closest movie theater, a large cineplex, was thirty minutes away and about as personable as a highway. Reopening the theater would not only offer local entertainment, but it would also provide employment opportunities and hopefully stir up the economy for the small town. But those weren't the main reasons he'd purchased it.

"It came on the market a few weeks before I got back to town. I had no idea we'd find each other again beyond a quick hello when you were here to visit. Breathing new life into historic buildings is what I do for a living. This theater might not be designated as historic, but it's an iconic landmark to the area, and to me. I feel *good* when I'm here. Some of my best memories took place right behind this theater. Why *wouldn't* I try to buy it?"

"It's just surprising, that's all. Suddenly you're back and

you're buying up property. My mother said you were some type of historic preservation expert, but…"

"I don't know about *expert*, but I love what I do," he said humbly, downplaying the fact that he'd been one of the leading preservationists in Michigan. None of that mattered. He hadn't become an expert for notoriety. He'd followed his passion.

"I couldn't pass up a chance at restoring this beauty. The deal isn't sealed yet, but I'm hoping it comes through. It's the perfect project for Roy and me to kick off our business." He'd purchased it on his own, but if this deal came through, Cross and Son would be known for making it shine. "But I don't want to spend our time talking about work. Tell me what you were about to say back at the creek."

Her eyes shifted away again.

"Come on, Gracie. Since when have you shied away from speaking your mind?"

"Since speaking my mind means bringing up the things that hurt most."

He reached for her other hand, and she didn't try to pull it away, which surprised him. "All the more reason to get it out in the open. We're either going to be friends or we're going to be lovers, but we're *not* going to be enemies."

She shook both hands free and set them on her hips with an appalled expression. "When did you get so full of yourself?"

"I'm not full of myself. We said we weren't going to hide from the truth. I'm just throwing it all out there. Here, you want me to start with the hard stuff?" He pushed a hand through his hair and paced a few steps before stopping and meeting her gaze again. His chest constricted, but he wasn't going to let that stop him from finally saying the things he never could.

"It sucked that you chose college over me, but I get it. Maybe I didn't then, but who can process that at eighteen? I loved you, Gracie. When you left, you tore my heart out." He shrugged, pained by the hurt in her eyes, but he was tired of harboring bad feelings and tired of the bullshit he'd put up with in Michigan. He was never going to live his life in the dark again.

"Then why did you tell me you wouldn't ever leave this place?" Her voice escalated, and she crossed her arms.

"Because I didn't plan on leaving. I didn't *want* to leave."

Her fingers pressed into her flesh. "Right. That's why you left less than a month later. At least I was strong enough to be honest and end the relationship. You hid behind what you *really* wanted to do." Her hands flew out to her sides. "Why couldn't you have just told me that you didn't want to be with me anymore? Why did you play that stupid game and pretend like you wanted me to follow my dreams? To make it easier for you to do what you really wanted?"

She'd totally lost him. "What are you talking about?"

"Don't play games with me, Reed. *You* wanted to talk about this."

"You're damn right I do." Irritation surged within him. "You can't seriously believe I ever wanted anything but to be with you. I *told* you I'd wait for you. It was *you* who said I'd be wasting my time."

"Because I never wanted to make my life *here*!" She accentuated her statement by pointing at the ground.

"Right. So why are you pissed at me?" He stepped closer, searching her eyes for a hint of what he was missing.

"Because you *left*, Reed! You hightailed it out of here as fast as you could! You couldn't leave for me, but someone or something made you *feel* enough, or *love* enough, or—" Her eyes glistened with tears, and she turned away.

"Grace…"

"*Don't.* Is this what you wanted?" She faced him again, tears streaming down her cheeks, and his heart cracked open. "To see that you hurt me?"

"Hell no." He reached for her, but she pulled away. "Gracie, stop. You've got it all wrong."

She swiped at her tears. "It's not hard to see the truth. You should take me home."

He pulled her into his arms, resisting her struggles. "No. You can be as mad as you want, but I'm not leaving until you hear the truth."

"I didn't come with you tonight to relive everything."

"Then why did you come with me?" he challenged, and when she stared him down without responding, he said, "I'll tell you why, Grace. Because whatever we felt in that creek tonight is too goddamn big to ignore. We were kids back then, but we weren't too stupid to know that this"—he tugged her tighter against him, and the air rushed from her lungs. Her fingers dug into his sides—"was *real.* First love or not, I've never felt anything like I did when I was with you. And when we kissed tonight? *Damn,* Grace…"

He released her, but she didn't let go, her eyes imploring him. His arms circled her again. "I didn't leave for anyone else. It was the last thing I wanted to do. But I *had* to get the hell out of here. Staying here was too fucking hard. I saw you *everywhere.* Every time I got in my car, it was your perfume I smelled, your laugh I heard. When I went to the creek, it was you I remembered splashing in the water with. I get why you left, why you *needed* to leave. You did the right thing, Grace. I know that now, but you took a piece of me with you, and I have tried to find that feeling again, but…"

"You haven't found it," she said in a voice full of wonder, as if she'd been chasing the same ghosts.

He shook his head. "Not once."

"My heart broke when you left town. I know that's not fair. I was going away to school anyway, but I thought—"

"Whatever it was, you thought wrong, Gracie." He moved his hands up her back, bringing her even closer, leaving her no room at all. "You broke me when you left, even though you'd always said you were destined to be a city girl, and I knew you meant it. I wanted it for you, for all your dreams to come true. I expected it. But it still tore me apart."

"It broke me, too. I just couldn't admit it, or I'd never have left."

"After you were gone, I couldn't see two feet in front of myself without seeing you, and once I left for Michigan, all of that made it hard to come back and visit, which is a whole other story. We both loved and lost, and I know I promised I wouldn't kiss you again, but I want t—"

She went up on her toes and pressed her lips to his in a surprisingly gentle, tentative kiss. Her tethered desire was a fierce aphrodisiac, and he slid his tongue along the seam of her lips. When she opened her mouth, he pushed both hands into her hair, intensifying his efforts. Their kisses turned messy and urgent, both of them giving and taking in equal measure. Everything else slipped away, until there was only him and Grace and their mind-blowing connection.

They came away as slowly as they'd come together. Grace's hands slipped from his sides. One covered her mouth, and the other touched her stomach. Her gaze drifted around them as if she was as dazed by their powerful connection as he was.

"It's still real, Gracie."

She looked as conflicted as he'd felt when he'd first seen her. "I shouldn't have…We can't do this."

He took her hand in his and said, "We can."

"It can't go anywhere," she said half-heartedly.

He couldn't stop the grin he felt tugging at his lips. "I can think of several places it can go."

A nervous laugh slipped from her lips, and he was glad to see her smile.

"Reed…" She took a step back and looked at their joined hands. "I think you should take me back to my parents' house."

As her hand slipped away, he said, "Grace—" But his voice was lost as she headed for the truck.

The drive to her parents' house was tense and quiet, each lost in their own thoughts. He parked in the driveway, and for a minute they sat in silence, reminiscent of those last days before they'd broken up. Old ghosts coming back to haunt. Back then Reed had been a boy on the cusp of manhood, about to have the rug pulled out from under him. He wasn't that boy anymore, and there was no rug to pull.

He came around to the passenger side and opened Grace's door. When she turned to step out, he took her in a slow, sensual kiss, the way she used to love. He felt her go soft against him, and maybe it made him a prick, but he used the ability to read her body language to his advantage and took the kiss deeper. He kissed her until she was barely breathing, and then he continued making love to her mouth until she trembled in his arms. Only then did he draw away, leaving a trail of light kisses in his wake.

Grace's eyes remained closed.

He slid his hand to the nape of her neck and whispered, "Breathe, Gracie. I'll always be your greedy boy when it comes to your kisses." She used to call him *greedy boy* because he could never get enough.

She blinked several times, as if she were trying to bring him back into focus, and then, without a word, she stepped from the truck. He walked her to the door, wondering what she was thinking. Hell, he didn't know what *he* was thinking.

When they reached the porch, he leaned in to kiss her cheek, and she put her hand flat on his chest, stopping him from coming too close.

Flashing a shy smile, which felt familiar, and somehow also way too distant, she reached for the doorknob and said, "Thank you for tonight," and walked inside, leaving him to wonder what she was thanking him for. The talk? The ride? The kisses?

As he opened the truck door, he glanced at her childhood bedroom window and caught her peeking out. His chest constricted as the curtains swished into place.

Welcome home, Gracie.

Chapter Six

GRACE TURNED OFF the hair dryer Sunday morning, and her sisters' voices floated in through the bathroom door, which was ajar.

"Finally," Sable said.

Groaning inwardly, Grace ran a quick brush through her hair and began putting on her makeup. "Don't you have auto work to do?"

"Not on Sunday."

Morgyn? Grace pushed the door open with her foot and found Morgyn lying on her stomach in the middle of the bed reading Grace's *Theatre Arts* magazine, her hippie skirt a colorful sea puddled around her knees. Her booted feet hovered precariously close to Grace's pillow, and her long blond hair cascaded over her shoulders, pinned to her forehead by a slim tie-dyed headband. Beside her, Sable sat on the edge of the bed in cutoffs, boots, and a skintight red T-shirt, flipping through Grace's stack of scripts. Even though she'd grown up with several no-boundaries siblings, after living on her own for so long, she found the intrusion jarring.

"Hey, M," Grace said. "What are you doing here?"

Morgyn grinned. "You left the party with a very hot, very

available man last night. Brindle said she'd kick my butt if I didn't tell her all the details."

It was bad enough that Grace had kissed Reed and hadn't slept worth a darn. Did she have to face an inquisition, too? "Where is Brindle?" She leaned closer to the mirror as she applied eyeliner.

"She left the party with Trace last night," Sable explained. "Right about now she's either having an orgasm, going down on Trace, or they're breaking up again. It's a toss-up, really."

Grace finished putting on her makeup and stalked into the bedroom. She took the script from Sable's hand and set it on the nightstand. "I noticed you weren't here when I got home last night."

"The party ran late," Sable said as her gaze slid down Grace's body. "Whoa. Looks like someone got a taste of the sausage buffet and wants seconds. You look *hot!*"

Grace felt her cheeks flush and glanced down at her gray stretchy miniskirt and pink short-sleeve sweater. "It's comfortable."

"It's *fuckable*," Morgyn said. "And those are killer ankle boots. I bet they cost you a pretty penny."

"They're nothing special," Grace lied. They cost a bundle and she usually only wore them on special occasions. While she wouldn't exactly call seeing Reed a special occasion, it was *something*.

"You definitely dressed for *Renovation Man*," Sable said.

Grace didn't want to talk about why she'd picked out her outfit. It was none of their business that she'd woken up hot and bothered, taken a cold shower, and still felt his lips on hers. Or that she remembered how much Reed used to love when she wore her short cheerleading skirt.

"Hey, I don't blame you," Sable said. "That guy can hammer me anytime."

"Sable!" Grace pointed to the hallway.

Sable laughed. "Don't worry, sis. *Sisters before misters* and all that. I'd never go after your man."

"So, it wasn't just a hookup?" Morgyn sat up next to Sable. "You and Reed Cross?"

Ignoring Sable's smirk, Grace said, "No, not me and Reed Cross. He's a *friend*. I knew him in high school."

Morgyn tucked her hair behind her ear, gazing innocently up at Grace. "Oh. I just assumed that since you two were inspecting each other's tonsils in the creek you knew him more intimately than that. My bad." She pushed to her feet, all innocent eyes and sisterly tease. "From the look in your eyes, either you have no recollection of kissing him, or you thought we hadn't seen you."

"I..." *Remember every blessed second of his hot mouth on mine.* She cleared her throat, struggling to push those memories aside, and said, "We were pretty good friends."

A knock sounded on the glass door that led to the deck, and all three of them looked at the curtains.

"Mom and Dad are with the dogs and Brindle's with Trace," Morgyn said. "My guess is that your *pretty good friend* is here for a *pretty good* booty call."

"Oh my God, you're as bad as Sable," Grace said, and tore the curtains back. Her stomach flipped at the sight of Reed's boyish smile and his unmistakably manly physique. What was it about a man with a tool belt that made women go stupid?

Sable pushed past her and pulled the door open. "Hello there, Reno Man."

"Sable," he said casually, his eyes never leaving Grace's.

"How're the Montgomery girls this morning?"

Grace's pulse raced beneath the heat of Reed's stare. She couldn't spit out a single word. Her mind had taken a journey back to the creek, revisiting their first kiss in forever.

"Some of us are functioning better than others," Morgyn said as she slipped out the door. "I've got to run. I'm going to the fair with Haylie and Lindsay."

Haylie was Chet Hudson's younger sister. She was a single mother and the administrator for the new community center, No Limitz. Lindsay was Sophie's younger sister, which made Grace wish Sophie were there instead of in New York. Sophie had been there for her long before Reed had entered her life. She'd helped pull Grace through the ups and downs of childhood, through Grace and Reed's breakup, and during every life-changing event ever since. Sophie would talk her out of this ridiculous infatuation, or whatever it was that was driving her to act like a teenager with a crush on the bad boy.

Sable crossed her arms and leaned against the doorframe, watching Grace and Reed as if they were there for her entertainment.

"Sable, don't you have something better to do?" Grace asked with a not-so-subtle glare.

"What could be better than watching something a decade in the making come to life?"

Reed pushed a hand into his tool belt and withdrew a big bag of M&M's. "Grace, I assume this is still your breakfast of choice?"

"You remembered?" she said too breathily.

"You're hard to forget."

"*Okay*," Sable said flatly, pushing from the doorframe. "This is *way* too mushy for me. I'm outta here."

Reed stepped aside to let Sable pass, his gaze still locked on Grace, making her more nervous than it should. She dealt with all sorts of people in her job, from the wealthy to the famous. How could a small-town guy like Reed make her mind turn to dust? She glanced down at her fingers absently tearing open the bag of goodies, and her heart thumped a little harder.

Oh yeah, that's how.

He knew her better than she knew herself. He'd *assumed* she'd want to see him, when although she'd dressed the part, she'd been debating until the moment she'd seen his handsome face. The face that starred in her naughtiest fantasies and kept her from ever letting go with another man.

One look was all it took, and then there was no question. She wanted to see him. Heck, she wanted to *kiss* him. She shoved a handful of chocolate into her mouth to quell that urge and held out a few for Reed. "Want some?"

"Yes," he said evenly. Then his eyes smoldered, dark as night and hot as fire, and he added, "But not what you're offering."

She laughed, and it broke the tension building up inside her. "Why are you so set on this?"

"I'm not set on anything. But it'd be a waste to ignore our chemistry. Don't you think?"

She'd gone without *chemistry* for a very long time. So long, she barely remembered how to spell it. Ignoring it was not an option. But she and Reed spelled heartache, and she liked living in her lonely bubble without any new slashes through her heart. Okay, maybe she hated that lonely bubble, but she definitely liked safeguarding her heart. "What I think is that we barely know each other anymore."

Reed stepped closer with a wicked look in his eyes.

"Why are you always invading my personal space?"

"Because there are some things that don't change, like your reaction to my being close to you." He paused long enough for the space between them to ignite.

Grace stood firm, refusing to admit defeat by her weakening knees.

"I'm going to venture a guess that other things haven't changed either," he said in a low voice. "You were never one for flings and always one for knowing what was next on your agenda. You're probably thinking about how you'd like to see if we're still compatible, but you're only here for a visit and then what?"

"I'm here for only three weeks, Reed. Like I said before, this can't lead anywhere."

His lips curved up in a cocky smile, and his fingers brushed the back of her hand. "And like I said, I can think of plenty of places this can lead."

"Holster your hammer, playboy."

"I'm no playboy, Grace. Never was, never will be." He leaned closer, his minty breath filling her senses. "But you already know that."

"I knew that before, but I have no idea what your personal life is like now."

"Then it's time we changed that. Go out with me."

She glanced at his tool belt. "You're working, and I have scripts to read through."

"Tonight, Grace. We always wanted to go to the fair together. Now we can."

"Grace!" her mother called from the yard, where she and Grace's father were working with the dogs. "Come see how good the pups are doing!"

Had they been watching her the whole time? Grace took a step away, and Reed put his hand on her arm, his invitation hanging between them like the apple in the Garden of Eden.

"Tonight, Gracie," Reed said, as if it were already decided.

She sighed, knowing she didn't stand a chance of turning him down. "Okay."

"I'll pick you up at seven." His gaze coasted down her body, bringing rise to goose bumps. He pressed a kiss to her cheek and said, "Something else hasn't changed. I still love your legs."

And you still make them weak as noodles.

She kept that tidbit to herself as she went to join her parents. Reba and Dolly bounded toward her, and she crouched to love them up. They were all snarfs and slobbery kisses.

"Hi, darlin'," her father said as she rose to her feet and he embraced her. Cade Montgomery was careful by nature, meticulous and detail oriented like Grace, Pepper, and Amber, and when it came to his daughters he'd always been a tad overprotective. Not overbearing, just stern enough to set guys in their places before they took any of them on dates. "You look nice. Do you have plans?"

"Just working, making phone calls. You know, the norm."

"I thought you gave up M&M's for breakfast," her father said, motioning toward the king-size bag in her hand.

"Oh, um...I did, when I'm in the city. But here, you know." *I'm hoping chocolate will make me forget how much I want Reed.* "Nostalgia, I guess."

Her mother made a *hm* sound. "You and Reed looked pretty friendly. He's a nice man, Gracie."

Grace sighed, feeling the age-old guilt that had plagued her as a girl when she'd hidden their relationship from her parents and friends. "Yes, he's very nice."

"You know, you're here for three weeks," her mother said as she tossed a ball for the dogs to fetch. "That's long enough to go on a few dates and have some fun. You never know what might come of it."

"Mom, I'm not moving back." Her mother was always trying to get Grace and Pepper to move back home. She'd given up on Axsel moving back, at least for a few years. According to her mother, he was still sowing those young-twenties wild oats.

Her mother shrugged. "A mama can hope. What's so bad about living here, anyway? You could do theater right here in town, where the people who love you could be part of it."

"*Mom.*" Grace shook her head, unwilling to have this discussion again.

"Marilynn, if you're not careful, she'll stop visiting," her father warned. He smiled, and it brightened his blue eyes. "And, Grace, you can't blame your mother for trying. She misses you."

"I know, but I've got a life in New York and an amazing career." *Even if it drives me batty most of the time and sucks away my free time.* It's what she wanted, what she'd chosen. What being a top producer required. "I've moved past community theater and small-town productions. You know that."

"I'm proud of you, honey," her mother said. "You had a dream when you were just a girl, and you followed it. But what if you miss out on the best dream of all by living your life in a cycle of work? You're always saying the men in the city are too prissy or materialistic. I thought spending time with Reed would be a refreshing change."

The single men Grace knew were exactly as her mother described, or worse. The actors were divas, and often worse than the actresses. She knew it was a gross generalization to say "men in the city," but she worked in the arts, and meeting men outside of that industry was difficult when she worked most of the time.

"Then you'll be happy to know that Reed and I are going to the fair together tonight."

Her mother's eyes widened, along with her smile. "Really? That's wonderful!"

"Don't start planning our wedding, Mom. We're going as friends, and that's all we'll be when I leave and go back to the city." Her cell phone rang, and she pulled it from the pocket of her skirt, glad for the excuse to end the conversation. "It's Sophie. Excuse me for a sec."

She walked away as she answered, speaking quietly into the phone. "Your timing is perfect."

"I got your message. Sorry I didn't call back earlier, but Brett and I were...*working out*."

"You forsook my despair to get down and dirty with your husband? Now I know how far on the totem pole I've fallen," Grace teased. Sophie was eight months pregnant. She and her husband, Brett Bad, had built a house in Oak Falls, where they planned to return and spend Sophie's maternity leave. Her family was throwing her a baby shower next weekend, and Grace was looking forward to seeing her.

"Hardly. You've always come after sex with Brett." Sophie laughed. "Oh my gosh, that sounds so dirty, like you *come* after *we* have sex!"

"Listen!" she said between giggles. "Be serious, Soph! I have a problem."

"Okay..." Sophie laughed again.

"Sophie, *please*. I have a feeling my dry spell is in jeopardy. Not that that's a bad thing, but I'm going to the fair with Reed tonight."

Sophie squealed.

"You're not helping!" She paced the grass a good distance away from her parents, watching them play with the dogs. Her parents enjoyed their lives so much, sometimes Grace wondered if her mother was right and she was missing out on *living* her own. Sophie's recent free fall into matrimony and impending motherhood had also piqued those worries.

"Oh, come on, Grace! You need sex before your girly parts close up, and you have *never* gotten over Reed."

"But—"

"Before you try to deny it, remember I was with you when you got your tattoo, *and* I know the name of your vibrator."

Aw, shit.

"Uh-huh. *Mr. Greedy.* If you think I don't know that's Reed, you don't give me enough credit."

Grace squeezed her eyes shut. "I wasn't going to deny it. I know I've never gotten over him, but..." She glanced up at the porch and said, "The shirtless heart stealer is hard at work...*looking hot* and talking sweet and cocky."

"Just the way you like 'em," Sophie said.

"Mm-hm. I swear, when I first saw him I was thrown right back to that lovesick teenager."

"Of course you were. I wish I could have been there to see it. What did you tell me about Brett? To sleep with him and get him out of my system? It didn't work for me, but it was good advice. Maybe you should sleep with Reed and see if it sucks."

"If the way he kisses is any indication, he'll still fuck like a sex god."

"You *kissed* him? And I'm just now hearing about it? I want all the details!"

Grace told her about the creek party and the way his kisses

consumed her to the point of not being able to think. "He's still my greedy boy, Soph, only everything feels magnified. And the way he talks…I swear his voice is pure seduction."

"Remember how he used to look at you? You'd melt every time."

"The way he looks at me now is that look on *steroids*."

"Oh shit," Sophie said just above a whisper. "You don't stand a chance."

"I know. And he brought me M&M's. I don't trust myself, Soph. I wish your baby shower were today, so you could chain me to my bed or something."

Sophie giggled. "I'm sure Reed would be more than happy to help you out with that."

A shiver of desire tickled up her spine. "That's what I'm worried about. Did you not hear me say *I don't trust myself?*"

REED SPENT THE day trying to focus on the porch renovations and not watching Grace, who had decided to park her gorgeous ass on a lawn chair in the yard and work in the sun. Needless to say, it had taken him twice as long as it should have to get through his tasks. When he'd wrapped up there, he'd come back to his place and spent a few hours working on his own kitchen renovations. He'd gotten a bargain on the old house overlooking the creek, and though he still had some work ahead of him, the four-bedroom house already felt like more of a home than his house in Michigan ever had, which wasn't saying much. Something was still missing, and no matter how much he fixed it up, he couldn't pinpoint what it was.

After a quick shower, he threw on a white T-shirt and jeans, pulled on his boots, and headed out to pick up Grace for their date. As ridiculous as it seemed, he'd missed out on doing so many things for her back in high school that he was excited about finally picking her up for a proper date. He stopped for flowers on the way and had a fleeting thought about the guys she probably went out with in the city. He gripped the steering wheel tighter and wondered if he should have worn a button-down shirt. He hated button-downs and wore them only when he absolutely had to. He parked in front of her parents' house and rubbed the scruff peppering his cheeks. He probably should have shaved, too.

The front door opened, and those thoughts went out the window as he stepped from his truck, taking in Grace's insane figure in a pair of black skinny jeans, what looked like ankle-high biker boots, and a black silky top. Holy shit, she was hot as *fuck*.

And she was ripping him off.

"What are you doing?" he called out to her as he came around the truck and joined her on the walkway, holding the flowers behind his back. *Man*, she smelled incredible. "Get back in that house, woman."

"*Excuse* me?" she said with wide eyes.

He held the flowers tighter to keep from reaching for her, because once she was in his arms, he wasn't going to let go. "I have never had the opportunity to pick you up for a real date. I'm not missing out on that again. Now, get your fine ass back in the house and let me knock on the door like a gentleman." He smacked her butt and said, "Go."

"That's *not* very gentlemanly," she said with a sexy laugh.

"Neither are most of the things on my mind right now, so

you'd better take the chivalrous acts when you can get them."

She glanced over her shoulder before walking inside, and in that split second, his world tilted on its axis. Grace was here, within reach, and right that second nothing else mattered.

He tried to clear his head, but it was no use. Grace had taken up residence. He knocked on the door and her father opened it, a smile at the ready.

"Hello, Reed. I hear you sent my daughter back inside."

Reed nodded. "Yes, sir. When I take a woman on a date, I like to pick her up properly."

"I told you I liked him," Marilynn said as she came to Cade's side. "Reed, come in, please."

Grace stood off to the side, watching with amusement as he stepped inside. He'd seen the inside of their home when he'd first started working on the porch, but Grace made it look even brighter.

He smiled and handed her the bouquet of pink and white orchids. The same flowers he'd left anonymously on the porch by her bedroom door on every thirty-day anniversary while they were dating. "You look gorgeous, Grace."

If a melting heart had a face, it would be Grace's at that very moment. She lifted the bouquet to her nose, smiling as she smelled them. "They're beautiful."

He was aware of her parents exchanging a glance but didn't want to miss a second of Grace to catch it. "I've been wanting to get you flowers since"—he noticed the warning in her eyes, but he was done hiding. He'd just have to be creative in his honesty—"I first saw you standing on the sidelines of the football field back in high school."

Another dreamy look washed over her. "That's a long time."

"It is." Reed couldn't resist stepping closer, vaguely aware of

Marilynn reaching for Cade's hand. "But some things are worth waiting for."

Grace lowered her gaze, her cheeks flushing.

"Why don't I put those flowers in a vase so you two can get on your way." Her mother took the bouquet from her.

Reed put his hand on Grace's lower back and said, "I won't have her back too late."

"Keep her as long as you want her. Overnight if you'd like," Marilynn said.

"Mom!" Grace said with a laugh. "Nothing like offering your daughter up for a good time."

"You take care of my girl, you hear?" Cade said with a friendly wink.

"Yes, sir."

Once they were alone on the porch, Reed hauled her into his arms and kissed her deep and slow, until their mutual laughter turned to passion. She was so sweet, so eager, he didn't want to stop, but they were on her parents' porch. Clinging to her arms, he reluctantly drew back.

"Thank you," he said, and pressed his lips to hers again in a quick, tender kiss.

"For the kisses?"

He took her hand in his and said, "For allowing me to experience what I was never able to all those years ago."

Chapter Seven

THE AIR BUZZED as rides soared up toward the night sky, alive with bright colored lights, their riders screaming, arms flailing, mirroring everything Grace felt as she and Reed meandered through the crowds. For the first time in forever, Grace felt carefree and truly happy—and it scared the heck out of her because where would she be three weeks from now when she went back to New York? She couldn't go through another heartbreak, but being with Reed, even just being around him when he wasn't kissing her dizzy, was everything she'd remembered. He was real, and he didn't put on a front, pretending, or *hoping*, to be something he wasn't. She'd always admired that about him.

They stopped for cotton candy, and Reed pulled a piece of the sticky sweetness off and held it up to Grace's lips. "Open up, beautiful."

She opened her mouth, and he set the cotton candy on her tongue. "Mm. I haven't had cotton candy in ages."

He gathered her in his arms and lowered his lips to hers, the sugary goodness giving way to his unique, heavenly taste.

"Well, well, well, look at my big sister making out like she's not Miss Buttoned-up City Girl."

Grace tore her mouth from Reed's at the sound of Brindle's voice. She tried to step away, but Reed's grip tightened, keeping her close. He didn't flinch, didn't blink, as he cupped her jaw, keeping her attention focused on him as he placed a tender kiss to her lips and said, "No hiding, Gracie."

How could he be so calm when her insides were whirling?

Reed brushed his thumb over Grace's cheek and turned slowly toward the others. Brindle was tucked beneath Trace Jericho's arm like she was sewn there, her eyes dancing with delight at catching Grace in a compromising position. Trace was a strappingly large cowboy, with dark hair and eyes and an ever-present arrogant smile. Beside him, two of his four siblings, Shane and Trixie, who helped him run their family ranch, were talking with Chet, who carried his four-year-old nephew, Scotty, on his shoulders.

A slow grin spread across Reed's lips as he said, "How's it going?"

"Apparently not as well as it is for you guys," Trixie said with a smile. "I'd hug you hello, but it looks like your hugs are all spoken for."

Grace couldn't suppress her smile, even though she hated the snarky look on Brindle's face. "Hey," she said, then chided herself. *Hey?* How long had it been since she'd replaced *hello* or *hi* with *hey?* She'd worked too hard to shake off those country ways to fall back into them. If that's what Reed's kisses did to her, she'd have to rethink things.

As if he could read her mind, he leaned in, touching his cheek to hers, and whispered, "Doesn't it feel good to be *us* in public?"

Maybe *country bumpkin* wasn't so bad after all, because heck *yes*, it felt amazing!

"Oh my gosh! I just figured it out!" Brindle waggled her finger at them. "This is why you freaked out the other night. How long have you two been secretly hooking up?"

"Wouldn't you like to know?" Reed winked at Brindle, and Grace glared at him. He pressed his lips to hers. "Guess they figured us out, huh, Gracie? No more hiding."

Taking his much-needed hint to avoid any further questions about their past, she said, "You caught us, Brindle. We've been having a secret long-distance, torrid affair for years."

Brindle seemed to think about that for a minute, her brows furrowed, nose wrinkled, in that adorable way she had that Grace had always envied.

"Man, that sounds perfect," Shane said. "Long-distance means you see each other often enough to make the most out of each visit without having time to get sick of each other." He was every bit the cowboy, like Trace and the rest of his brothers, but he was three years older than Trace and had never been as cocky.

Grace liked all the Jericho siblings, but Shane had a certain gentlemanly way that made him one of her favorites.

Trixie tugged at the knot in her flannel shirt, which was tied above her belly button, leaving a glimpse of tanned flesh above her denim shorts. "We're going on the Ferris wheel. Want to come?"

"Hell, yes," Reed said. "I've been dying to kiss Grace at the top of it for years."

Her stomach flipped. He really was going for no more hiding. She made a mental note to define borders on their newfound relationship, like *please don't out me to my family.* She'd never been a liar, except where seeing Reed was concerned, and she knew she needed to come clean to her family about their past before they heard about their fake multiyear relationship from Brindle.

Falling into step with the group, Trixie nudged Grace's arm. "Those boots are wicked cute. Aren't you worried about ruining them?"

Grace looked down at her black leather ankle boots, which were already covered in dust, and she winced. She'd forgotten how dirty the fairgrounds were, and she'd been so swept up in Reed, she hadn't given a thought to anything other than looking cute for him.

"You should have worn Mom's boots," Brindle said.

As much as she hated to admit it, Brindle was right.

Reed glanced down at her boots. "I'll get those cleaned up for you back at my place. No worries."

Butterflies swarmed in her belly at the prospect of going back to his place, *and* at his confidence that that was exactly where they were heading. But weren't they? Hadn't she spent the whole evening trying to ignore that she was secretly hoping for the same? Apparently Brindle didn't miss that comment either. She was grinning like a Cheshire cat as they made their way into the Ferris wheel line.

They finished their cotton candy, sharing with everyone as they waited their turn. Chet set Scotty's feet on the ground. His face and hands were pink and sticky.

"Be right back." Reed gave Grace a quick kiss, then ran out of line to a nearby food vendor. He returned with a bottle of water and a handful of napkins. "Give me your hands, buddy." He poured water over Scotty's hands and cleaned them off.

"Dude's making your uncle look bad, Scotty," Chet teased.

"Nah," Reed said as he tousled Scotty's hair. "I did some work with kids in Michigan. I'm used to sticky hands."

Holy cow. "You just got ten times hotter," came out before Grace could stop it.

Reed pulled her close again with a frisky expression. "If that's all it takes, maybe I should tell you about the time I dressed up like Santa Claus."

He touched his lips to hers, and Trixie said, "I've gotta find myself a long-distance lover."

"Over my dead body," Trace said.

"And once he's dead, you'll need to take me down, too," Shane said, bumping fists with Trace.

"I'm so glad I don't have a pack of brothers," Brindle said. "Trix, you go to Maryland enough. Just pick one up there. Or come help with my drama club play. There are lots of single dads there."

"There are?" Trace gave her a stern look. Brindle laughed and rolled her eyes.

"No single dads for me," Trixie said. "I need my freedom."

Brindle smirked. "I hear ya, sister. Being tied down is not in my plans, either."

Reed gave Trace a look that clearly asked what was up with that comment.

"No strings," Trace said with a wink. "That's what life's all about."

Brindle nodded in agreement. Even though Grace knew Brindle had no interest in settling down with any one man, it still made her sad to know she was okay with the idea of Trace being with another woman. She had no idea how she and her siblings could have been raised by the same parents when they were different in so many ways.

Scotty tugged on Brindle's shirt and said, "Mommy said I can be in your play when I'm bigger." He pushed his mop of blond hair from his eyes for the umpteenth time, and it flopped right back down.

"Darn right you can, little man," Brindle said. "That reminds me. Grace, can you stop by rehearsal one afternoon this week? I'm having some trouble with the script. We start at three thirty. I could use your insight."

She and Brindle might not see eye to eye with their personal lives—Brindle flirted shamelessly, while Grace had always been very careful in that department—but when it came to their careers, they were equally as passionate. Brindle gave her all to her students.

"Sure. I'd love to. My class starts tomorrow and runs from four to six, Monday, Wednesday, and Friday at Amber's bookstore. Why don't I come by Tuesday?"

"That's perfect," Brindle said.

Reed squeezed Grace against his side. "If you ever need help with the sets. I can squeeze in a few hours here and there." He kissed Grace's temple and said, "If my girl's there, it'd be even more of a priority."

His girl? Everything about tonight should worry her, but being with Reed had always been easy. It was the hiding that had been torture. Warnings screamed in her head, *Tread carefully! Heartache up ahead!* But maybe her mother was right. She had three weeks, and it had been a long time since she'd been this happy. Why not enjoy it?

Brindle looked up at Trace, who towered over her and said, "See? Some guys make time to help."

"Babe," Trace said, "I've got a ranch to run. But if you want to spend the time we have together building sets, instead of"— he glanced at Scotty and cleared his throat—"our *other* extracurricular activities, that can be arranged."

"Nope! Never mind," Brindle said, and promptly changed the subject.

The line moved faster than expected, and before Grace knew it, it was their turn. They climbed into their car, and Grace's pulse quickened. She loved rides, but they always made her nervous. Reed hauled her against him and pointed to Scotty safely tucked beneath Chet's arm.

"There's nothing sexier than a man who watches out for children," Grace said.

"I was pointing to Scotty, not Chet," Reed growled.

"I know you were. And I was talking about *you*."

"Aw, Gracie." His lips touched hers in a feather of a kiss as the ride began and they were lifted into the air. "I've missed you."

"I've missed you, too," she said honestly, and was surprised at how much she felt herself opening up to him. "I want to know all the great things that have gone on in your life."

As their car sailed toward the sky, Reed pointed beyond the fairgrounds. "See that road over there? It leads to the theater, where I lost my virginity to a *very* special girl. That's also where I first told her I loved her. See the high school? The football field? That's where I first saw her."

Grace snuggled closer, the breeze stinging her eyes. Or maybe it was nostalgia. It had been so long since she'd felt anything other than rushed and lonely, she couldn't decipher which. "I was there for all those things. I want to know what's happened since then."

He gazed deeply into her eyes, and she felt the emotions she saw there climbing beneath her skin and burrowing in.

"Don't you get it, Gracie? You're all that matters."

THEY HUNG OUT with their friends, riding roller coasters and bumper cars, and raced down an enormous slide in burlap bags. They played darts, and Trace won a small stuffed dog for Brindle. When Grace gushed over it, Reed spent fifty bucks playing a shooting game until he won her an enormous stuffed bear. She hugged it tight, looking cute as hell.

"Show-off," Trace teased.

"I love it!" Grace exclaimed as she tried to figure out how to carry it. "What should I call him?"

Reed stole another kiss and said, "Greedy Boy, of course. That way you'll think of me every time you see him."

She tugged him down by his shirt for another kiss. "Thank you. How will I be able to *not* think about you again after such an amazing night?"

"You won't, if I can help it." He hoisted the stuffed animal onto his shoulders and put his arm around her as they followed the others toward another ride. After a while they parted from their friends, and *finally*, Reed had Grace all to himself again.

"I love being here with you," she confessed. "We missed out on a lot as kids, but I think it made our relationship deeper because we spent so much time alone, really getting to know each other."

"We'll make up for those missed things," he assured her. "I have to admit. I was jealous of the little things we didn't get to do, like going on real dates and wearing those boyfriend-girlfriend beaded bracelets everyone had. I would have loved to see you wearing one of my football jerseys on game day, too."

"We missed prom, the homecoming dance…"

"We'll make new memories," he promised.

"One dollar! Guess your weight or height!" a man called out from beside a tall scale.

Grace dragged Reed away from it. "Give that man a wide breadth. That's the scariest thing at the fair."

He chuckled as they ducked into an arcade tent and made their way to the photo booth. Surprisingly, there was no line. He set the stuffed bear in the booth and they climbed inside, closing the curtain behind them. Serenaded by whirring machines and ringing arcade games, he pulled Grace down on his lap, and a sense of completeness flooded him. It had been so long since he'd felt anything remotely close to that, it took him a second to identify it.

"Remember the pictures we took in the photo booth in Wishing Creek?" The town of Wishing Creek was about half an hour away from Oak Falls. They'd gone there when they were younger so they could spend time together without worrying about their friends seeing them.

"I still have mine," she said happily.

"Me too." He pulled out his wallet and withdrew a few bucks for the pictures. Then he handed Grace the wallet. "Look inside."

She opened it with a confused expression.

"Go on. Look through these." He pointed to the plastic credit card holders.

She flipped through them, pausing with uncertainty.

"Keep going," he said.

A small sound escaped when she came to the pictures they'd taken in Wishing Creek. They were gazing into each other's eyes, with smiles as bright as their newfound love.

She ran her finger over their faces. "We were so young."

"And you were so beautiful." He withdrew the picture and unfolded it, revealing another picture of them kissing and a third of them making silly faces.

"You've carried them all this time?" she asked.

"No. There was a time I didn't, right after we split, but I always had them with me. When I decided to move back, I put them in my wallet. The universe must have known we weren't done."

He fed the money into the slot and slipped the picture back into his wallet, tucking it into his pocket. "Time to make new memories."

They pressed their faces close together. Grace smiled for the camera, but Reed was too taken with her to look anywhere else. And when her green eyes met his, their mouths came together hungrily. Her lips were warm and sweet as he took the kiss deeper. The flash went off around them a few times, and then there was only the darkness, the curtain to the booth buffering them from the outside world as they made out like they had all those years ago, groping and kissing like they'd never get enough of each other. He lifted her up and she straddled his lap, holding his face between her soft hands like she never wanted to let him go—and man, he hoped she didn't.

"Come home with me, Grace," he said between kisses.

"Okay," she said, and pressed her lips to his. "One more kiss."

By the time they stumbled out of the booth with their enormous bear, Reed's body was on fire. They made out on the way to the truck, stopping every few minutes to maneuver around the bear. He tossed the stuffed animal behind the seats and they tumbled onto the front seat in a flurry of lasciviousness. His body pressed down over hers, and he pushed his hand beneath her blouse, filling his hand with her womanly curves. She moaned, breaking through his lust-addled brain.

He ground out a curse. "Not here, Grace. I want you naked in my arms, and I don't want to worry about who might see or hear us."

"Oh! Right!" she said, and then worry rose in her eyes. "Brindle saw us together. We'll be the talk of the town tomorrow, if we're not already."

"That's not what I mean," he said, laughing softly as he stepped out of the truck and helped her sit up. "I'm glad they saw us." He went around to the driver's side and hauled her across the seat until she was pressed tightly beside him. "Talking is one thing. Giving them a show is another. Let them talk all they want. Pretty soon nobody will remember a time when we weren't together. Most of all, *you*."

They kissed at every light on the way to his place, and when they turned off the main road, Grace said, "Remember when we used to dream about owning that Victorian on the road where Sophie's parents live?"

"Mm-hm." The nearer they got to his house, the clearer his thoughts became. He was pushing for no more hiding, and that meant being honest about *everything*. Including Alina. He hated the idea of bringing her up and hated even more having to admit to Grace that he'd almost married the wrong woman. But she trusted him, and he didn't want to keep anything from her.

"Sophie built a house there. She's coming home for her baby shower next weekend, and—" She stopped talking when he turned down his *and* his new neighbor, Sophie's, road. "Reed...?"

He turned into his driveway, which was lined by tall oaks, and his pulse kicked up as the house came into view. He parked out front, the headlights illuminating the house.

"You bought it? This is *yours*?" Her gaze sailed over the wide front porch that abutted the turret on the left, then drifted up to the two windows on the third floor.

He cut the engine and stepped from the truck. "Fate's got a strange way of making things work out. This Painted Lady came on the market at the right time. How could I *not* buy it? It's a piece of history"—*ours and its own*—"and has all the hallmarks of the things I treasure. Check out the gingerbread trim, the wide porch, and octagonal tower. And the steep, multifaceted roof is true Victorian. Not to mention the memories I have of us ogling the place." He glanced at Grace and caught her watching him with a wondrous expression. "Sorry. I get a little carried away."

"No, it's nice to see you haven't lost that romantic touch. You always got carried away about houses and things other kids paid no attention to. It was one of the things that I admired about you. You were different from everyone back then. I guess you still are."

As they headed for the front door, she said, "It's gorgeous. It looks the same, only different. Better."

"I fixed up the siding, replaced the gingerbread around the peaks, had it painted. I fixed up the whole porch and was able to use most of the original pieces. Wait until you see the inside. It's even better than we imagined."

"You painted it white, lavender, and pale green," she said with a smile.

"I was never very good with colors." It wasn't really true, but Grace had loved those colors, and when it came time to paint, he figured, why not? "You had a great eye for that."

"I'm sure I sound shell-shocked. I can't believe you bought

it." She ran her hand up the railing as they ascended the steps.

"I've still got a little work to do in the kitchen, and I need to paint the living room, but it's getting there."

He pushed the door open, revealing high ceilings and archways leading into the living room and kitchen and restored carved woodwork along the lower half of the walls and stairs to their right. Grace smiled appreciatively as she took in the results of his hard work. She stepped into the living room, which opened to the dining room.

"The kitchen's around back, and there's a great morning room that overlooks the creek."

"Wow. This is gorgeous." She ran her fingers over the complex moldings and glanced up at the ornate chandelier and intricate medallion on the ceiling. "Did you do all of this work?"

Pride rose inside him. "Yes."

"It's really stunning. And what's going on over there?" She pointed at the color samples he'd painted on the wall.

"I couldn't decide which colors would look best. Which do you like?"

Her brow wrinkled in concentration, her head tilting to one side, then the other. "I really love this one." She pointed to his favorite, pale seafoam green. "It ties in with the outside of the house. It's vivid and somehow also soft, but it might be too much for the whole room. I'd probably go with something like this one." She pointed to the next sample. "It reminds me of buttercream, and white trim would make it *pop*. It also goes with anything." She looked around the room. "Not that you have anything to match it to. Where's your furniture?"

"I have the necessities, a mattress and dresser, a kitchen table. Until now I haven't needed anything else. Other than when I showed the house to my aunt and uncle, you're my first guest."

"With a house this special, don't you want to show it off?"

"Not really. I'm rehabbing it for myself, not so other people can gawk at it."

"Well, you've done an impressive job, and it brings back memories. It smells like the houses your uncle used to work on," she said, lacing her fingers with his.

That simple act of claiming him, letting him know she was still right there with him, brought a streak of happiness. "The houses we used to sneak into to make out? I have a faint memory of that smell you're referring to, but mostly I remember your sweet scent knocking me off my feet."

"Reed," she said with a bashful smile.

"I can't help it, Grace. I remember it all, the way we kissed, lying beneath the stars and never wanting our nights together to end. Texting until three in the morning when you'd fall asleep and leave me hanging more often than not."

She buried her face in his chest with a groan.

"My girl needed her beauty sleep."

"Your girl needed to go to the same school as her boyfriend so she could have seen you every day without worrying about what anyone else thought."

"Rivalries were awful back then, weren't they?" He remembered too many kids who had gotten into fights to prove their school was the best and girls who had been called horrible names because they dated guys from other schools. He never would have risked that happening to Grace. "It's not that way now around here. Did you know that? Everyone gets along, regardless of which town they're from."

She nodded. "That's what I hear."

"I wanted to be with you every second. You had to know that, Grace." Her gaze was soft and alluring, drawing him deeper into her. "And right now I want to carry you upstairs and make love to you until nothing else exists."

"I like that plan," she said softly.

He knew what he had to do next might ruin this moment, but to keep Grace's trust, he'd take that chance.

Chapter Eight

GRACE'S INSIDES WERE trembling. She couldn't believe she was really standing in Reed's house, agreeing to go upstairs and make love to him after all these years. But she felt so good when she was with him, she couldn't imagine anything stopping her from taking the next step.

Reed touched his lips to hers in a whisper of a kiss that left her wanting more. "Gracie, I want you more than I have ever wanted anything in my life. But I can't look into your trusting eyes and have anything left unsaid between us. You asked about my life, and I want to know about yours. Let's have a drink and talk."

She exhaled a breath she hadn't realized she was holding and realized she was terribly nervous. "A drink is probably a good idea."

She admired the ornate crown moldings and elegant, antique chandeliers as he led her through the dining room to a large kitchen with gorgeous marble countertops and gaping holes where the stove and dishwasher should be. A table for two sat beside glass doors overlooking the backyard. Even in the darkness she could see moonlight reflecting off the creek.

He pulled a bottle of wine from a cabinet and untied a red

ribbon from around the neck. "Compliments of Roy and Ella."

He grabbed two wineglasses from a cabinet, and poured them each a glass.

"Here you go." He handed her one and led her through the kitchen to another set of stairs.

She followed him up to the master bedroom, where a single antique dresser sat against the far wall. A king-size mattress lay atop gorgeous hardwood floors by a wall of nearly floor-to-ceiling windows. Grace swallowed hard. Was that their talk? The few seconds in the kitchen? Her nerves kicked up again.

"Come with me." Reed led her through the bedroom and out a set of glass doors to a veranda. He flicked a switch, illuminating tiny white lights wrapped around iron railings, a U-shaped, deep-cushioned seating area with a few soft-looking blankets. A small round table for two sat in the corner by a fireplace.

The view of the creek took Grace's breath away. She imagined Reed spending most of his time out there. They'd had no place to go when they were dating, so they had spent a lot of time in secluded outdoor spots, like behind the theater, down by the creek, and in local parks. She realized now how little time she spent outside when she was in the city.

"This is beautiful. I remember you used to say you wished you had a tree fort but you were too old for one. Is this your version of an adult tree fort?"

"Something like that." He reached for her hand and guided her to the couch.

"Is this where you bring all your dates? To your bachelor pad, with romantic lights and a make-out couch?"

He pulled off his boots, giving her a *don't be ridiculous* look. "Hardly."

He slipped off the cushion, kneeling in front of her, and began taking off her boots, making her even more nervous.

"I'll clean these for you, as I promised. But right now let's just be comfortable."

"I can clean them tomorrow."

He set her boots aside and nudged her legs open, kneeling between them, his arms circling her waist. He smiled, tugging at all the lonely pieces of herself she'd been starving for years.

"I need to tell you something, Gracie, and it might hurt to hear it, but I don't want any secrets between us."

"That's not exactly the best line to get a woman into bed."

"I know, but you need to hear this. I've been trying to figure out how to tell you, and the weird thing is, I know it's going to bug the hell out of you, but you should know, it doesn't bother me."

"Reed, just spit it out, because you're making me nervous."

"You asked about my life, and what I said on the Ferris wheel was true. With the exception of the business I started and sold, nothing I've done matters more than coming back together with you. After we broke up, I headed to Michigan. Roy's brother, Joe, lives there. I went to college, and he hooked me up with a historical preservation company. I worked through school, which is where I met Thad, who eventually became my business partner. After college we made a name for ourselves in the industry, and within a couple years we were earning seven figures and things were going well. About two years ago I met a woman, Alina, and we dated for a while. She wanted to get married, and even though I knew something wasn't right between us, I was considering it. Six months ago, I came back from a business meeting early and caught her in bed with Thad. Two months later Roy suffered his heart attack. I sold my half of the business to Thad, sold my house with all the furnishings, and came here."

Grace struggled to find her voice. "You were *engaged* six months ago?"

"No. *Almost* engaged, if you can even call it that. Our relationship wasn't what it should have been, so I never took that last step. Something was always missing."

She pushed to her feet, feeling gutted. "Not what it *should* have been? What does that even mean?" She was breathing hard, and somehow she still felt like she was choking. "How can you say you feel so much for me, when you were in love with another woman only six months ago?"

Reed stood and closed the distance between them. "Grace, I wasn't in love with her. I never felt for her what I felt for you, or what I feel for you now after only a few days of seeing you again."

"You were never engaged to me, so you must have felt *more*." She turned away, staring out at the creek, trying to dodge the pain zinging through her.

"Bullshit. I never even introduced her to my family, and in four months I've never once felt the need to talk about her to *anyone*. No one here even knows about her other than Roy and Ella. Doesn't that tell you something? I have *never* felt more for anyone than I've felt for you. I spent a decade *not* feeling, Grace. Do you have any idea what that's like? I gave up hope of ever finding what we had again. I *gave up*, Grace. I figured, I might not be *all in* with her, but she wanted to get married. I hoped that someday I'd get over whatever was holding me back, so I considered it. There was no ring, no proposal, no 'I can't live without you.' Do you know why?"

She crossed her arms, struggling to hold back tears she knew he didn't deserve. Why did it hurt so much to know he'd almost married someone else?

"Gracie, please look at me. I'm trying to be honest with you. We've never lied to each other, and I wasn't about to start now."

She turned, and a tear broke free. He wiped it away with the pad of his thumb, the love in his eyes boring into her chest.

"I never said it to her because I never felt it. You weren't as broken as I was. You must have had other relationships. Don't tell me you never came close to settling down."

"I didn't! I might have, if I'd met the right guy, but…" She blinked away tears, thinking of how few guys she'd actually gone out with and how disappointing they'd all turned out to be. "No one was right. No one was *you*, and I was so angry at you for that, because I was hurt that you left town after telling me you never would."

He reached for her. "But now you know why I left."

"I *know*," she snapped, feeling foolish for crying. "And I don't have any idea why I'm so upset, or why it hurts to know you almost married someone else, but it does."

"Because you still love me, Grace." He wiped her tears and gathered her in his arms. "You still love me, the same way I still love you."

She tried to push the hurt aside, struggling with the truth of his statement.

"I know that was hard for you to hear. It was just as hard for me to say, and not only because I knew it would upset you, but also because I didn't trust my feelings enough to get out of that relationship long before it imploded. I'm not willing to make that same mistake again and live in the dark. You're it for me, Grace. You *always* have been. This coming-clean business, and the ten years prior, were hard. But loving you has always been easy."

"We were never easy," she reminded him. "We had to sneak around."

"That's *seeing* you, not *loving* you. I'd have gone to any length to see you because I loved you."

Her heart climbed into her throat. "But we're temporary again."

"We don't have to be. A long-distance relationship can work if we want it to. I'll never ask you to give up your dreams."

She thought about her busy life back in the city and how difficult it would be to maintain a full-time relationship when she was working long hours and weekends. Could they manage a long-distance relationship? Maybe that way they could actually enjoy the time they had together without the stress of either of them feeling second-rate to their careers on a daily basis. Hope bloomed inside her.

"You never asked me to give up my dreams back then," she said as realization dawned on her. "You never asked me to stay in Oak Falls. If anything, you pushed me toward college and New York."

"Because I loved you. I wanted you to be happy, and I knew you never would until you caught that rising star and rode it all the way to the moon. That's who you are, Gracie. You were the girl with big dreams, and now you're the woman who has achieved them. I'd never want to take that away from you. If the only way we can make this work is long-distance, I'll take it. I'm not pushing you away this time. I'm asking to be *part* of your life, however we can fit it in."

His honesty, endless faith in her abilities, and his support touched her so deeply. She didn't want to dissect their future or wonder if all the pieces of herself she felt shifting into place were real or only in her head. All she wanted as she went up on her toes and touched her lips to Reed's was *him*.

FOR THE FIRST time in years, Reed wasn't thinking about the job he had to do or his next project. With Grace's eagerness, he didn't want to think at all. He claimed her mouth with fierce possessiveness, his hands traveling over her lush curves. She arched into him, and he clutched her ass, groaning with the inferno it ignited inside him. He took the kiss deeper, rougher, holding on to his control by a fraying thread.

"Grace—" he said between frantic kisses, needing to know this wasn't all in his head, that she wanted him as desperately as he wanted her.

"Don't ask. *Know*," she said eagerly. "You've always known."

Their mouths crashed together as they stumbled toward the couch, their lips parting only long enough to strip off their shirts. Reed's breath caught in his throat at the sight of her glorious breasts straining against black lace.

"Damn, Grace. Don't move. Just let me look at you." He'd fantasized about her too many times to count, but nothing—*nothing*—compared to having her in his arms. Gone was the young girl he'd fallen in love with. She was *all* woman, curvaceous and seductive. "You're stunning."

Her skin flushed as he ran his hands over her waist and up her ribs, brushing over the rough lace as he lowered his mouth to the swell of her breast. He tasted his way across one warm mound, to the dip of her cleavage, where he lingered, kissing until she was moaning and needy. He unhooked the front clasp on her bra and pushed it off her shoulders, kissing her again, slow and sensual, as he filled his hands with her breasts, his thumbs teasing over her taut peaks. She gasped into their kiss, and that sinful sound sent bolts of lightning to his cock. He pressed her breasts together, kissing and nipping at her heated flesh until she trembled with desire. She still reacted to his every touch, his every kiss, but her reactions were more powerful, more *sensual*. She clutched his hips as he lowered his mouth over one nipple and sucked hard.

"Oh *God*," rushed from her lungs. "That feels good."

He took the nub between his teeth, tugging gently, and she went up on her toes, her fingers digging into his sides.

"Reed," she panted out.

"I've got you, baby, and there's no way I'm going to rush through this."

He devoured her neck and took her in another savagely intense kiss. He was rock-hard, ready to take her, but first... "I'm going to enjoy driving you wild."

Holding her gaze, he dragged his tongue along her lower lip and cupped her face, taking her jaw between his fingers and thumb. He kept her mouth open as he kissed her, until she gave up trying to kiss him back, allowing him to thoroughly love every dip of her mouth until he knew it by heart. He'd always gone mad over her sweet, sexy mouth, the way she panted and sinful noises slipped from her lips even as he kissed her.

"I love your mouth, baby." He released her cheeks, taking her in a slow, intoxicating kiss.

She was barely breathing as their lips parted. "Love all of me, Reed."

"I do, and I will," he promised, kissing her again.

They made out with reckless abandon, stripping off the rest of their clothes and falling to the couch, naked and panting between feverish kisses. He laced their hands together, soaking in the feel of her thighs against his, his cock nestled against the tuft of hair between her legs, the needful look in her eyes pulling him in. He brushed his lips over her cheek and mouth, in a series of light kisses. She smelled heavenly feminine and hauntingly familiar. He welcomed the memories as she spread her legs to accommodate his hips and rocked beneath him.

A smile tugged at his lips as he released her hands and moved down her body, nipping and tasting as he went. She writhed beneath him, arching and digging her fingers into the cushions as he placed openmouthed kisses just above the juncture of her thighs. Her hips rose as her knees fell open wider, a wicked invitation he couldn't resist. He sealed his mouth over her glistening sex, and her essence spread over his tongue, sweet and hot and so fucking perfect.

"Oh God. *Reed*," she said with a shaky breath.

The plea in her voice snapped his remaining control, and he feasted on her, teeth, tongue, and fingers teasing and plundering until she was shaking and gasping. His cock throbbed to get in on the game, but he wanted to see his Grace strung out with pleasure before they finally came together, and he knew just how to do it. He reached up with one hand, groping her breast, while he teased her sex with his fingers, drenching them in her arousal. She moaned and rocked, and he slid his hand beneath her bottom as he loved the very heart of her with his mouth. He couldn't resist looking up at his beautiful girl, and their eyes connected.

"*Yes*," she said breathlessly, her hips gyrating. "Love all of me."

And he did, taking her right up to the clouds, his name flying from her lips like a prayer. As she came down from the peak, he sent her soaring again, loving her with his mouth and hands until she collapsed, spent and smiling, beneath him. Only then did he move up her body, slowing to love her breasts again.

He reached for her hands, lacing their fingers together again, and rubbed his erection against her wetness, earning another string of sexy pleas that nearly sent him over the edge.

"Gracie, do you trust me?"

"More than I trust myself."

The honesty in her voice brought his lips to hers. He kissed her until they were both rocking and moaning.

"After I caught my ex with Thad, I made sure I was clean. I haven't been with anyone since. Please tell me you're on the pill."

"I am, and I want all of y—"

Her words were smothered with the hard press of his lips as their bodies came together. He filled her completely, just as he always had, and he knew they were made for each other. They both stilled, gazing deeply into each other's eyes.

"Can you feel it, Gracie? How much I love you?"

"Yes. Now *show* me."

They made frantic love, clawing and biting, kissing and moaning as they found their rhythm, moving in perfect harmony. They made love until they both gasped in sweet agony from pure, explosive pleasure. And then they moved into the bedroom, becoming one again, slow and tender, their love binding them together like a never-ending ribbon.

Grace fell asleep in Reed's arms. He lay awake feeling the soft rhythm of her breath against his skin, filled with a sense of peace he'd never before experienced. His gaze ran down her body as he reached for the blanket, and he noticed a small tattoo of an orchid on the back of her thigh. *You never forgot.*

Time moved slowly, but it seemed to go too fast. With morning approaching, the last thing he wanted to do was move an inch, but he knew he had to do the right thing.

He brushed kisses over her cheek and whispered, "Gracie, baby."

"Hm?" She snuggled deeper into him.

He kissed her then, drawing strength to do what he didn't want to.

"As much as I want to wake up with you in my arms, I don't want you to feel funny tomorrow around your parents, or for them to think this is just a fling. I think I'd better take you home."

She turned in his arms, a sleepy smile on her lips. "Really? I'm so comfy."

He pressed his lips to hers. "Me too, but I want you to wake up tomorrow smiling, not wondering how to face your parents." He kissed the tip of her nose and said, "I know you, Gracie. You're a private person, and you'll be embarrassed to get home after dawn. I want your parents to know I love you enough to do the right thing."

"Trust me," she said with a seductive smile. "You did *all* the right things."

She touched her lips to his, and her expression turned serious. "You also did the right thing by telling me about what happened in Michigan. You always do the right thing, even when it's hard."

"Because that's what you do when you truly love someone. You put their well-being before your own."

Chapter Nine

GRACE AWOKE REFRESHED and rejuvenated despite so few hours of sleep and being sore in places she hadn't known she could be. It was a deliciously good soreness, and she didn't regret having made love with Reed one bit. She reached for her phone, and a text from him told her he didn't regret it, either. *Good morning, beautiful. My sheets smell like you. I'm having withdrawals. Can I see you tonight?* She smiled as she responded, *I'd never deprive you of your next hit.*

She rolled over, nearly squishing Clayton, and hugged Greedy Boy, thinking about Reed's confession. She had been so upset hearing about his *almost* engagement, she hadn't slowed down enough to think about what he'd gone through and how much that betrayal must have hurt. She glanced at the curtains, wishing he were there so she could talk with him about it.

She grabbed a handful of M&M's from the nightstand and shoved them in her mouth. She reached for another handful and stopped herself. If she was going to eat like this, she needed to sign up for a gym. Three weeks of eating junk would add at least five pounds to her hips.

Unless Reed and I can work it off.

Pleased with that idea, she ate a few more M&M's, deciding

she'd start running tomorrow morning. Even if they worked off the junk food, she was used to exercising in the mornings, and she might go stir crazy if she didn't.

She scrolled through her other texts and read one from Sable—*Hank just came into my shop. He said the café's buzzing about you and Reed.*

Great. Hank and his wife, Pearl, owned the Stardust Café. Now that they were in their late seventies, their daughter, Winona, basically ran the place. Reed's voice sailed through her mind. *Let them talk all they want. Pretty soon nobody will remember a time when we weren't together. Most of all, you.* He was so sure of himself, and he always had been. It was one of the many things she loved about him.

She sent Sable a quick reply. *Thanks for leaving the front door open for me. I was afraid I might wake the dogs.*

Sable's reply came seconds later. *I took care of that when I got in at 2.* Her text ended with a winking emoji. Sable flaunted her sexuality like a flag, much like Brindle.

She read a text from Sophie next. *Did you get your GREED on last night? I want all the details!* Instead of texting, Grace called.

Sophie answered on the second ring. "That good, huh?"

"You have no idea, Soph. I'm still recovering." She went into the bathroom and turned on the shower.

"It's about time you fed your hunger for that man."

She wasn't even going to pretend she hadn't compared every man she'd gone out with to Reed. "You know I'm all about being careful and making sure I know where I'm headed."

"That's why we're besties. We could have come from the same womb."

"Then tell me if I'm crazy, please. You can't tell anyone this, but he was almost engaged, and she cheated on him. He says he was never in love with her. Am I nuts to believe him? When we're together, it's like the past decade was a blip in our lives and we were meant to find each other again. But that only happens in fairy tales, right? I'm being stupid?"

"God, I hate cheaters, and *no*, you're not crazy or stupid. You're following your heart. You followed it to New York City, and you made your dreams come true. Why not enjoy Reed? You know he's your forever-kiss guy." Sophie's family had a long-running belief that the person someone was destined to be with was the one whose kisses lasted long after they left the room.

Reed's kisses had lasted for years. "Maybe so."

A call beeped through, and she saw Amber's name on the screen. "That's Amber. I've got to take it. I start teaching the class this afternoon. I'll text you later."

"I forgot to tell you, Nana signed up for your class. Have fun with that! Bye!" Sophie's grandmother, Nina, who everyone called *Nana*, was like a grandmother to Grace, and she was known around town for celebrating *every* holiday and event as if it were her last. She also had absolutely no filter. Sable and Brindle could have been her daughters.

Grace switched over to Amber's call. "Hey, Amb. Don't worry. I'm going to be there well before the class. I was thinking I'd come over a little early to get set up."

"Sounds good. I wanted to let you know we had a fifth signup. My friend Janie, the erotic romance writer, will be joining you."

"That's great. This should be fun. Janie is blind, right?"

"Yes. That's why I was calling. She said if you email her the documents, she has a program that can read them to her. Are there any materials that will need to be handled differently?"

"No. That's perfect. Other than the class outline, everything is verbal and done in class on the computers. Send me her email address and I'll send her the information."

They talked for a few more minutes, and after ending the call, Grace took a shower and got ready for the day. She took extra time with her hair and makeup, excited to see Reed this morning, glad he was working on her parents' porch. She peeked out the curtains, but the porch was empty. She smelled the flowers he'd given her, which sat on the nightstand beside the bed, where her mother must have put them after they left for their date. Feeling like she was walking on air, she dressed in the cute navy miniskirt and white silk tank she planned to wear to class and slipped her feet into a pair of strappy sandals. She snagged her phone and messenger bag with her work for the day in it and headed down to the kitchen for coffee.

Reba greeted her with a nose to the crotch. Grace shifted sideways and pet her. "Good morning to you, too, Reba. Where's your sister?"

"Sit, Reba," her mother said.

The pup plopped down on her butt, her tongue lolling out of her mouth as Grace set her bag on the counter.

"Dolly went with Dad to the library," her mother said, and handed Grace a cup of coffee. "How are you, sweetheart?"

"Fine. Thanks for the coffee." She took a sip and glanced out the side door, looking for Reed's truck. He wasn't there yet. She thought about texting to see when he would arrive, but that felt a little clingy, so she turned away from the door.

"Looking for Reed?" A spark of curiosity rose in her mother's eyes.

"Mm-hm. Sorry I got in so late last night."

"I'm not," her mother said with a mischievous smile. She sat down at the kitchen table. Reba padded over and sat by her feet. "Sit and chat with me for a minute. We haven't had any time to visit."

Grace's nerves tingled, which was ridiculous considering she was an adult.

"I take it your date with Reed went well?" her mother said, clearly fishing for more information.

A thread of guilt wound through her. "Yes, very well, actually. The fair was fun, and we went to his place afterward."

Her mother raised her brows. "How *nice*. I hear he bought the Carmels' house. Angel said he's done quite a bit of work, at least from what she'd seen of the outside of the house." Angel was Sophie's mother.

"He has, and the work he's done so far is really amazing."

"Like him." She sipped her coffee, watching Grace over the rim.

Grace crossed her arms, readying for an inquisition. "Go ahead, Mom. Ask whatever it is you'd like to know."

"I don't want to pry." Her mother set her coffee cup on the table.

"Yes you do."

She smiled and leaned closer. "You're right, I do! Oh, Gracie, he's such a nice man! And the way he looks at you..." She fanned her face dramatically. "That man couldn't hide his feelings for you if someone gave him a mask. He'd burn right through it."

"Mom!" Grace felt her cheeks flush.

"Oh, honey, *please*. If you think I was kidding about him keeping you overnight, you're dead wrong. It's about time you found a man who knew a good thing when she was standing right in front of him."

Grace heard Reed's truck door close in the driveway, and she jumped to her feet, one hand covering her racing heart. Reba lifted her head, panting happily.

"Well, it looks like you and Reed *both* know a good thing when you see it."

"Why am I so nervous?" she said more to herself than to her mother.

"Because it's been a long time since you've received *orchids*, and it scares you."

Grace felt her eyes widen.

Her mother stood and put her hand on Grace's shoulder. "Mothers always know, baby girl. You were happy then. You're even happier now."

"Did Dad know?"

"Some things aren't meant for a father's ears."

All that time she thought she was being so careful. How could her mother have known if her siblings hadn't? The realization that her mother had kept her secret made her heart feel impossibly fuller.

"It must have been difficult for both of you, keeping your relationship a secret," her mother said. "Although I'd imagine at that age there was a certain thrill to it, too."

Grace remembered both the thrill of sneaking around and the longing not to. "There were so many times I wanted to tell you and tell everyone else. Gosh, just about every day. I remember being so jealous at get-togethers when my friends brought their boyfriends. It was hard not telling anyone. Sable knew, and so did Sophie, but that was it. I'm really sorry, Mom." She didn't want to mention Reed's aunt and uncle knowing, because it felt like a betrayal that she and Reed had trusted them and not all of her family, though she knew it would have been too big of a secret for most of her siblings to keep.

"To be honest," her mother said, "I was glad you had each other, regardless of how it happened. I'd never seen you happier than when you were with him. I did worry that it might stop you from going to college, and when it didn't, I worried you might be too distraught to do well. But you've always been strong. Reed, however, had a harder time of it. The emptiness in his eyes after you two ended things could have drowned an Olympic swimmer. I always wondered if that was why he left town."

Grace's heart hurt anew.

Reed tapped on the screen door. He flashed a smile that made her insides tumble and said, "Mornin', Gracie."

Her mother whispered, "Couldn't hide it if he tried." She raised her voice and said, "Reed, come in, sweetheart. Have some coffee."

Reed stepped inside and made a beeline for Grace. "I think I'll have my sugar without coffee this morning, thank you." He pressed a kiss to Grace's cheek, earning an approving smile from her mother. "Grace, can I borrow you for a minute? I want to show you something."

He took her hand, leading her out the door and around to the far side of his truck, where he wrapped her in his arms and lowered his lips to hers, taking her in a kiss so hot it should have been preceded by a warning sign. She came away a little dizzy and a *lot* turned on.

"I COULDN'T WAIT another second," Reed said, and went for more. His hands moved down her hips as the force of their kisses drove her back against the truck. Her softness conformed to his hard frame. They'd always been insatiable, but everything felt amplified, stronger, more real. He wanted to lift her into his arms and take her right there against the truck. He reminded himself they were in her parents' driveway and reluctantly drew back. But the fire in her eyes and her grip on his shoulders brought his mouth to hers again.

When they finally parted, he pressed his hands flat on the door, caging her in. It was safer than his hands on her body, which would have made him want to spend the entire day making up for lost years.

"I didn't get a wink of sleep," he admitted. "Every time I closed my eyes I saw you."

Her lips were enticingly pink from the force of their kisses, and when they curved into a sexy smile, he touched his forehead to hers to keep from kissing her again. "What have you done to me, Gracie?"

"I think you mean what have we done to each other. Whatever it is, I don't want to stop. And, Reed, I owe you an apology."

He drew back so he could see her face more clearly. "For what?"

"Last night when you told me about what happened with your ex and having to sell your business, I was so wrapped up in my own head, I didn't slow down enough to think about how it must have made you feel. The betrayal alone must have been horrible, but coupled with selling the business you worked so hard to build? I can't imagine how devastated you were."

"It's over, Grace. Leave it in the past."

"I thought we weren't hiding from our pasts anymore. By the way, my mom knew about us. She just told me, but she said she never told my father, which is really…*big*."

"How did she find out?"

Grace shrugged. "I don't think it was Sable, and if any of my siblings knew they'd never have been able to keep it a secret. Mother's intuition, I suppose. But can we circle back for a second? I need you to know you can talk to me about what happened in Michigan and I promise I won't get upset this time." She took his hand in hers and said, "I don't want to skip the things that made you the man you are. I don't want anything left unsaid."

"Talking about Alina is the last thing I want to do."

"Then don't talk about her. Tell me about *you*."

"Gracie…"

"You don't have to, but I know it had to hurt."

She embraced him, and her comfort felt so good, the truth came without effort. "Oh, Grace. When you and I broke up, I didn't really feel *betrayed* because even though I gave my all to our relationship, we both always knew where you were heading after high school. We knew what was coming. But with her, I never gave my all to the relationship. So when she cheated, the betrayal was cutting, but I knew I'd dodged a bullet. The betrayal of my business partner was far worse than the betrayal of my ex. Thad and I had a bond I had given one hundred and ten percent to for years." His fingers curled into fists. "That pissed me off to the point of no return. That's why I sold him my stake in the business. I'd have come home either way to help my uncle, but I worked my ass off to build that business, and Thad's actions negated everything. He broke my trust, and I knew I'd never want to work hard enough to repair it."

"Do you miss the work you did there?" she asked.

"Sure, but there's nothing I can't do. I'll rebuild here. I've got my eyes on a few projects." He touched his lips to hers. "When I first moved back to town, I went into Morgyn's shop to buy a gift for my aunt, and we got to talking. When she heard I'd just moved back to town, without knowing anything about the reasons, she said, 'The universe has a plan for you, and once it shows itself, you'll know you did the right thing.'"

Grace laughed. "That sounds like Morgyn. She's all about leaving things in the hands of fate."

He gazed into her eyes, his heart so full of her his past felt like a story he'd heard about someone else. "Don't you see, Gracie? She was right."

Chapter Ten

AS GRACE DROVE down the main drag of Meadowside toward Amber's bookstore Monday afternoon, tingles of anticipation crawled up her limbs and chest. Meadowside was a quaint small town, much like Oak Falls, known for its rural setting and close-knit community. But to Grace it would always be *the place where Reed lived.* As a kid, she'd get shivers of anticipation about the possibility of running into Reed when she was out with her friends or family. Just catching sight of him had been enough to hold her over for hours back then. But now, if this morning was any indication, catching sight of him would never be enough again.

Grace parked in the lot beside the drugstore and walked down the block to Story Time, Amber's bookstore, which was located between the Catch Up Diner and Magnificent Gifts. Amber's storefront window displayed a mix of recent releases, a select few of her customers' favorite books, and a mix of bookish gifts and dried flowers. As much as Grace had always wanted to escape small-town life, most of her siblings never had. Amber embraced it and had dug her roots so deep in both Oak Falls and Meadowside, it was a wonder she hadn't begun sprouting saplings. She had a knack for making everyone feel as though they were an integral part of her bookstore, holding contests for the front-window displays, sending birthday wishes, and taking every customer suggestion to heart. She put energy into the community in the same way Grace put energy into each of her productions.

A bell chimed above the door as Grace walked in, greeted by hints of cinnamon and the kick-off-your-shoes-and-read-for-a-while aura Amber had expertly created.

"Hey, Gracie," Amber said from behind the counter, where she was ringing up a purchase for Haylie Hudson, Scotty's mother. "I'll be done in a sec. Make yourself at home."

"Hi, Grace." Haylie embraced her. "I heard you're teaching a screenplay writing class. I *wish* I could take a fun class like that, but between the center and Scotty, I barely have time to breathe during the week. But Boyd's fiancée, Janie, is excited to attend. Her first romance novel was a huge success. She's so creative. She's always trying to hone her craft." Boyd was Haylie and Chet's brother.

"I can't wait to meet her," Grace said. "It's great to see you."

Amber handed Haylie her bag of books and came around the counter wearing a cute pair of jeans and colorful leather boots. Reno pushed to his feet and ambled over.

"Thanks, Amber." Haylie smiled at Grace and said, "Scotty mentioned seeing you and Reed at the fair. Are you two going out? He's a great guy."

"We are." It felt wonderful to admit that so freely.

"Does that mean you're moving back?" Haylie asked.

"No," Grace said quickly. "My life is in New York now." Her *annoying* life, as of this morning. A director she adored and had hoped to work with for the next production had spent the morning trying to push her into taking a huge risk on an unknown playwright. He swore the production would do well, but Grace had been down iffy roads before, and they usually led to more headaches than they were worth. She wasn't sold on the idea and had left things up in the air.

"Long-distance relationships can work if you want them to, but I think it'd be tough after a while," Haylie said. "I have to get back to the center before they think I ran off for good. Good luck with the class."

After Haylie left, Amber said, "So it's true? You and Reed are an item?"

"Yes. It's true." She trusted Amber, and she was bursting at the seams to share her happiness, so she said, "Please don't tell anyone, but we dated in high school. I need to tell Dad at some point. Apparently Mom knew the whole time, but for some reason I'm really nervous about telling Dad I lied to him."

"Because you're not a liar." Amber smiled and said, "But you kind of *are*! Oh my gosh, Gracie. You and Reed had a secret fling?"

"Not a fling, no. He was my first love, and I swear, not much has changed. Does that make me sound ridiculous?"

Amber sighed. "No. It makes you sound happy." She hugged Grace. "I wondered why you hadn't found a real boyfriend in New York after all this time. I mean, you're gorgeous, smart, and successful. You could have any man you wanted. Sophie once told me you were just too picky. But that wasn't it, was it? You were waiting for Reed."

"I wish I could say that romantic notion was true, but I wasn't *waiting*," she admitted. "Or at least I didn't know I was. But the second we kissed, it was fireworks all over again."

"I want that!" Amber said with wide eyes. "I want fireworks. Just *once* in my life I want a kiss that makes me see stars."

"You'll get one, Amber. And if my life is any indication, it'll happen when you least expect it."

"I hope so." She took Grace by the arm and led her toward the back of the store. "Come on. Let me show you your options."

While the front of the store boasted floor-to-ceiling shelves, with several rows of bookcases in between and a few displays, the back of the store was more casual. The children's section took up the right rear corner, with a cylindrical bookshelf made out of stacked wooden crates. The top of the shelving unit was home to a multitude of potted plants and ivy, giving it a treelike appearance. Over the years, Amber had added fake vines and flowers, which made it feel eclectic and alive. There were dozens of small carpet mats that children could move around and sit on to read.

A nook of comfortable couches and mismatched armchairs took up the center of the rear of the store, surrounded by more bookshelves and displays.

"There are three places where you can teach. I have several lap desks in the storage closet, so if you want to teach in the reading nook, you can. But I also set up this table." Amber walked around the couch and motioned toward a long wooden table with several chairs. "This offers a little separation from the rest of the store, and a place for everyone to sit. But if you want more privacy, you can use my office. I set up a table in there, too."

Her office was separated from the rest of the store by a wall with bookshelves on the bottom and glass on the top, giving Amber a view of the shop from inside.

"You didn't have to go to all this trouble. Why don't we start in the office, just to make sure everyone is comfortable. I'll have a better idea of what will work after the first class. I hear Nana's coming."

"Oh, *yes.*" Amber tucked her hair behind her ear and said, "Don't make the same mistake I did. I called her *Nina*, because that's the name she used when she signed up, and she gave me a ten-minute diatribe about how 'kids' my age are only allowed to call her *Nana*. She signed up with her friend Hellie. You know how wild those two can get. I heard them talking about what they wanted to write about." Amber smiled and raised her brows. "It's either going to be wicked fun, or you'll have more trouble with them than the high schoolers who are coming."

"After the morning I had arguing with a director..." Grace rolled her eyes. "I can use a little fun to remind me why I got into this business in the first place."

They headed into her office, and Amber said, "I have no idea how you can keep so many balls in the air with each production. I have a hard time with my one little shop, and you've got to oversee financing, casting, choosing the script, sets, and Lord only knows what else over and over again, like an endless sea of decisions and headaches."

"Oh, please. You do just as much as I do." She set her messenger bag on the table. "I hope you're not disappointed with the size of the class. I know you hoped this would bring more attention to the bookstore."

"Don't be silly. I'm thrilled that you agreed to do it, and with so many people reading ebooks, I think any attention I can bring to the store is good. Besides if five people have fun in the class, they'll talk about it, and you know how gossip spreads. Maybe we can make it an annual thing. You never know; it could be the next best thing in Oak Falls."

Her enthusiasm made Grace glad she hadn't let her down

and gone back to New York. The bells chimed over the door to the shop, and Grace said, "I really hope it helps. I'm going to set up. Go ahead and do your thing, and, Amber, thank you. I'm glad we're doing this together."

Amber hugged her. "Me too!"

As Grace prepared for the class, setting documentation in front of each seat and mentally going over her plans, she grew more excited by the minute. She found herself thinking about her eleventh-grade English teacher, Ms. Devonshire. Grace had always enjoyed theater. She had taken part in drama club throughout elementary, middle, and high school. She had dabbled in writing, but she hadn't taken it seriously until Ms. Devonshire had challenged her to do an extra creative writing assignment and write a play for the elementary schoolers. Grace hadn't realized it until years later, but it was Ms. Devonshire's nudge in that direction that had fueled her love of creative writing. Ms. Devonshire had since retired and moved south, but Grace never failed to send her a holiday card. It was amazing what the attention of one person could do for another. She was excited to pay it forward and help others find their creativity.

"Gracie!" Nana said as she came through the door, carrying a large fabric bag that said GOT LIFE? in big red letters. Hellie was right behind her. Nana looked like a sweet and proper grandmother, dressed in a stylish pair of linen pants and a smart top. Her short, layered hair was mostly white, with a few strands of blond mixed in. She hugged Grace too tight and stood back, visually appraising Grace from head to toe.

"You are even more gorgeous than you were at Sophie's wedding. I hear you and Reed Cross are an item." Nana waggled her brows. "If you're smart, which I know you are, you'll give that hunk of a man anything he wants. He is too fine to pass up."

"Mm-hm," Hellie agreed, tossing her wild silver locks over one shoulder. Her long colorful dress, caramel-colored skin, and hazel eyes gave her an exotic look. She and Nana had grown up in Oak Falls, and they knew all the town's secrets.

Grace suddenly wondered if Nana knew hers. She'd never given Grace any indication of knowing about her and Reed, but Grace knew better than to rest on her laurels around Nana. She ushered them toward the seats as two teenage girls arrived, chatting as they entered the room.

"Hi. Is this the screenplay writing class?" the taller of the two asked. Her pitch-black, pixie-style hair was highlighted with streaks of vibrant blue, and her eyes were made up as dark as her black shirt and shorts. Her lace-up leather boots added a big-city, trendy touch to her rebellious outfit.

"Yes. Come in. I'm Grace, and I'll be teaching the class." She motioned toward the seats. "Sit wherever you'd like. What are your names?"

"I'm Phoenix," the raven-haired girl said. She nudged the freckle-faced redhead beside her, who was busy texting, and said, "This is Lauryn."

Lauryn looked up, and her soft green eyes widened. "I'm so excited to meet you. My parents took me to see *Summer Fever* two years ago, and it was so good!" *Summer Fever* was a play Grace had written and produced. It had won several local awards and ran for more than a year.

"Thank you," Grace said, glad to see she wasn't like many teenagers, solely focused on her phone. "That was a really fun play."

As the girls settled into their seats, Janie, a cute curvy blonde, and her guide dog arrived. Grace's mother had trained her dog.

"Janie? Hi. I'm Grace. It's nice to meet you in person."

"Thank you for sending the documentation early," Janie said. "I'm excited to get started. Do you have room for Friday, my dog, near my seat?"

"Absolutely." She showed Janie to her seat. "Everyone is sitting around this table. You each have plenty of space."

Janie began setting up her laptop and braille device, and Grace helped her find the outlets. Once Janie was settled with her pup at her feet and the others were prepared, Grace said, "I think we're all here. Let's go around the table and introduce ourselves. I'd love to know what brought you to the class and if you've done any other sort of writing. I'll start. You all know I'm Grace Montgomery. I grew up in Oak Falls and always had a love of theater and later developed a love of creative writing. I've been producing in New York City for a number of years, and I'm excited to share my knowledge with you. Janie, would you like to go next?"

"Sure," she said cheerfully. "I'm Janie Jansen, soon to be Janie *Hudson*." She held up her left hand, displaying a gorgeous engagement ring, which everyone admired. "I'm sure you noticed my guide dog, Friday. He's very friendly, but he's trained to hang out beside me. If you'd like to pet him, feel free as long as I'm not roaming around and needing his help. I'm an erotic romance writer, and my second novel is being released later this year."

"Hi, Janie. It's me, Nana. I loved your first book, *Sinful Fantasies*," Nana said with a waggle of her brows. "I wonder, do you and Boyd do hands-on research? Because that would explain those steamy sex scenes."

Janie laughed. "Nana Roberts, that is *not* something I want to admit to in public."

"You two know each other?" Grace asked.

"Honey, I know *everyone* in this room," Nana said proudly. "I changed Lauryn's mother's diapers, got Phoenix out of trouble when she was caught making out behind the Stardust Café, and Hellie and I knew Boyd's parents before Boyd and his family lost them in a fire, the poor things. That was devastating. Janie's a big deal to most people because she's an author, but to me she'll always be the girl who brought Boyd back home to his family, where he belongs."

Janie smiled. "Thank you, Nana, but I'm still not going to answer your research question."

Everyone laughed, and they continued with introductions.

"I'm Phoenix. I'm a junior in high school and I just like to write." She nudged Lauryn again.

"I'm Lauryn, also a junior. I write for the high school newspaper, and I hope one day to move to the Big Apple and follow in Grace's footsteps."

Grace was touched by her admiration. "Wow. Thank you. I'm sure you'll do better than I ever have. Hellie? Would you like to introduce yourself?"

"Like Nina, I've lived here forever, so I pretty much know everyone. I'm taking this class because Nina was bored and wrangled me into being her writing partner. I'm excited to see what we can come up with."

"And I need no introduction," Nana said. "All you need to know is that with your help, I'm going to write a kick-ass script. Now, let's get to it. Time's a wastin'!"

"Good idea. I know you're excited to write something wonderful, and you will. But much of your actual writing will happen on your own time, and then we'll discuss and critique it in class, so you can get hands-on, practical experience."

"Janie's got a leg up on the hands-on stuff," Nana said with a smile, earning laughter from everyone, including Janie.

"Hey," Hellie said. "We've got hands-on experience, too. I don't know about you, but just because the chimney's got snow on it doesn't mean there isn't fire down below."

The girls giggled, and Grace tried to circumvent an inappropriate tangent. "I can see we're going to have a lot of fun. Before we get too sidetracked, let's talk about the topics we'll be discussing, such as structure, character arcs, dialogue and themes, conflict, style, tone, and cinematic syntax…"

Grace fielded questions and found her teaching groove, enjoying every second of the two-hour class. She felt invigorated, and remembered just how exciting the whole creative process was. She gave her class a homework assignment to come up with a short description of what they hoped to write.

As everyone packed up to leave, the air was filled with excitement. "Can we team up to write?" Lauryn asked on her way out the door.

"Sure, if you'd like to," Grace said as she grabbed her bag.

"Oh good!" Lauryn lowered her voice and said, "I want to see if Nana will write with me. I *love* her!"

"I'll write with you," Nana said, apparently eavesdropping on their conversation. "But I don't want to write anything sappy."

"There's enough sap in real life," Hellie said. "We're going for badass characters."

"Sounds fun," Phoenix said. "Maybe we should do a group project."

"Only if Janie agrees to sex up our characters," Nana chimed in.

Janie laughed as she hoisted her bag over her shoulder. "Now you're speaking my language."

They left in a group, tossing out ideas one after another. Grace pulled her phone from her bag to check her messages, and Amber appeared in the doorway.

"It sounds like they had a great time." Her sister walked around the table pushing in chairs.

"So did I. It was awesome." She opened and read a text from Reed. *Hope your class went well. I'm running late and got stuck in the middle of a project. Can you meet me at my place? Wear something that can get dirty.*

Amber peered over her shoulder. "Reed?"

"Yeah. We were going out to dinner, but he's running late. What do you think he means by 'wear something that can get dirty'?"

"If you were Brindle, I'd say wear sexy lingerie. If you were Sable, I'd say wear a grease monkey suit. And if you were me, I'd say prepare to garden or something like that. But since it's you, I have no idea. Did you guys used to do anything dirty?"

Laughter burst from Grace's lungs. "We *did!*"

"I didn't mean *that!*" Amber blushed. "I don't want to know that about you!"

"Sorry." She tried unsuccessfully to stifle another laugh and hugged her sweetest sister. "Seriously, I don't remember doing anything particularly *messy.*"

Amber glared at her.

"I'm sorry! This time I really wasn't trying to be sexual." She hitched her bag over her shoulder. "Although…"

"Don't!" Amber put up her hand.

Grace pretended to zip her lips.

"Let's get back to your question. Since Reed is friends with the Jerichos, maybe you should dress for horseback riding or four-wheeling?"

"Oh boy. Maybe I'll go with sexy lingerie and see if I can sidetrack him."

Chapter Eleven

THE SOUND OF Grace's car drew Reed's attention from the living room wall he was painting. He climbed down from the ladder and leaned the brush on the paint tray, hoping her class went well. Earlier in the day he'd gotten a glimpse of the strong businesswoman she was, while she'd paced the yard, talking on the phone as he'd worked on her parents' porch. He hadn't eavesdropped, but it would have been hard for anyone to miss the determined set of her stride and the calm though firm sound of her voice.

"Knock, knock," Grace said through the screen door, ogling his bare chest.

Reed made his way to the door. He'd been thinking of her all day. Her familiar scent had still lingered in his bedroom when he'd come home, and as he'd painted, he'd felt her presence all around him, rousing his emotions. Now, as he opened the door and she stepped forward looking innocent and sensual at once in her miniskirt and blouse, he drew her into his arms and his heart poured out.

"Welcome home, pretty girl." He closed the door and lowered his lips to hers, kissing her with all the passion that had been building up all day. He intensified his efforts, and the bag she was carrying dropped to the floor.

"Can I go back outside and knock again? I like this greeting."

"How about you stay right here and I kiss you until those gorgeous legs of yours don't have the energy to take you anywhere?"

"Yes, please," she said in a sultry voice, and rubbed her body against him.

He took her in a slow, sensual kiss that brought fire to his veins. Her hands moved up his back, keeping him close as he nipped at her lower lip.

"Damn, Gracie. How can I miss you this much after only a few hours?" He kissed her neck, and she leaned to the side, giving him better access.

"I don't know, but I think we need to spend a few hours apart every day just so I can come back to this."

He brushed his lips teasingly over hers. "That can be arranged."

"I'm interrupting your painting," she said between kisses.

"I thought I'd be done before you finished your class, but since I wasn't..." He ran his tongue along the shell of her ear, his hands moving up her sides, brushing against her breasts. "How do you feel about a painting date?"

He sank his teeth into her neck, and she gasped.

"Yes," she said breathlessly.

He touched her pretty blouse, then ran his fingers along her thighs as he kissed her again. Her skin was warm and soft, and painting was the last thing on his mind. "This isn't really *getting dirty* attire."

"I think it's working pretty well," she said, and looked down at the streak of cream-colored paint on her leg.

He glanced at her leg, then at the paint on her blouse and cringed. "Sorry, babe. I'll pay for that to be dry cleaned."

"Maybe I should take it off." She began unbuttoning her blouse, eyes trained on him. "Oops." Her hands stilled on her buttons. "I might distract you too much to finish painting."

"Distract me, baby." He kissed her deeply, but as he'd come to expect, it wasn't enough for either of them. Their kisses turned urgent and messy as he fumbled with her buttons and she worked open his belt buckle.

"I swear I don't only want you for sex," he said. "I want to hear about your class."

"It was fantastic."

She kissed his chest, her nimble fingers playing over his pecs as he struggled with her buttons. She flicked her tongue over his nipple, driving him out of his mind. He managed one more button and stilled at the sight of her full breasts restrained by a skimpy pink bra. A heavy groan escaped before he could stop it.

"*Christ*, Gracie. You know how much I love you in pink lace."

"Then you'll probably enjoy the matching bottoms." She blinked flirtatiously, gazing up through her long, dark lashes as she lifted the hem of her skirt, revealing sexy pink lace panties.

He crashed his mouth to hers, and then their hands were everywhere at once. She grabbed at his head and shoulders as he groped her ass, loving the combination of lace and her hot flesh against his palms. She rocked her hips, and he slid his hand between her legs from behind, his fingers brushing over her damp panties. Another groan escaped as he pushed his fingers beneath the wet material and into her tight heat.

"Oh, *Reed*—" she said, and tugged at the button on his jeans.

He grabbed her wrist, and her eyes flew open, dark and ravenous. "First I take my fill." He tore her panties down and dropped to his knees to remove them. He pushed her legs apart, holding her thighs, pinning her against the wall, and slicked his tongue over her glistening sex. The air rushed from her lungs. She grabbed his head, her nails digging into his scalp as he devoured her sweetness. She writhed and moaned as he worked his magic, her sexy pleas spurring him on. Her legs flexed and her body trembled as he brought his fingers into play.

"Don't stop," she panted out. "Please don't—"

He sealed his mouth over her sex, using his fingers on her most sensitive pleasure point, and a long, surrendering sound left her lips. He quickened his efforts, sucking and licking, nipping and burrowing his tongue deep inside her. He thrust his tongue in and out of her tight heat. She met each thrust with a rock of her hips, a tiny gasp, and then her body bowed from the wall, quaking as she cried out, "Yes, yes, yes!"

Her sex pulsed as she rocked and pleaded. He stayed with her, loving her through the very last shudder of her orgasm. As she came down from the clouds, he shoved his jeans to his knees, lifted her into his arms, and drove into her in one hard thrust. Their tongues tangled and danced. He loved that she didn't pull away at the taste of herself. Her nails dug into his flesh as he lifted and guided her up and down his shaft, each thrust more powerful than the last, until their bodies took over, blinded by passion. She was so fucking hot, so tight and eager, there was no holding back. He pounded into her, his balls drenched with her arousal, nearly sending him over the edge. He fought for control, wanting—*needing*—to feel her lose herself in him again. It took only a few seconds before she was crying out his name, ravaged by another intense climax. He sank his teeth into her shoulder, sucking hard enough to earn another string of sinful, erotic pleas as their bodies ground together. Heat streaked down his spine with every upward slide along his cock.

"Oh God...*Reed*...."

Another climax tore through her. She clawed at his shoulders, and he followed her into blissful oblivion, capturing her passionate pleas with more hungry kisses as they rode the waves of their love.

He held her so tight he didn't know where she ended and he began, kissing her as their bodies began to calm.

She rested her cheek on his shoulder, her warm breath coasting over his skin as she said, "We were never very good at waiting."

He could hear the smile in her voice and pressed a kiss to her neck as a car door sounded outside.

She lifted her head, eyes wide. "Who's that?"

"Probably the pizza delivery guy. Good thing we came before he did."

"Reed!" she snapped as he set her on her feet. She grabbed her panties and the bag she'd brought. "What if they'd caught us?" She didn't wait for an answer as she bolted up the stairs.

He hiked up his jeans and called after her, "Then I'd say they got a pretty big tip!"

After paying for the pizza, he set it in the living room and went upstairs to wash up. He followed the sound of Grace humming and found her in the master bathroom. She held the hem of a dark T-shirt in her teeth as she zipped up a pair of cutoffs. Her hair curtained her face, and she looked eighteen years old again. She tucked her hair behind her ear as she released her shirt, lifting sultry eyes to his.

He wrapped his arms around her and kissed her softly.

"You smell clean," he said, nuzzling against her neck.

"And you smell like *me*."

"My favorite scent." He lifted her onto the sink and played with the fringe on her faded shorts. "I remember these shorts."

"I can't believe I still fit in them. When you said to dress in something that could get dirty, I wasn't sure what you meant, so I grabbed some of my old clothes from my closet, and…"

Her gaze trailed to the bag by his feet, and he followed it down, noticing a few pieces of silk and lace. His cock twitched again. "If you keep showing me your lingerie, I'll never finish painting."

"Good point." She slid off the sink. "Besides, you had *dessert*, but I'm starved."

"I've got your *dessert* right here, baby." He grabbed his junk.

She laughed as she headed for the stairs. "I like whipped cream on my desserts."

He chuckled as he turned on the sink and made a mental note to buy a case of whipped cream.

MUSIC STREAMED FROM Reed's phone as they ate dinner and painted the living room. Grace was surprised to see he'd chosen the colors she liked best. He'd already painted the trim white, and he'd also painted the center of the raised panels below the chair rail a pale seafoam green. The room looked warmer and brighter. Reed listened intently as they rolled paint on the walls and she told him about her class.

"They want to work as a group, which is really cool, because collaborative writing can lead to even more creativity. And you know how Nana is," Grace said. Reed knew Nana, Hellie, and Janie from around town. "Can you imagine if she put all that sass into a play? Oh my gosh, Reed. Maybe I should have told her to keep it rated PG or something."

"Nana is hilarious. When I first moved in and was working on the exterior of the house, she'd drive by really slow and watch me work. Sometimes she'd bring me a pitcher of iced tea or a muffin. She said she had some women in mind for me and proceeded to tell me about a litany of women, including Sophie's sister, Lindsay, who according to Nana is *shamefully single*."

"She used to always try to set up Sophie. She was scoping you out."

"Whatever," he said with a laugh. "If your class is even half as excited as you are, then it sounds like you're really making a difference."

"I don't know about making a difference," she said as she dipped her roller in the tray again. "I mean, it's too early to tell if they'll even stick with it. Three weeks is a long time. But their enthusiasm reminded me of what I was like when I first went into the business. I had that same level of excitement about everything I did."

He lowered the paint roller to the tray and asked, "And you don't now?"

"I do, but it's different. I thought producing would be like it was when I was in school, only on a much bigger scale. But it's like being the CEO of a huge, complicated corporation. There's a lot of babysitting, hand-holding, placating..."

"What exactly do you do as a producer?"

"What *don't* I do?" she said sarcastically. "I'm an independent producer, so I initiate the production, which means finding the script and hiring the director. Sometimes I handle casting, and other times I only approve the cast. I develop and handle the budgets, secure funding, create marketing and advertising strategies, set ticket prices, performance times. And, lucky me, most of the time I get to deal with the divas and snooty actors, too."

She set her roller in the tray and sighed, thinking of the hoops she'd had to jump through to get the lead actor. Keagen Thorpe was a hothead who thought he shit gold, which he just might, given how much money he earned. The investors had insisted on using him, and she counted herself lucky that so far he'd played by the rules.

"This is going to sound silly, but I miss being excited over productions the way I used to. Is every career like that?" she asked. "Does the joy go out of it once you've done it for a while?"

"Mine never has. Well, that's not true. After what happened in Michigan, just the thought of working on any of the projects I'd been doing with Thad made me sick. But that was because of him, not the work. I love what I do. Every project is unique and holds its own challenges. Restoring old buildings to their original beauty restores memories and history, and it feels like I'm giving back to the communities in which they're built."

The thrill in his voice was palpable, making Grace realize how sorely it was missing from her own. She began painting again. "That's something else I miss. Everyone in my business is take, take, take. And that's cool. I get it. It's a tough industry, and everyone wants to get ahead. But I miss giving back to people who appreciate what they're being offered. When I went to college I volunteered at a high school helping their drama club. The kids were so excited about every little thing—the routines, the rehearsals, the friendships."

"I remember, and you were in drama club in high school. I always assumed you continued doing those things in college. Can't you volunteer at a school in the city?"

"Not with my schedule. These three weeks are an anomaly for me. But even when I take time off, I don't really get it. I have one production that's running smoothly and an assistant who's taking care of things while I'm here, but this time in between is when I typically get started with the next show. Unfortunately, the director I was hoping to work with is giving me a hard time. I'll either have to convince him to go with a script I like, or I'll have to hire a new director. But that's just a headache, not overwhelming. I think slowing down these past few days has really shown me how much of a hamster wheel my life has become. Do you know that Sophie and I can't even meet for dinner more than once a month because of my schedule? We work out together, but even that's rare these days. It's crazy, and there's been no time to write, which is my true passion. I used to love writing in Central Park in the mornings. I'd sit on a bench or on a blanket in the sun and write until I had to start my day. The outdoors is so inspiring. But between work, exercise, and sleep, that time has just disappeared. Other than these past few days, I don't think I've even *relaxed* since college."

Reed set his roller down and came to her. He set her roller aside and laced their fingers together. "I watched you on the phone this morning. You're obviously business savvy, and you always had a knack for figuring things out. Can't you find a way to produce less and write more?"

She shook her head. "It doesn't really work that way unless I take a hiatus, and then I have the struggle of trying to get back into the game. Don't get me wrong. I still enjoy producing, and I'm grateful for all that I've achieved. The class today just sort of amplified how much enthusiasm I've lost, and I want to get that back."

He gathered her in his arms and pressed his lips to hers. "Let's brainstorm. What makes you happiest? What's missing?"

This. "A number of things."

"Give me an example."

"Besides time to breathe?"

He rubbed his whiskers over her cheek, sending titillating tingles all the way to her toes. "Come on, Gracie. I want to help."

"Orgasms," she said with a playful smirk.

"Well, I'm glad to hear that, since I haven't been there with you. We'll have to make sure you go back fulfilled and have lots of FaceTime trysts in between visits."

"FaceTime trysts? I can't..." *Can I?* She was surprised to realize she wanted to. She shivered with the idea of doing something so naughty with Reed.

"Baby, there's nothing we can't do together." He brushed his thumb over her cheek, and his eyes darkened seductively as he dragged that thick digit over her lower lip. "You can, and we will."

"Okay," came out easily, surprising and exciting her at once.

"Now, focus on your job for a second. How can I help you find that excitement again? Do you want to figure out a way to teach? I know you want to write. Can you do that on your lunch hour, or on the weekends?"

"You're such a fixer," she said, smiling, because he'd always tried to fix things for her when she was younger. It didn't matter if it was an argument with a sibling or trouble memorizing her lines for a play, he was there by her side trying to figure out a solution.

"And you've always been too stubborn to let me help. But why was that? Is it because you're the oldest and you think it's your job to help everyone else? Let me in, babe. Let's talk about it."

She'd seen needing help as a sign of weakness for as long as she could remember. She prepared to tell him that he had no idea of the magnitude of her schedule and that if she couldn't figure it out how could he, but she forced herself to slow down and take a step back.

She'd felt this way about her job for the last several months, and she'd done nothing to make it better. Maybe talking it out would help her see things more clearly. *Maybe if we'd taken the time to talk through all of our options before I'd gone to college, I wouldn't have jumped to the wrong conclusion and spent a decade carrying around unnecessary hurt. Maybe you never would have left town. Or maybe you would have come to New York at some point.*

She squeezed his hand and said, "Do you have any wine?"

Chapter Twelve

TUESDAY MORNING GRACE got up early, ate a handful of M&M's, and pulled on her running clothes even though she and Reed had probably worked off enough energy last night to negate the caloric content of the candy. After they'd talked about her crazy life in the city, she'd felt much better. Not that they'd come up with any firm answers, but they'd come up with some ideas for her to think about. More importantly, she'd been handling her own issues in such a vacuum for so long, it was cathartic to share her innermost thoughts with someone who cared about *her* without any ulterior motives toward her work or trying to get her to move back home. They'd finished painting the walls, ended up naked, painted, and intertwined on the tarps in the living room, and then they'd taken a shower together, where they cleaned each other up only to get down and dirty again.

She was lacing up her running shoes when Sable sauntered into her bedroom, wearing the same outfit, from boots to Stetson, she'd worn yesterday. She walked past Grace, grabbed a fistful of M&M's, then sat beside her on the bed. Grace glanced at the time—6:02—and bit back the urge to tell her to find her own boyfriend and eat his M&M's.

"Who was the lucky guy last night?"

"Nobody got lucky." Sable shoved the candy in her mouth and flopped onto her back. "After band practice we went to JJ's Pub and hung out until it closed. The only guy who piqued my interest was a certain fireman who's blown me off too many times for me to try again."

"Who?"

Sable gave her a deadpan look. "How many hot firemen do you know that would blow me off?"

Grace pushed to her feet and began stretching, uninterested in guessing, but knowing one for sure. Chet Hudson had never given Sable the time of day, which made him the ultimate challenge for her ballsy sister. "I'm surprised you didn't find some other hot guy to hit on."

"I did, but I wasn't into him."

"Maybe you're getting tired of hookups."

"Bite your tongue. I was sidetracked. I've been working on some new ideas for songs, so I sat out on the hill and tried to get inspired, but…" Sable sighed. "I'm just not feeling it. I've been having a hard time with that lately. I even spoke to Axsel for a while. He's so good at opening my creative pathways."

While Grace never liked to ask for help, Sable preferred people not to have *any* inclination that she might even need it. Grace was glad to see her easing up on the typical tough-as-nails vibe she gave off and not only turning to Axsel but sharing with her, too. It helped Grace feel closer to the one sister who had always made her feel a little unnecessary. Her mind traveled back to her conversation with Reed about her predicament at work. He'd had some good suggestions, like cutting back from three productions a year to two and trying to work in a few more afternoons off once each production was up and running.

She'd been on such a fast track for so long, the idea of taking any time off just to rejuvenate had somehow become slated as wasted time. How had that happened? Time off to sneak in some writing or enjoy a long weekend with Reed was definitely *not* wasted time. She had a lot to consider.

She caught the tail end of something Sable was saying and realized she'd zoned out. Trying to play catch-up, she said, "How is Axsel?" Axsel was just shy of six years younger than Grace, and he traveled so much, she saw him only once or twice a year.

"Has he ever *not* been great? *Chill boy* is always good. He never gets rattled. He's back in L.A., and bummed he's not here to hang with you."

Grace laced her fingers together and stretched her arms above her head. "I miss him and Pepper, but I guess there's always Christmas."

"Speaking of Pepper. Mom invited her to the barbecue next Friday night, but she can't make it, of course. She said something about a research project."

"Pepper is always researching, but what barbecue?" She shifted, stretching her hamstrings, thinking about how infrequently she saw her scientist sister.

"You two are more alike than you might think," Sable said with an air of boredom. "Last night Mom said she's throwing a family barbecue next Friday night after Reed finishes the porch. Oh yeah, you're supposed to invite him, and I was supposed to text you and let you know. Sorry."

"*Great.* That should make him run for the hills." Her family was a lot to handle in small doses. As a group they could be downright overwhelming, especially to a guy who was used to quiet.

Sable smiled and closed her eyes. "It's best to indoctrinate him to the chaos earlier rather than later." She set her hat over her eyes and said, "You don't mind if I just crash right here, do you?"

Normally Grace would kick her out of her room, but she didn't want to close the door Sable had only begun to unlock. She pulled off Sable's boots and set them beside the bed. "Get some rest. I have to go run off my junk food."

She wrote a quick note for Reed—*Sable is sleeping on my bed, so don't go in and whip off your clothes or anything. I went for a run. Xox, Grace*—and went to the kitchen to find tape. She found it in the family junk drawer and put a piece on the top of the note. Then she grabbed a pen, crossed out *Grace* and wrote *Gracie*.

Humming, she went outside and taped it to the outside of the glass door that led to her bedroom. Reed had done a gorgeous job on the porch so far, and she was happy that her childhood home was being lovingly restored.

Remembering the mornings she and Reed had secretly met by the football field before the sun came up, she took off jogging in that direction.

As she rounded the corner toward town, energized by thoughts of Reed, she realized her childhood home wasn't the only thing being lovingly restored.

REED STOPPED BY Roy and Ella's to catch his uncle up on his progress at the Montgomerys and check on the delivery status of the materials for his kitchen, which Roy had offered to handle. They were sitting at the table enjoying breakfast when he tapped on the kitchen door and walked in.

"There he is," Ella said as she rose to greet him, and promptly ushered him into a seat. "I'll get you a plate."

"It's okay, Ella. I didn't come for breakfast. Sit down and relax."

"You know that isn't gonna go over very well," Roy said under his breath.

"A working man has to eat." She set a cup of coffee in front of him and patted his shoulder before turning back to the stove. "You just relax."

"Thank you." Reed took a drink.

"Cade said you're almost finished with the porch," Roy said. "He's mighty pleased with your work, of course."

"That's good to hear. I'll be finished by the end of next week."

"More importantly," Ella said as she set a plate of pancakes in front of Reed. "Why are we the last to hear that you and Gracie are together again?"

Aw, hell. He'd forgotten how quickly word moved between towns. "You're not the last to hear."

Ella sat beside Roy and set her napkin in her lap. "According to my friend Rosie, who saw Hellie at bingo last night, the whole town knows about you two." She sipped her coffee, her smiling eyes peering at him over the rim. "Are we done keeping secrets?"

Reed chuckled and stabbed a hunk of pancake with his fork. "We are definitely done keeping secrets."

"Well, thank goodness for small favors," Roy said. "You can't ever find honest love when you're shrouded in secrecy. Life doesn't work that way."

Reed focused on his breakfast and not the message his uncle was really sending, which had landed loud and clear. When he'd returned to town, they hadn't been pleased to hear that he had been serious enough to almost have been engaged to a woman they'd never met.

Ella reached across the table and touched his hand, bringing his gaze up to hers. "Honey, we understand why you had to keep things hush-hush when you were in school. Kids can be cruel, and you wanted to protect your girlfriend. You did the right thing under the circumstances. And as far as that last woman goes, well, I can only assume she hadn't yet kissed your heart for you to keep her a secret. But moving forward, we'd really like for there to be no more secrets."

A spear of guilt pierced Reed's chest. "No more secrets," he agreed. "And I'm sorry for keeping them in the first place."

"That woman was a stopgap, son," Roy said as he cut his pancakes. "Someone to hold you over until the time was right for you to come back home and find your true soul mate."

Reed's fork stopped midair. "That makes me sound a little callous, Roy. I didn't think of her as a stopgap. I just wasn't capable of giving her all of myself."

"That's not what I meant, Reed, so put out those fumes." Roy sat back and exhaled a long, slow breath. "Love's a funny thing. When it hits, there's no keeping your distance or wondering if you should do something to fix whatever feels off. That's how we knew you and Grace were meant to be together, and that's why we kept your secret, when the proper thing to do would have been to make you stand up to your friends and her friends and pick her up properly at her daddy's house. The *stopgap* I spoke of had nothing to do with you treating that other woman badly, or making a bad judgment call. I meant you were filling the emptiness inside you. That's only natural, just as it was only natural for her to feel the weight of another woman in your heart."

Reed set his fork down on his plate. "Roy, did you know Grace was coming back to town?"

"I *may* have heard she was scheduled for a visit," Roy mumbled, and filled his mouth with pancakes.

"Ella?"

"My memory is not what it used to be." She patted her mouth with her napkin.

They ate in silence for a few minutes while Reed processed that new information. Were they matchmaking? He dragged an assessing gaze over Roy's face, wondering what else he might have kept to himself.

"Most of your appliances are being delivered Thursday," Roy said a few minutes later. "Are we still on for starting your kitchen after you're done with the Montgomerys?"

"Yes. I'm looking forward to working together, although Grace and I have already gotten some of the painting done. There's not much left to do beyond the kitchen." He eyed the two people his father had trusted with his life. The two people who knew what he needed even before he did, and he had to ask the burning question. "When did your doctors give you the okay to return to work?"

Ella choked on her coffee.

Roy stilled, staring at his plate.

Reed's gut clenched tight as shock tore through him. "*Roy?*"

"Well, heck, Reed. What do those doctors know? My body needed the rest, and you were here anyway. We still hadn't settled the new corporation paperwork, and the jobs we were bidding on hadn't come in yet. It made sense for you to take on the Montgomery job."

"He really did need to rest, Reed," Ella added. "You can see how much stronger he is now."

"I can, and I'm happy to do the work." Reed finished eating and carried his plate to the sink, stewing over, and touched by, their efforts. "I sure am glad we're done with secrets."

Ella's gaze darted to Roy.

"Aw, come on, Ella. What more could there possibly be?"

She glared at Roy.

"Gosh darn it." Roy tossed his napkin on the table and said, "You know how I said that *most* of your appliances would be delivered Thursday? I transposed the numbers on your stove and accidentally ordered a bright red one. But it's *handled.*"

Ella stood up and reached for Roy's plate. Roy slid an arm around her waist and pulled her closer. "And for the record, your aunt gave me hell for being less than up-front with you about work. But the stove order is fixed, so don't you worry about that."

Reed chuckled. "That's all right, and speaking of fixes..." He kissed Ella's cheek and patted Roy's back. "I have to go get my *Gracie fix* for the morning. Love you, and I appreciate you watching out for me. Not just now, but...well, you know."

"Yeah, we know," Roy said. "Now get your lazy ass over to that job before your girl thinks you've forgotten her."

Twenty minutes later Reed pulled into the Montgomerys' driveway and was greeted with the most spectacular view of a fine ass, an ass he'd know anywhere. He stepped from the truck as Grace unfolded her gorgeous body and reached her fingers toward the sky. She turned, smiling brighter than the morning sun, and holy smokes, her black running pants rode low on her hips, clinging to every inch of her like they were painted on.

And her running bra did some sort of cross-over thing that pressed her breasts together, creating cleavage so deep he wanted to crawl in and live there. Her hair was pinned up in a high ponytail, exposing her long neck and cute ears he liked to nibble on. Her cheekbones looked even higher with her hair pulled back, her eyes looked greener, and her skin glistened with a sheen of sweat that made her appear oiled up and scorchingly sexy. He was catapulted back to the days of watching her cheer for the opposing team and was reminded of how jealous he'd been over the guys who had been lucky enough to watch her practice on a daily basis. She had womanly curves now, and her eyes were sharper than that of a naive girl, which made her that much more attractive.

As he reached for her, his heart tumbled inside his chest, and he sent up a heap of silent gratitude that his relatives had known him well enough to keep their secret about Grace's visit. Had he known she would be there, he might not have taken on the job.

"You have never looked more beautiful than you do right now," he said as he gathered her in his arms.

"I'm all sweaty," she warned.

He guided her arms around his neck and said, "I don't care if you've rolled in horse manure. You'd still look and smell better than any woman on earth, because you're mine, Gracie, and I adore you."

He pressed his lips to hers, soaking in her sweetness. He ran his finger along her side, and she shivered in his arms. "I didn't know you were a runner."

"I usually run at the gym, but I haven't gotten a temporary membership at one here yet," she said as they made their way to the porch. "And if I keep eating M&M's and pizza, I'm going to need to go twice a day or buy bigger clothes."

"I would love to get you *out* of those clothes," he said as they climbed the steps and followed her toward her bedroom door, earning an adorable blush. "Why would you work out in a gym when you can enjoy sunshine and fresh air? Help me today. You'll get a great workout, and I'll get to spend the day with you. Win-win."

Her brows knitted. "You just want me to hold your *tools*."

Just hearing her say that got him going. "Baby, I always want your hot little hands on my *tools*." He pressed his hips to hers and said, "But I'm pretty sure your parents wouldn't appreciate the show."

Her cheeks pinked up again, and he couldn't resist pressing his lips to them.

"You don't have to help me." Knowing how competitive she was, he egged her on, hoping to spend the day with her. "It's a man's job, anyway."

Her jaw dropped, and just as quickly her eyes narrowed and she took a step back. "A *man's* job? Let me get my dad's tools..." A smile lifted her lips, and she wrinkled her nose. "Actually, let me get *Sable's* tools. I promised Brindle I'd stop by her play rehearsal later, but I think I can show you up before that."

He hooked his arm around her neck and laughed. "You're really hot when you're trying to prove a point." He gave her a chaste kiss and noticed a note taped to the door and snagged it. "Is this for me?" He read it aloud. "*Hey, big boy, come on in. I'm ready and waiting.* Damn. I wish I hadn't stopped to see Roy—"

She ripped the note from his hands and scanned it. She gritted her teeth, fire in her eyes, as giggles floated out the kitchen window, where Brindle and Morgyn were cracking up.

"I'm going to kill them," Grace seethed, crumpling the note in her fist as her sisters came out the kitchen door, laughing hysterically, with Reba and Dolly on their heels.

She shoved the note in his hands and bolted off the porch toward them. Brindle and Morgyn screamed and ran into the yard. Reba and Dolly chased after them, barking up a storm.

"I'm going to kill you!" Grace hollered.

"Not if you can't catch us!" Morgyn yelled back as she raced, full speed, toward the barn.

"Don't get me dirty!" Brindle screamed as Grace grabbed her. "I have to go to work!"

Grace's bedroom door opened, and Sable walked sleepily out. "What's going on?"

Reed watched Grace tackle Morgyn to the ground, both of them laughing. "I think Gracie is finding her way back to her roots."

Chapter Thirteen

AFTER THE MORNING chase, Grace's sisters left for work, and Grace changed into a pair of the sexy cutoffs Reed loved, and then they went to work on the porch. She worked through the morning like she'd been building porches her whole life. She was as meticulous as Reed was, and he got a kick out of her refusing to let him carry the planks or do much of anything *for* her. *With her*, however, was another story. Reed taught her how to use the chop saw and nail gun, gave her a lesson in leveling and shaping, and she listened so intently, he knew she didn't miss a word. Together they measured, cut, and hammered. He had a field day making sexy comments about her *screwing* the boards, which earned a few blushes and a lot of laughter.

"You're going to owe me a full-body massage after this," Grace said as they lined up a plank.

"If you think that's a threat, you're sorely mistaken." He swept her into his arms and kissed her, with an accompanying "Mwah!" earning another heart-melting laugh.

"It looks like you two make a great team," Cade said as he came around the side of the house with Dolly and two glasses. He handed them each a drink. "I thought you could use some iced tea. With Axsel gone, it's nice to have a man around again.

I'm a bit outnumbered in the estrogen castle."

Reed laughed. "You are a bit outnumbered." He took a drink and knelt to love up Dolly.

"I don't know, Dad," Grace said as Dolly wound around her legs. "Sable's kind of like a guy sometimes."

"Sable's a tough cookie," Cade agreed. "But beneath that tough exterior, she's a real sweetheart. She's got a softer side. Always has. She just needs a man who's strong enough, and patient enough, to find it."

"Good luck with that." Grace tipped her face up to the sun, eyes closed, looking like a goddess despite the sweat she'd earned and the dirt she'd acquired. How many women would spend hours doing manual labor in the hot sun when they could be doing any number of other things? Not to mention doing it with a sense of humor. But Grace had never been afraid of hard work.

Reed had always thought she was more afraid of not standing out as her own person than of the work it might take to get there. He didn't know for sure, but he thought that might have something to do with having grown up with so many siblings. The reason didn't matter. He loved Grace for her determination and her insecurities. She was as real as a woman could be, and he knew he was one hell of a lucky man.

"You raised strong daughters," Reed said. "Sable's no stronger than Grace. They just show it in different ways."

"I'd agree with you there," Cade said.

Marilynn and Reba came out of the barn, and the minute Reba saw them, she bounded across the grass and joined Dolly. The two pups smothered Reed with kisses. Grace took Reed's glass and set it on the deck beside hers, then sank down to the grass with them. Reba immediately crawled up her body and licked her cheek.

"This is their playtime," Marilynn said as she came to Cade's side. "But I can call them off with one command if you'd like."

"I love dogs." Reed grabbed Reba's head and pressed a kiss to the end of her snout. "Won't you be sad when you've trained them and you have to give them up?"

Marilynn and Cade exchanged a knowing smile.

"We miss them all, but if we kept them we'd have to buy a bigger house," Marilynn explained.

"It's hard to let them go, no doubt. But we raise them to be independent and to make a difference in other people's lives, just like our children," Cade said as Grace pushed to her feet beside him. He put his arm around her, love brimming in his eyes. "It's nice to see you doing something other than working, darlin'. I made lunch for you and Reed. It's in the fridge."

"You didn't have to go to all that trouble," Reed said as he rose to his feet.

"No trouble at all. I threw together a few sandwiches and cut up some fruit. No great shakes. It's the least I can do, considering you've got my girl sticking around without her nose in a script."

"*Dad.*" Grace rolled her eyes. "What would you have me do? Be barefoot and pregnant?"

"Now we're talking!" Marilynn said with a smile. "I could use a grandbaby or two."

"Stop!" Grace said.

"Don't worry, sweetheart. I'm taking your mama out for a trail ride." Cade reached for Marilynn's hand. "She won't be able to marry you off this afternoon."

"Reed, why don't you ask your aunt and uncle to join us for

the barbecue next Friday evening," Marilynn suggested.

Reed glanced at Grace. "Barbecue?"

"Oh, shoot! I was supposed to tell you about it," Grace said. "I got a little sidetracked with—" She glanced at his shirtless body. "All the work we're doing."

He chuckled.

"Work? Is that what they're calling it these days?" Marilynn teased.

"Mom! Dad, take her away. *Please.*"

As Cade led Marilynn toward the barn, her mother said, "Please ask Roy and Ella if they'd like to come next Friday evening. We're celebrating the completion of the porch, and Sable moving out."

"I'm sure Sable will be happy to know you're celebrating her leaving," Grace teased.

Her mom spun around as if to say something, and Cade hauled her against him, silencing her with a kiss.

"I really like your parents," Reed said as he gathered Grace in his arms.

"Yeah, they're pretty cool, aren't they?" She pushed her fingers into the waist of his jeans. "Are you hungry?"

"I could eat."

"Me too," she said in a voice as smooth and intoxicating as a shot of whiskey. She began walking backward toward the doors that led to her bedroom, tugging him with her by her grip on his jeans.

"Grace, what about your parents?"

"We figured out years ago that 'trail ride' was code for Mom and Dad needing make-out time." She yanked open the door and pulled him into her bedroom. After closing *and locking* the porch door, she drew the curtains, and then she shut and locked the door to the hall. With a fierce, sexy look in her eyes, she worked his belt buckle and button free and said, "This is *your* lucky day," as she unzipped his jeans. "I happen to be famished, but not for lunch."

He was already hard, but when she pushed her hand into his briefs, her strong grip on his cock pulled a groan from his lungs.

"My lucky day was the morning you walked out of this bedroom in those slinky little pajamas and back into my life."

"We'll see if you still feel that way in ten minutes." She yanked his pants down in one swift tug, and then her lips touched the tip of his cock. "Hello, big guy. I've missed you."

She lowered her mouth over the head, teasing him with her tongue in a slow, mind-numbing rhythm. When she cradled his balls and took him to the back of her throat, he moaned and tangled his hands in her hair, but allowed her to set their pace. She sucked and licked, her hand sliding along the length of him in perfect, tight tugs. Her hair brushed over his thighs, and she moaned around his cock. The illicit sound vibrated through him, and when she quickened her pace and grabbed his ass, using him for leverage so she could take him deeper, he just about lost it.

"Gracie," he said through clenched teeth. "You're going to make me come."

She drew back, still working him with her hand, and there was no mistaking the desire in her eyes as she said, "I should hope so."

She dragged her tongue from base to tip and then worked her magic. The world sped by as her glorious, hot mouth sent him soaring. She stayed with him through the very last pulse of his release, and then she rose to her feet, and he gathered her in his arms, pouring all of his love into passionate kisses.

"We were both wrong, baby," he said into her ear. "Every day we're together is luckier than the last."

LATER THAT AFTERNOON, Grace went to see Brindle at her drama club rehearsal. What was it about elementary schools that made her want to either stand up straight or run down the hallway? She'd never run down the hallway as a kid and couldn't imagine why that even popped into her head as she made her way toward the all-purpose room. While half of her siblings' rebellions were wild and crazy, short of lying about seeing Reed when she was in high school, Grace's rebellious acts had been few and far between. She'd once faked being sick and had gone to the nurse's office. They'd called her mother, who had come to pick her up early from school. On the way to the car, Grace broke down in tears and told her mother she wasn't really sick. She'd then marched herself directly into the principal's office, despite her mother trying to convince her that taking half a mental health day wasn't such a bad idea. Grace had pleaded her guilt to the stunned principal and assigned herself detention. That was the first and last elementary school prank she'd ever pulled.

As she entered the all-purpose room, the children's voices brought memories of her drama-club days. She'd sat in this same room beside Sophie, reading lines for plays and giggling with their friends. This was where her enjoyment of theater first began, fed by the support of teachers and classmates. She leaned against the wall, observing Brindle sitting in a circle with the children and what looked like a few high-school-aged helpers, as the kids recited their lines. She rarely got to see Brindle teach and took a moment to watch her. Brindle's blond hair cascaded over the shoulders of her pretty sheer blouse, which she wore over a simple white camisole. Even sitting cross-legged in jeans and sandals, like the kids, Brindle looked elegant, professional, and nothing like the girl who just a few hours ago had been racing around their parents' yard.

Brindle listened carefully, offering suggestions when the children missed a line and complimenting each one as they finished. It was interesting seeing her flirtatious, risk-loving sister acting so serious, interjecting information about what the kids can expect when they went onstage.

One of the children glanced at Grace. Brindle's gaze followed, and a smile lifted her lips.

"Kids, this is my sister Grace. She's going to help me make the play a little shorter," Brindle said, and all the kids cheered.

"Thank you!" shouted a towheaded boy.

"Not too much shorter," pleaded an adorable girl with braids.

"Nat, can you please take over?" Brindle asked one of the teenagers.

"Sure," Nat said. She was a studious-looking brunette with dark-framed glasses and stick-straight posture, and she reminded Grace of herself at that age.

"Thanks for coming. Let's sit down." Brindle pointed to the bleachers, eyeing Grace with a curious expression. As they walked across the room, she said, "I guess Oak Falls really is good for the soul, like Mom says. You look amazing, like you're...I don't know. Refreshed? Happy?"

"That probably has more to do with Reed than Oak Falls," Grace said as they sat down. "I helped him with the porch this morning." She felt her cheeks burn with the memory of what else she'd helped him with.

Brindle gasped, her eyes filling with amusement. She leaned closer and whispered, "Grace! Did you have a *nooner*? At Mom and Dad's?"

Grace laughed softly and admitted, "Mom and Dad went for a *trail ride*." She'd never shared her sex life with Brindle and had no idea why she was now, except that she was so happy with Reed she wanted the world to know—about her happiness, not their intimacy. That had just slipped out.

Brindle let out a tempered squeal and hugged her. "I'm so proud of you!"

"Stop!" She pushed her sister away with a smile. "We're *not* talking about this," she said firmly.

"Well, *you're* not, but oh my gosh, Gracie!"

"No, Brindle," she said with a glare. "You are not speaking about it either. I don't want to hear about this from Morgyn or Sable or anyone else."

Brindle sighed. "Fine! You are no fun at all." A smile lit up her eyes as she leaned closer and whispered, "But you totally *are* fun! This is so good! I'm happy you're not an ice queen."

"*Ugh!* Can we work please?"

Brindle's expression softened. "I didn't think you were an ice queen. That was Sable. I'm just glad you proved her wrong, because, you know. You're always so proper around us, and I'd be sad if you missed out on taking advantage of our parents' make-out session."

A laugh slipped out before Grace could stop it. "Thank you. *I think.*"

Brindle gazed out at the kids with a look of admiration. "These kids are so smart, Gracie. They've got the whole play darn near perfectly memorized, and we're still a few weeks out."

"Then what's the issue?"

"These are my third and fourth graders, but we have kids from first and second grade in the play, too. They're rehearsing in one of the classrooms with two of the high school volunteers. The play's an hour long, and it's too much for them. They get restless, and I want this to be fun for all the kids. I think the only way to find a happy medium is to cut it back to thirty or, at the most, forty minutes. But I tried, and it's like I'm married to every word of the story."

She handed Grace the script, and Grace skimmed over it. "I've never heard of *Beans, Buttons, and Bullies*."

"Nat wrote it. She's in my English class at the high school, and she's so creative. I remembered the story you wrote for the elementary schoolers when you were in high school. You said Ms. D really inspired you to take your creative writing seriously. I thought I'd borrow that tactic." She did her signature Brindle-happy shrug, wrinkling her nose and smiling, and said, "I think it's really working. She's already writing another play. She wanted to take your class, but it interfered with our rehearsals."

Grace was impressed and strangely touched by her sister's interest in helping her students succeed. She had worried about Brindle going into teaching, as teaching was a challenge for anyone and Brindle had never been a particularly focused student. Even in college Brindle was a wild child, and Grace had told her there was no place for *wild* in a teacher's professional life. Brindle had sworn that teaching was her calling because she felt she could relate to kids of all ages—and she'd proven herself many times over. Her students loved her because she was down-to-earth, but she was also firm enough to demand respect. Grace was happy to see that attitude had carried over to the drama club.

"Maybe I can find a way to mentor Nat long-distance," Grace offered. "In fact, I'd like that."

"Really? She'd be thrilled. Thank you. I'll introduce you after we're done. Do you think you can rewrite the script?"

Grace watched Nat, who obviously patterned her behavior with the students after Brindle, as she was every bit as supportive toward them. "This is Nat's script. I think you should discuss rewrites with her."

"I did, but she said she didn't know where to start."

"Looks like the mentoring can start today. Can you spare her for an hour?"

"Absolutely! Let me go get her." Brindle jumped to her feet and hugged Grace. "I can't thank you enough. It's so hard to find kids who look beyond partying, and Nat's really excited about this project."

Grace had to laugh. "Says the girl who never met a party she didn't like."

Brindle held her finger over her lips. "Shh. They don't need to know that."

"You do realize this town's got ears in the ground, right?"

"Yes! But they know better than to comment on it, and I've gotten really good at being discreet with my personal life."

Grace arched a brow.

"Okay, *more* discreet," Brindle said softly. "Besides, there's only been Trace on and off for a while now. But don't tell him that. The man's ego is bigger than his…" She glanced at her students and said, "*Heart.*"

As shocked as Grace was to learn Brindle had only been with Trace, she knew better than to hope her wild sister might tame her ways while she was in Paris for six weeks this summer.

Brindle put another teenager in charge of the class while she introduced Nat to Grace.

"I'm so excited to meet you," Nat gushed. "I really wanted to take your class, but I also wanted to be here for the kids, and my mom said it was more important to see this play through than to work on another project."

Nat spoke fast, fidgeting first with her glasses, then the hem of her shirt, then her glasses again. Grace found her nervousness endearing and her excitement inspiring.

"I know she's right," Nat said, "but I wish I could have done both."

"I admire you sticking with the play. Your mom was definitely right about that. In the arts, seeing your dream become a reality is a tricky and exciting process. The more control you have, the better."

As they made their way down the hall to the classroom Brindle suggested they use, Grace realized that achieving her dreams had also been tricky for other reasons. She'd lost a lot of the joys of life in the process. She wondered if there was a way to slow down, and if so, what ramifications it would have on her career.

If I don't, what will it mean for me and Reed?

Why did it seem like everything good in life required a painful choice?

Chapter Fourteen

THE NEXT FEW days flew by in a blur of conference calls, teaching, and mentoring during the day and laughter and loving at night. Grace's love for Reed blossomed into a love truer and deeper than anything she'd ever known. Friday afternoon as she taught the class at the bookstore, she couldn't believe tonight marked the end of her first week at home. How had the time moved by so quickly? She and Reed had gone furniture shopping Wednesday evening, and once they'd gotten past needing to cuddle and kiss on every sofa—*just to be sure they were comfortable*—he'd bought a beautiful dark blue couch and love seat that had an antique feel, a glass coffee table with leather around the edges, and a plush throw rug. They'd also picked out a dining room set made from refurbished barn wood, which fit the relaxed yet elegant feel of the room perfectly. The furniture had been delivered last night, and it had completely transformed the already gorgeous house into a warm and inviting home. Grace couldn't help feeling like they were building a home together, but she tried not to get drawn in by that aspect, because it was Reed's home, and she had her own to return to in two weeks. But she enjoyed setting up his home with him. He had a keen, artistic eye.

She looked around the table at the other artistic individuals she was spending time with, huddled together discussing character arcs and plots. Wednesday's class had been even more thrilling than the first. They had been hard at work creating an outline of the script they wanted to write.

"Okay, ladies," Grace said. "Are we ready for our discussion?"

"Yes!" they said in unison.

"Wonderful. Who's going to present the story?"

They exchanged looks among themselves, and Lauryn whispered something to Janie.

"Sure, I'm happy to," Janie said. "Do the rest of you want me to start?"

They all agreed, and Janie said, "Our script is called *I Ain't No Cinderella*. Our heroine is sharp, rebellious, and is *not* about to wait around for her prince."

"And the prince is not badass enough for her, so she's going to snub him and hit on a biker," Nana interjected. "*He's* badass."

"Mm-hm," Hellie agreed. "The prince is a sissy. Our girl needs a real man, and she's not about to wait around for him to come to her."

"That biker's going to have his socks knocked off," Janie said. "There's a big community barn dance, kind of like the monthly jam sessions the Jerichos host."

Phoenix narrowed her green eyes and said, "And the stepsisters are total bitches, but Cinder, that's our heroine's name, is going to put them in their places right off the bat."

"And the stepmother is kick-ass from page one. We all agreed that we hate that stereotype of the wicked stepmother," Lauryn explained. "But it's normal for sisters to annoy each other, regardless of if they're step or bio."

Grace's pulse kicked up at such a unique idea. "The premise sounds fantastic, but it's all going to be in the writing. There's got to be more than just rebellion. What can you tell me about your character arcs?"

"Oh! I can tell you about Cinder!" Lauryn chimed in. "She's been through the ringer. Her mother was a drug addict, father was pretty great, but he died right before the script starts. She was never a real daddy's girl, but she always had him watching out for her."

"He had her back," Phoenix added.

"Yes," Lauryn agreed. "But she's never really let anyone take care of her. So she has a hard time letting her stepmom do it, and she fights her every step of the way."

"And there's a big blowout with the sisters, where they call her on not letting them be part of her life in any real way, and that's why they're so bitchy," Janie explained. "That comes in Act II."

"Those are great twists for not only Cinder, but the sisters, too." Adrenaline coursed through Grace at the prospect of an angsty script. They discussed the other characters, setting, and structure. She wished Nat could be there. She'd love being part of this group, and the direction of their story, too. Grace had given her guidance about how to shorten the play, and she had been emailing revisions to Grace to review. It was coming together beautifully.

Amber peeked her head into the room and said, "Excuse me, Grace, but I'm closing up early and heading out to meet Aubrey Stewart. She's got some great ideas for expanding the shop. Can you set the alarm when you're done?"

Grace glanced at the clock and realized they'd run almost an

hour over their designated class time. She was supposed to meet
Reed at seven fifteen for dinner.

"Sure. Sorry we ran so late," she said to Amber. "Give Aubrey a hug for me."

Amber had gone to Boyer University just outside of New
York City, and she'd connected with a group of girls who all
shared a love of writing. They'd rented a house where they'd
lived like a sorority and had started their own sisterhood called
the Ladies Who Write. Aubrey and two other house sisters now
owned a multimedia corporation, LWW Enterprises, with
offices across the United States—and they had since purchased
that sisterhood house to use for LWW retreats. Grace was glad
to see Amber put as much effort into her friendships as she did
her work. *Lord knows I don't do that often enough.*

"Stay as long as you'd like," Amber said. "Aubrey's just
passing through, so it'll be a quick hug."

As she ducked out of the office, Grace began gathering her
papers. "We should wrap up for the day, too. When you have
your first few pages ready, we'll begin critiquing the dialogue."

"We're already done writing Act I," Janie said. "We've been
getting together for a few hours each day, and these ladies are
brilliant."

"Oh, please!" Hellie said. "We're *all* brilliant. Janie, it's your
expertise that finesses our ideas into magical moments."

"Wait a sec. You're *done* with Act I?" Grace asked.

"And halfway through Act II," Janie explained.

"We've been working hard while you've been playing house
with your hunka hunka burning love," Nana said, and pushed a
stack of papers across the table to Grace. "I have to get out of
here before Poppi chows down on Ho Hos for supper. You
know how much of a sugar fiend that man is."

"I'd better go, too," Janie said. "Boyd and I are going out."

"I have a hot date with my flute." Lauryn glanced at Phoenix and said, "I've *finally* convinced Phoenix to play her banjo at next Friday night's jam session at the Jerichos."

Phoenix rolled her eyes and pushed to her feet. Today she sported black-and-silver biker boots, black jeans, and an Aerosmith T-shirt. Her eyeliner was bright blue, and she had a pink feather hanging from a tiny braid on the right side of her head. "She wants me to show my inner hick. But I only agreed because she promised to play her flute."

"Hey, girlie." Nana pointed at Phoenix. "You watch your mouth. I'm proud of my inner hick, my outer hick, and everything in between."

"I'm sorry, Nina," Phoenix said.

Nana glared at her.

"*Nana*," Phoenix corrected herself. "I'm not trying to be disrespectful, but not everyone's cut out for small-town life, right, Grace? I mean, just look at Grace's outfit. She looks like she stepped out of a fashion magazine with that awesome, drapey black shirt and that skirt with the slanted silver zipper pockets. I'd *kill* for those black leather heels with silver buckles. I mean, if you pair them with a black leather skirt you'd look all BDSM, but with that tan skirt, it's totally chic, like you're going out to a five-star restaurant or something. Nobody dresses like that here. I don't think anyone would ever think Grace was from around here."

Grace glanced down at her outfit. It was one of her favorites, and Phoenix was right about the heels. In fact, that's why she'd bought them, because they could be office chic or nightlife sexy. She suddenly realized that around here the outfit just made her look like she thought a lot of herself. Or like she wanted other people to stop and take notice. The thought made her woozy. That was not who she was, and she hoped other people didn't see her that way.

"Everyone appreciates different things in life," Grace finally said with a stab of discomfort, as if she were somehow dissing her family by agreeing. Suddenly she wondered if her family, or the people who knew her, thought she'd been putting her family down all along by trying to run from her roots.

On her way out to her car, she tried to convince herself she was overthinking her appearance and pulled out her phone to text Reed and let him know she was late. There was a message waiting for her. *You. Me. Under the stars. Tonight.*

That sounded like the perfect night. She sent a quick reply telling him she was running late. She still had a hard time believing that he was in her life again.

As she climbed into her car, she found a single wildflower on the passenger seat. She smelled it, remembering how he used to leave a single flower for her in the funniest places. She'd found them in her cheerleading bag and on the field before a game. Even though he'd never left a note, she'd always known they were from him, even the very first time when she'd come outside before school and found one under the windshield wiper on her car. And when her sisters had found them, she'd turned the situation on them and questioned which of their boyfriends had left them a flower.

On the drive to her parents' house, her emotions skidded and whirled between thoughts of Reed and stewing over her revelation about how she might have hurt her family's feelings. By the time she arrived, she'd gotten herself upset about being called out for not looking like she was from Oak Falls, despite the fact that she'd worked hard to achieve exactly that.

Dolly and Reba greeted her at the kitchen door with wagging tails. "Hey, girls," Grace said as she wound around them toward her mother, who was chopping vegetables. Her hair was pinned up in a ponytail, giving her a youthful appearance.

"Hi, sweetie. Did you see how much Reed got done on the porch? It's so beautiful. How was your class?"

Grace had been too distraught to notice the porch. "Class was great. I loved it." She snagged a piece of cucumber and bit into it.

"But…?"

She took another bite and said, "No *but*."

"Maybe not about the class, but I know you, Grace, and there's a but hanging in there somewhere trying to get out."

Grace sighed and leaned against the counter. "Someone said I don't look like I'm from here."

"Mm-hm." Her mother handed her a piece of a carrot. "And?"

"It just bugs me. You know I'm not embarrassed by you guys, right?"

"Ah, there's the *but*." Her mother set down the knife, and her expression turned serious. "Grace, you've always wanted more than what this town had to offer, but that doesn't mean you wanted a different family or that we're not good enough for you. We know that, honey."

She let out a relieved sigh. "Thank goodness."

"But…" A small smile curled her mother's lips. "People change, honey. Just because you have what you thought you always wanted doesn't mean you always have to want those same things."

"I love producing." She heard the lack of enthusiasm in her own voice and knew her mother had, too. She'd already pissed off the director she'd wanted to hire by telling him she didn't want to use the script he'd presented. And now she was back at square one, trying to figure out which script had the most potential for funding and the best chance at sought-after actors. Even the thought of dealing with entitled actors who might have once been driven by their passion but whose passion had become twisted and driven them to be some of the most annoying people on the planet made her less enthusiastic about pouring her heart and soul into each production.

"If you say so." Her mother began chopping again. "If you want to talk about it, I'm here."

"I know. Thanks, Mom. Do you mind if I stay at Reed's tonight?"

That earned the brightest smile she'd seen since Reed had picked her up for their first date. Her mother set the knife down and wiped her hands on a dish towel. "Mind? I'll help you pack."

Grace laughed as her mother grabbed her arm and dragged her toward her bedroom with the dogs on her heels.

"I can't believe you've waited this long." Her mother went to the bed and picked up the big stuffed bear. "Are you taking Greedy Boy?"

She'd told her mother she'd given the bear that name because Reed had greedily eaten the majority of their popcorn at the fair. Her mother had bought it hook, line, and sinker. Now she wondered if she really had…

"No." Grace opened her smallest bag and began packing. "He'd take up the whole bed. I'm not moving in. I'm just staying for a night or two."

"Mm-hm."

Grace's cell phone vibrated. She snagged it from the

nightstand and read Reed's text. *I'll be right over.*

"I assume that's your man?" her mother asked.

"Yes. He doesn't know I'm bringing an overnight bag. I wish I could be there when he reads this text." She typed out a reply, unable to quell her grin. *Wait there. I'm packing a few things to stay overnight. I'll meet you at your place.* Her phone rang seconds later.

"Oh! Someone's happy," her mother said. "I'll leave you alone to chat."

Grace mouthed, *Thank you,* and answered Reed's call. Before she could say a word, he said, "You're staying over?"

"Unless you mind?"

"Does a bear mind hibernating in the winter?"

She tried to tamp down the thrill skittering through her. She couldn't afford to get caught up in a fantasy, but she refused to let her temporary stay keep her from enjoying every minute she could with Reed.

"Well, make room in the cave, because I'm just going to take care of a few things, and then I'll be on my way."

REED WAS PACING the porch when Grace pulled into the driveway. He'd spent the last two hours getting ready for their date, and knowing she was staying over offered the perfect end to what he hoped would be an incredible evening. When she stepped from her car, he lifted her off her feet, kissing her as he twirled her around.

"Tell me you're staying again," he said, but before she could answer, he kissed her one more time.

"I'm staying."

"I think I've waited my whole life to hear you say that." He brushed his lips over hers and realized he *had* been waiting, but he wanted a hell of a lot more than a night. "I'm actually going to wake up with you in my arms tomorrow?"

"For as many tomorrows as you want until I go home."

He was torn between elation and heartache, knowing their relationship had an end date. Or at least a *pause* date. One look in her loving eyes and elation won out. He set her down and led her to his truck.

"Where are we going?" She hurried to keep up in her high heels.

"We'll bring your stuff inside later. I have a surprise for you." He helped her into the truck. When he climbed in on the other side, she scooted over next to him. That simple move made his heart sing. He was dying to give her the news about his contract being ratified for the theater, but he'd planned a special way to share it.

He drove to the Majestic, and as he parked out front, he said, "I know how much you love this theater, so I thought we'd finally see a movie here." He grabbed the cooler and backpack he'd prepared and led her through the long grass to a blanket and the equipment he'd set up behind the theater.

"Is that a projector? We're *literally* watching a movie here?"

"Yup. The projector runs off my computer and projects onto the back of the building. Beckett clued me in to these awesome speakers, which will give us the feel of being at an outdoor theater."

"This is going to be *so* fun! But what if we get caught? People will see the lights from the road."

The theater sat at an angle, hiding the far side of the rear from view. Making out had never been a problem, but she was right; people would surely find out they were watching a movie. He didn't care who knew as long as he had this special night with Grace.

"It's okay. I hear the owner's a great guy."

"If you say so. I guess the worst that can happen is someone tells us to leave. I can't believe you set all this up. When did you become so tech savvy?"

"I didn't. Beckett helped me. That guy knows computers as well as he knows numbers."

"That's not surprising. Most of his business is online. I can't believe you left your equipment out here. Anyone could have stolen it."

He chuckled. "You're not in the city anymore, sweetheart. No one's going to steal my shit." He held up a note he'd left on the projector that read TOUCH MY PROJECTOR AND YOU'LL NEVER WALK AGAIN. THINK TWICE. REED CROSS.

"Who's going to mess with *you*, after all?" she teased.

"Nobody smart, that's for sure." He smacked her ass. "Sit your pretty ass down and let me woo you with my dating-Grace expertise."

"Aren't you eloquent." She took off her heels and sat on the blanket.

He visually devoured the flash of smooth thighs her skirt revealed as she tucked her legs beside her.

"Hey, *greedy boy*," she said, bringing his eyes up to hers. "No *dessert* before dinner."

He leaned forward and kissed her. "Bet I can change your mind."

"Did you bring whipped cream?"

He swore under his breath, although it was just for show.

He had no intention of getting naked with her right then. When they were kids, they could barely contain themselves long enough to get undressed, and short of the field behind the theater, his uncle's truck, Grace's car, or the empty houses his uncle worked on, there weren't many places they could go to be alone. That was no longer a problem, and he wasn't about to chance giving anyone a peek at their intimacy.

"I don't have whipped cream, but I did run over to Wishing Creek. Tonight we're celebrating."

"What are we celebrating?"

He handed her a burger and fries from the Creekside Diner where they used to eat. "You'll figure it out."

She gazed down at the telltale wrapping, which had pictures of Wishing Creek on it. "Bacon cheeseburger?"

"What else is there?" He reached into the cooler and withdrew a to-go cup. "And one, probably soupy, half chocolate, half vanilla milkshake. Know what? I did bring whipped cream. There was some under the lid, but I think it's probably melted by now. I know you're probably used to being wined and dined, and I wrestled with having a restaurant deliver here, but—"

"Reed, this is beyond perfect. You know what you get with being wined and dined? Pin-straight posture, *pleases*, and *thank yous*." She grabbed his shirt and tugged him forward, taking him in a fiercely passionate kiss. When their lips parted, she flashed a sinful smile and said, "That's what you get when you do the most romantic thing in the world for me. I love that you remembered, and I love that you won't let me forget who we were—who *I* was—because you know what? All my best memories were made here, too."

Chapter Fifteen

REED AND GRACE sat on the blanket eating dinner as the title, *Mrs. Henderson Presents*, appeared on the back of the building.

Grace gasped. "I *love* this movie! Have you seen it?"

"Yes. Do you mind watching it again?" The movie was about a woman who inherited an old run-down theater. She reopened it as a performance hall, and it goes down in history. Reed had assumed Grace would have already seen the movie, as she had always been a movie buff, but it was the ideal movie to help reveal his exciting news.

"Not at all. It's hilarious." She popped a fry in her mouth. "Mm. I haven't gone to the Creekside Diner since I moved away. The fries are so salty and delicious."

"It takes me back to those vinyl booths, where we'd share fries and kiss like we *weren't* sneaking around." He leaned in and stole a salty kiss. "Sneaking around was hot, but..." He kissed her again, deeper and longer. "Kissing you whenever I want is fucking insane."

"Is that what we're celebrating? That we're not hiding?"

"Nope." He took a bite of his burger as the movie began. "But if I owned this place, I'd be sure to serve salty fries just so I could get your salty-fry kisses."

They snuggled as they ate, watching the movie. Every so often Grace would lean closer and guess at what they were celebrating. "Our one-week anniversary?"

"No, but that's worth celebrating," he said.

A short while later a group of teenagers came out of the darkness from the direction of the parking lot.

"Hey," one of the kids called over. "Mind if we watch from the field?"

"Not at all," Reed said.

They continued walking deeper into the field, fading back into the darkness. Reed noticed that cars were slowing to crawls as they drove past, and he imagined the people inside craning to see what was going on behind the theater. He and Roy had checked out the interior together, and Roy had captivated him with stories of his youth and the good times he and Ella had at the Majestic. Reed found himself wondering if any of the people in the cars had been around long enough to remember when the theater had been open, more than thirty-five years ago.

A little while later, Grace tipped her face up to his and said, "It's not your birthday; that's in October."

He kissed her softly. "I'm glad you remembered."

She was quiet for the longest time, and he was anxious to tell her, but it was fun letting her try to guess.

A few more people meandered past, some asking if it was okay to join them, others simply assuming so. Reed didn't mind the intrusions. They kept their distance, and he had everything he needed right there in his arms. The world could explode around them and he'd go out a happy man.

Grace finished her fries—before her burger, just like he remembered—and said, "I've thought about you a lot over the years, even when I tried not to; you were always there."

"And I always will be."

He set his drink down and moved behind her, leaning her back against his chest so he could hold her closer. She cuddled into him and they watched in comfortable silence.

When the woman in the movie found out she'd inherited the theater, he dropped another hint. "It's so weird how theaters sort of drop into people's laps."

"Mm-hm."

A little while later, they were engrossed in the film, laughing at a scene, when Reed became aware of someone else's laughter in the air. Several people's, in fact. He glanced up at the road and saw a line of cars parked along the curb and people sitting on the grass.

He looked over his shoulder at the field behind them, where throngs of people were watching the movie. "Holy cow, Grace. Check this out."

She leaned around his body. "Oh my gosh. There must be more than fifty people here. How did we not hear them? This is awesome! Can you imagine what this would be like if your deal on the theater comes through? You could do this—" She sat up on her knees, and her eyes widened. "That's it, isn't it? Is that what we're celebrating? Did your deal on the theater come through?"

He laughed and pulled her into a kiss.

"Finally, baby. I've been trying to give you clues all night."

"Oh my gosh! Reed! This is going to be *yours*? Can you imagine all the things you can do with it? Outdoor movies, community plays! Can we go inside? I've never been inside. You've been inside, right? You had to if you made an offer."

She was talking a mile a minute. He spotted her sisters, a

few of the Jerichos, and a handful of other people approaching, but he didn't want to slow Grace down.

"I can't believe you held this in all this time, and here I was missing every clue. Theaters dropping in people's laps!" She laughed. "I'm so thickheaded. I was too into the movie and *you* to even think of anything like that."

"I can't believe you set this up and didn't even invite us," Sable said.

Grace spun around as their friends converged on them.

"Dude, what the hell?" Trace turned his palms up to the sky. "You've got a whole theater going on out here with all these Meadowsiders? What are we? Chopped liver?"

"No, man," Reed answered. "This was a date that got over-run."

Morgyn and Sable sat on the blanket. Sable reached for what was left of Grace's milkshake and said, "Awesome date night. Good thing you two weren't naked. Practically the whole senior class from Oak Falls is behind you."

"I saw Chet, Boyd, and Janie on the hill," Morgyn added. "And Mom texted, asking if I knew about someone holding movie night at the Majestic."

"That's it, Reed! Movie night at the Majestic! You have to do that!" Grace pleaded. "Think of it. Old-fashioned popcorn machines, soda fountains. You could show movies for families, romantic comedies for date nights…"

"Whoa, what do you mean *he* could?" Brindle asked.

"Reed's buying this place," Grace said, then immediately slapped a hand over her mouth. "Uh-oh. Was that a secret?"

"No, babe. It's fine." He explained that they'd just ratified the contract for the property and were set to close in a few weeks. "We've got a long road ahead of us to rehab the place, but the inside is gorgeous, and it has a lot of potential."

"Hey, Reed," Trace said. "If you're buying this place, I know Jeb will want to put in a bid for the stonework." Jeb was Trace's oldest sibling, a talented artist who worked with stone, wood, and metals, creating custom furniture and refurbishing antiques.

"I wouldn't want to bid or anything," Morgyn said, "but I'd love to help with the interior. I'd be happy to help with curtains, upholstery, and whatever else you think I might be able to help with. I'd love to be part of this type of project in any way I can."

"Thank you. That's great," Reed said. "I really appreciate the offers. And, Trace, I'll be sure to connect with Jeb when we get that far." He pulled Grace closer as the others made themselves comfortable to watch the movie.

"Thanks for helping Nat," Brindle said. "She showed me the revisions, and I think the play will be perfect."

"She's really talented, and the sweetest girl," Grace said. "You did such a good thing for her, Brin, and she raves about you. Whatever you're doing, keep doing it. I told her that when I'm back in New York I'll mentor her via email."

"I know," Brindle said, snuggling closer to Trace. "She's told everyone how excited she is. She's here tonight." She turned around and pointed to a group of girls by the streetlight. "She's with Phoenix and Lauryn, or as I've started calling the three of them, your *fan club*."

"Oh, stop." Grace shook her head.

They turned their attention back to the movie, but Reed was too swept up in Grace to pay attention to anything but the smile on her face as she put her arms around his neck and leaned closer, speaking loud enough only for him to hear.

"Sophie comes back next Saturday afternoon, and her baby shower is Sunday morning. Do you think we could try to do this with her and Brett? They'd love this. Brett is a huge theater fan. And maybe we can invite Roy and Ella? They'd probably love this, too. And if we don't invite my family, they'll probably show up anyway." She sat back and said, "Actually, we'd probably end up with everyone here anyway."

"Babe, we can do whatever you'd like."

"I have to go back to New York the following weekend," she said softly, the sadness in her voice inescapable.

"I know. We'll make it happen before that. Maybe the weekend you leave as a going away-party, so everyone has a chance to say goodbye."

"Okay." She was quiet for a second, resting her head on his shoulder. And then she pressed a kiss beside his ear and said, "I have a feeling you're going to hear this a lot from me, but I can't believe you're *buying* the theater. You'll forever own the property where we first...*you know.*"

"I do know, babe. And we'll make a million more memories that are just as great. We're making them right now." He lifted his chin in the direction of her sisters and their friends, just as her parents, Amber, and Reno, came around the side of the building carrying big bags of popcorn.

Everyone got up to greet them at once.

Grace laced her hands with Reed's, waiting her turn, and said to Reed, "I'm sorry our romantic night has turned into a party. This would never happen in the city."

"*Exactly,*" her mother said. "This would *never* happen in the city."

Chapter Sixteen

GRACE AWOKE TO the feel of Reed's lips on her ribs. She ran her fingers through his thick hair as memories of their evening came back to her. They'd hung out with friends and family long after the movie had ended, and she'd seen several of the people she'd gone to school with. Her visits home had been so quick over the years, unless she saw her friends while she was out with her sisters, she rarely caught up with anyone. But last night Reed had seemed happy to let her stay and chat as long as she'd wanted. They'd gotten home at nearly two in the morning and had made love until they were both too spent to move.

Reed nipped at her belly, bringing her thoughts back to the man loving his way up her body. He slowed to tease her breasts, and heat streaked like darts to the juncture of her thighs with every flick of his tongue. He moved over her, his chest hair tickling her skin as he perched on his elbows.

She smiled up at him. "I like waking up with you."

"I like doing everything with you."

He kissed her again, a long, sweet kiss that made her insides soft and him hard against her stomach. He brushed his whiskers along her cheek, alternating between kissing and abrading. Grace thought back to when she'd first seen him riding a horse at the Jerichos'. She'd fought so hard *not* to feel the emotions he'd stirred, and now, as his warm breath whispered over her skin, she couldn't imagine *not* feeling this way ever again. Worry tiptoed in as he laced their hands together and gazed lovingly into her eyes.

"What's going on in that beautiful brain of yours, Gracie?"

Not wanting to dwell on the fact that her life was hundreds of miles away, she tried to lead him astray. "I was wondering if you were ever going to buy a bedframe."

"Do you want a bedframe?"

"It's not my house."

His eyes darkened. "But you're in my bed." He kissed her chin. "Should I worry about why you're thinking about bedframes when I'm lying on top of you, naked?"

"No," she said lightly. "I was really wondering when you were going to finish your kitchen so you wouldn't have to eat out every meal."

His eyes went pitch-black, and he nipped at her lower lip. "I love *eating out.*"

A soft laugh escaped, and she whispered, "Me too. I wasn't really thinking about appliances."

"Ah, you've begun lying to me," he teased.

"Just avoiding the truth. I was thinking about how much I like this." She rose to kiss him, and he drew back with a tease in his eyes.

"This?" He rocked his hips, pressing his erection against her.

"Yes. But it's bigger than that."

"Hey, watch it."

"Not bigger than *that.* Being with you, falling asleep in your arms, waking up to your kisses. It feels like it's always been this way. Like life went on when we weren't together, but that all seems like a blip in time." Even though she wasn't leaving for another two weeks, she felt the end of her stay looming, making every moment they had together feel special and every moment with her family feel important in a way she'd never appreciated.

"When I first got to my parents' house, I wondered how I'd make it through three weeks with my sisters' drama, and then I saw you and my world turned inside out. But my sisters haven't driven me crazy. They've enabled me to do more of what I love, and they've shown me sides of themselves that I've never slowed down enough to appreciate. And you and I...well, the two weeks we have left doesn't seem like enough."

"Because it's not. Nothing will ever be enough, but it's not supposed to be. Love is supposed to grow stronger, not get easier."

"But we won't have *this*, Reed. Right now we have parts of every day. I mean, we'll have Friday and Saturday nights and Saturday and Sunday mornings. But I'll have to work some of that time, and if you're fixing up the theater, you'll need to be *here*."

"We'll figure it out," he promised. "All we have to know right now is that we both *want* to make it work. Do you want that?"

"Yes, very much."

"Good. Then let me ask you another important question. Do you"—he kissed the corner of her mouth—"think I should start here?" He kissed the other side of her mouth. "Or should I start at your pretty little toes and work my way up your gorgeous legs all the way to your lips?"

She giggled at his playfulness. "The second option sounds appealing, but I think I have an even better idea." She pushed on his shoulders, and he shifted onto his side. Then she moved, bringing her legs by his head, and she pressed a kiss to his ankle. "How about if we *both* start like this and we meet in the middle?"

She ran her fingers along his strong calves, pressing kisses to his legs as he did the same to her. His lips were warm and soft, and his hands were rough and insistent, squeezing the backs of her ankles and calves with each tender kiss, creating a dichotomy of heavenly torment inside her. She tried to concentrate on bringing him just as much pleasure, kissing and petting as she inched up his powerful thighs, and all her worries faded away. Then his mouth was on her sex, as rough as his hands were on her ass, holding her to him as his tongue shattered her ability to do much of anything other than lie there and gasp. She forced a moment of lucidity and wrapped her hand around his cock, but just as quickly he guided her leg over his shoulder and brought his magnificent mouth to her sex, sending sparks skating beneath her skin. His tongue plunged into her as he pinned her in place with one hand on her ass, his other teasing her sex, drawing a long, surrendering moan from her lungs.

His hips thrust to the same rhythm as his tongue, bringing her mind back to his thick, delicious cock. She glided her tongue along the wide crown and over the sensitive glans the way she'd learned he liked and followed his shaft all the way down to the base.

"Fuck, baby. That mouth of yours kills me."

She lowered her mouth over the crown, and he placed his hand over hers and squeezed tight around his cock, rocking through her fist. Every pulse of his hips sent his shaft deeper into her mouth, making him wetter, and soon she was lost in lust, stroking and sucking. His hand slipped away, and she continued devouring and loving, touching and taking, feeling like she'd never get enough of him. He sealed his mouth over her sex, sucking and tweaking as he clutched and licked. It took all of her focus to remember how to breathe as he shifted her onto her back. She tried to guide his cock into her mouth, but he did something with his teeth and tongue and heat shot through her like lightning. Her hips bucked as his fingers explored, and his hungry mouth sent her topsy-turvy world spinning away.

She fisted her hands in the sheets, her inner muscles pulsing so tight she moaned. "*More.* Don't stop," came rushing out.

His teeth grazed her sex as he feasted on her, taking her up, up, *up* and over the edge again. As her insides quivered and quaked, he came down over her and pinned her hands to the bed, kissing her hungrily. His mouth was wet with her arousal, but she didn't care, because the taste of Reed overrode everything else as he buried only the head of his cock inside her.

He drew back from the kiss, his eyes as intense as they were loving as he entered her so slowly she felt her body stretching to accommodate his girth, felt her heart welcoming him and her soul treasuring him.

Once he was deep inside her, he said, "You were my first love, Gracie, and I know that regardless of where we're living, you'll be my last."

LATER THAT MORNING, Reed made room in his dresser for Grace's things and took far too much pleasure in watching her put them away. It was hell not asking her to move back, to move *in*, but he held his tongue.

As they got ready to head out to the Stardust Café for breakfast, Grace stood in the foyer holding a pair of cute sandals, looking gorgeous in skinny jeans and a lavender top, with her hair twisted into some sort of knot on the top of her head. Several dark tendrils had already sprung free, sexily framing her face.

Reed embraced her from behind. "Are we bed shopping after breakfast?"

She turned and wound her arms around his neck, her sandals dangling over his shoulder. "You know I don't care if you have a bedframe or not, don't you?"

"A big-city girl like you needs proper furniture."

She swatted his arm, then bent to put on her sandals. "I do not."

He chuckled.

"I have to get Sophie's baby shower present. Can we stop by that new baby boutique in town?"

"Sure." He opened the door for her and followed her out.

"And I should really go for a run later. Will you go with me?"

"What is with you and exercise? You're gorgeous."

"It keeps me sane. Relieves stress."

"Why are you stressed?" He drew her into his arms again. Some people lived on deep breaths; he lived on moments with Grace.

"I'm not right now, actually. I just realized that. But I'm used to working out a few times a week, and *not* horizontally. Everyone has their crutches. You work with your hands all day—and *night*. My job is mentally taxing, and sometimes I feel like I need to give all that mental chaos a breather."

"I get it, and I'll go for a run with you anytime you'd like.

But it might be more fun to head out for a hike or, I don't know, play Frisbee or something."

"I love both of those ideas!" Her phone rang, and she pulled it out of her back pocket. "*Ugh.* Speaking of mental chaos, this is work. Sorry. I'll try to be quick." She stepped off the porch as she answered the call and walked toward his truck. "No, Satchel. That's not how this works." She held up one finger, indicating she needed a minute, and walked away, speaking sternly into the phone.

Reed locked up and sat on the porch steps. Ten minutes later he was still waiting. He walked down to the creek so she wouldn't feel pressured and sat in the long grass listening to the leaves rustle and the gentle trickle of the water. Most creeks had an earthy, pungent smell, but the creeks in Virginia had always smelled sweeter to him than those in Michigan. The same way the small towns seemed friendlier and the air felt crisper. None of that was true, of course. He was well aware of his bias toward his hometown. He'd missed the closeness of the community and the ease of the friendships while he'd been in Michigan. His life had been a race. First trying to outrun his heartache and later focusing on anything except the emptiness inside him. Losing Alina had been a relief, and though losing his business had been painful, looking back, that business had only been a mask, a safe distraction from what was missing from his life.

He felt Grace's presence behind him before he heard the swishing of grass or smelled her sweet perfume. He pushed to his feet, trying to read her troubled expression, and gathered her in his arms. "Whose ass do I need to kick?"

"You can't fix it that way. Besides, Satchel would take one look at you and run the other way."

"Satchel? What kind of name is that?"

"His real name is Samuel, but Samuel isn't exactly an artistic name. He's the casting director, and he's wonderful. But the lead actor in the play is apparently being a real numskull. He hooked up with one of the cast members, and he's decided to be a jerk to any guy who looks at her. What is wrong with men, anyway? It's like the minute they have sex with a woman they think they either own her or they're over her. There's no middle ground."

"Are you really asking me that? You don't think women are the same way?"

"Of course not."

He arched a brow.

"What? I'm not mean to women who look at you, and trust me, most every woman who walks by checks you out. Even my sisters."

"And how do you handle it? Do you say, 'Yeah, he's hot. Go for it.'"

She knocked him with her shoulder. "Seriously?"

"Don't tell me the minute we slept together you thought you *owned* me," he teased.

"We hadn't even slept toge—"

"Glad you see my point." He gave her a chaste kiss and draped an arm over her shoulder as they headed for his truck. "So, what did Satchel expect you to do about it from four hundred miles away?"

"He's just keeping me in the loop. In theory, the staff should be able to deal with and manage the chaos. In reality, it can be like herding cubs, and sometimes they'll only listen to Mama Bear."

"Just let me know if you need backup."

"I can handle it. But from now on I'm only hiring castrated

males and women who will agree to wear chastity belts."

Twenty minutes later they entered the Stardust Café. Every red vinyl stool at the counter in the casual, retro-style café was taken, and the booths were nearly as packed.

"Y'all come right in here and sit at the counter." Winona Hanson, a fortysomething redhead powered by enough sass to fuel a steam engine, waved them over. Speaking to a brunette sitting at the counter, she said, "Ali, would you and Walter mind taking that corner booth, please? I have a bone to pick with these two lovebirds."

"We can sit in the booth," Grace offered.

Winona crossed her arms, locking her forest-green eyes on Grace. "Oh no you *cannot*."

The brunette slid off the stool, revealing a very pregnant belly, and threw her arms around Grace. "Gracie! Ali Parker, remember me? Big Ali? Well, Ali *Larson* now. I haven't seen you in ages! The town's all abuzz about you two."

"Ali!" Grace's surprise was evident in the pitch of her voice. "Oh my goodness, you look incredible! And you're having a baby!"

"Thank you. I dropped nearly eighty pounds two years ago, thanks to Wally." Ali looked adoringly at the tall man standing beside her. "We met at a cupcake tasting. He's a baker and all. Then we started taking walks, and well…" She shrugged. "He taught me about moderation and all that." She leaned closer and said, "Then we got married, and I gained twenty back with *our* little cupcake." She rubbed her belly. "Our baby girl is due in just six weeks."

Grace's expression warmed. "You're having a girl? I'm *so* happy for you. Wally, it's nice to meet you. And this is my boyfriend, Reed Cross. He grew up in Meadowside and just moved back a few months ago."

Reed had wanted so badly to claim Grace as his girlfriend when they were younger that hearing her call him her boyfriend affected him way more than it should have at his age. But hell if it didn't give him a thrill. He shook Walter's hand. "Nice to meet you both."

"You're the guy buying the theater?" Walter asked.

"That's right. I guess the rumor mill has already started churning." Reed reached for Grace's hand.

"Okay, Chatty Cathies," Winona said. "Time to move along and sit on down. Y'all can catch up over lunch one day."

"Good idea! Let's do it soon," Ali said, giving Grace another quick hug. "I want to hear all about the play y'all are putting on."

"Play?" Grace asked.

"Oh, maybe I heard wrong. Pregnancy brain and all," Ali said. "I thought I heard you were producing a play here in town."

"Oh no. I'm teaching a screenplay writing class over at Amber's bookstore."

"Come on, baby." Walter put a hand on Ali's back. "We'd better sit down before Winona refuses to feed you any more pickles and cream cheese. It was nice to meet y'all. Enjoy your breakfast."

"I get the oddest cravings," Ali said over her shoulder as they headed for a booth.

Reed and Grace sat at the counter. Winona set two mugs in front of them, pouring coffee with a smirk on her freckled face.

"Go ahead, Winona," Grace said as she poured cream into her coffee. "Ask away."

"Oh, I will." She set the coffeepot down behind her.

A burly tattooed guy in the kitchen put two plates on the pass-through and hollered, "Order up!"

Winona grabbed the plates and set them in front of a customer at the end of the counter. When she returned, she leaned across the counter and spoke quietly, "Just tell me this. Have you been playing around with each other for all these years? Or was that a high school fling and now you're reunited?"

Grace blinked several times, as surprised as Reed was.

"You knew about us?" Grace whispered. "Does everyone?"

"Don't be silly. The only reason I know is that my cousin Tami works at the Creekside Diner. She mentioned you two smoochin' in there a decade ago when you were kids. Someone's gotta watch out for y'all."

"But you never said anything," Grace said with awe.

Winona winked. "And I won't now. I just wanted to know if it was true. But I can see it was. Everyone thinks I don't know how to keep a secret." She leaned closer again and lowered her voice. "Y'all did the right thing back then, with those crazy rivalries goin' on."

"Thanks, Winona." Reed put his hand on Grace's and squeezed. "To answer your question, no. Grace and I have just found each other again."

Winona's gaze moved between them. She pulled a pencil from above her ear and waved it at them. "And the rest of the rumors? I hear you had a community movie night and didn't even think to invite my parents, who have known you, Grace Montgomery, since you were nothing more than a hope in your mama's heart."

Grace smiled and shook her head. "That was a date that Reed set up for us. People saw the movie playing and stopped to watch."

"And Reed's buying the theater?" she asked.

"I am. And before you tell me what I have to do with it, don't worry; I got an earful last night. Seems everyone in town wants outdoor movies as badly as they want an indoor theater."

Winona nodded. "Heck yes, we do. Nobody wants to drive for thirty minutes to go to a cinema complex that they need a map to navigate. Now, I just have one more thing that needs clearin' up before I take your orders and leave you be." She set a serious gaze on Reed and said, "Tami told me about you moping in the diner after you two ended that secret thing we're not speaking of. Going weeks without eating." She waved her pencil at Grace. "Teenage heartbreak is the worst." She pointed to the graffiti wall in the back of the café. "You know nearly every kid who ever lived in Oak Falls has worked here for some period of time, and our *Let It Out* wall is full of *Joanie loves Chachis* and all sorts of matters of the heart. That's one thing, but I don't want any moping around here. If you two decide to part ways, there will be no sitting alone in a booth staring into a chocolate shake, ya hear?"

Reed chuckled. "Loud and clear, Winona." He pressed a kiss to the back of Grace's hand and said, "But we're not kids on our way to college anymore."

"No, you're ten times more complicated," Winona said. "Your hearts are so intertwined you couldn't help but find each other again, but your lives are now worlds apart."

"Haven't you ever heard *when there's a will there's a way?*" Reed asked.

"Sure I have," Winona said with a smirk. "That's how I ended up raising Shayla on my own. My man had the will, and his good-for-nothing trollop found a way." She pointed her pencil at Reed and said, "You do that to her, and I'll hunt you down myself. Now," she smiled brightly, "what can I get y'all for breakfast?"

THEY HEADED OUT to look for a bedframe after breakfast and meandered through the furniture store by the mall. "I don't think I've ever shopped for furniture like this," Grace said, looking around at the nearly empty store.

"You mean arm in arm with a guy who keeps grabbing your ass?" Reed tugged her against him.

"That and shopping in a physical store. When I went to college, the dorms were furnished, and when I got an apartment I bought furniture online. I'm surprised stores like this can stay open when people can shop from home. Everything is so…"

"Boring?"

"*Yes*, totally. You worked so hard to make your house stand out, and it's too pretty for this. This furniture would bring it down. At least the boutique where we bought the couches and dining room set had unique pieces. But nothing here feels special."

"You're absolutely right. This isn't us, Grace. Let's get out of here." He took her hand and headed for the exit. "There's only one place to look for a bedroom set worthy of my girls. The Barn."

She stopped cold. "Whoa. *Girls?* Plural?"

"Well, yeah. You and my Painted Lady. She's my other girl." He crushed her to him and said, "You'd better read up on Victorians, babe. Or you're going to need that morning run just from misunderstandings."

"I think we need to stop at the library."

They drove out to Jeb Jericho's place. He owned a few acres just far enough off the main drag to be private, but close enough to be found by consumers. Jeb ran the Barn, his appropriately named furniture shop, out of a big, blue, renovated barn, with his showroom on the first floor and his living quarters on the second. His workshop was in a separate stone building, which was once an old church.

"I can't believe we didn't think of coming here first," Grace said as they headed up the wide walkway.

"It must have been all that mind-blowing sex, followed by a full belly." He hauled her in for another delicious kiss. "You've made me dumb, sweetheart."

"That's weird. You've made me happy."

She snuggled into him as they climbed the granite steps. There was a note on the barn door that read IN THE WORK-SHOP and had an arrow pointing toward the old church building.

The shop was built of stone, floor to ceiling, with the exception of a few stained-glass windows on either side and near the peak of the back wall, where the altar must have once been. There were several large workstations with furniture in various stages of assembly littering the tops. Metal shelving units holding tools lined the walls, and some sort of fireplace or kiln was built into the rear wall, near a set of enormous double doors. They found Jeb in full protective garb, welding two large pieces of metal together. When he spotted them, he turned off his welding gun and took off his mask.

"Hey, guys. How's it going?" he said as he pulled off his gloves and stripped out of his protective jumpsuit. "I hear you might need some stonework done on the old theater."

He strode toward them in a pair of faded jeans and a blue T-shirt with COWS WON'T MILK THEMSELVES written on a round label with a picture of a cow at the top. Ever the farm boy, Jeb had always been proud of his roots. He snagged a baseball cap from a table and pulled it on. He had smallish, studious eyes that Grace had always felt saw far more than people wanted him to. Those watchful eyes took in the two of them. A hair over thirty, Jeb was a big man, known around town for his artistic talent and overprotective nature. Poor Trixie had a heck of a time trying to date with Jeb and her other brothers watching over her.

"Absolutely," Reed said. "I just got the word yesterday that the offer was accepted. I'm still processing it."

"It's a hell of a building. I'd have bought it if I'd had the money, but it's too rich for my blood. I'd love to be part of the project, though."

"You've got it," Reed said. "We'll set up a time to go out there and look around. We thought you could help us with a bedframe."

Jeb smiled, softening his sharp jawline. "Sure. I'm glad to see the rumors are true about you two. What'd you have in mind?"

The devilish look in Reed's eyes when he said, "Something *sturdy*," told Grace exactly where the conversation was headed. She yanked on his hand, and he pulled her closer and laughed.

"I'm kidding," Reed said. "Well, not really, but you know…"

After too many sexual innuendos and an equal dose of laughter, they left with a contract in hand for a custom-designed wood and iron bedframe, spent some time meandering around the shop and picked out two unique nightstands before heading into town to shop for Sophie's baby gift.

"I can't believe Sophie's married and having a baby," Reed said as they looked through baby toys. "Do you like her husband?"

"Brett's great, and he's madly in love with Soph. He's from New York City. The fact that he built her a house here and he's staying here for her maternity leave, which is, like, three months, I think, says it all."

"I'm glad she found a nice guy." Reed picked up a box and read the side. "Check this out. It's an activity gym, and it says it not only helps develop the baby's fine and gross motor skills, but this musical mobile will help enhance the baby's problem-solving skills and turn your baby into a little Einstein. What the…?" He showed her the box. "Who's thinking about enhancing their infant's problem-solving skills?"

Grace read the boxes of several other toys. "They all say things like that. Every toy is supposed to make your baby smarter. And here I was looking for something soft and cuddly."

"Oh no, you can't go soft and cuddly when there's this." He picked up a musical toy and read the box. "This one 'invites your little maestro-in-the-making to tune in to classical music.'" He set the box down and picked up another. "This one teaches cause and effect." He scanned another box. "And this one helps with identifying animals."

"All baby toys help babies learn." Grace picked up a stuffed puppy and brushed the silky ear over her cheek. "Feel this." She rubbed it on his arm. "This one teaches them about the importance of snuggling."

"We need sheets made of that." He waggled his brows. "Seriously, though, Gracie. We had sticks and rocks, and we turned out just fine."

"I remember making things out of paper cups and using my mom's pots and wooden spoons to make music with my brother and sisters."

"I need to call Ella. She obviously raised me wrong. I could have been as skilled as Mozart or as brilliant as Galileo if *only* I'd had these toys."

"When they're toddlers, it doesn't matter what toys you give them," she said. "They always like the box best."

"All infants need is love. To be held and talked to, to know they're wanted."

Grace's heart squeezed. Was he thinking about his father? Or was he thinking about having never been held by his mother? She wanted to ask, but just in case he wasn't thinking about those things, she didn't want to bring him down, so she kept those thoughts to herself.

"But when they're older, they'll get a spinning top," he said with a smirk. "Those things hardly ever spin, and when they do, they stop before you can get anyone to look over and see it. That's a lesson in frustration and self-control right there. I remember wanting to bean those things across the room."

"I remember wanting to bean my siblings across the room," she said jokingly.

"Yeah, but you love them. It's written all over your face."

"You think you can read my face?" She forced a serious expression. "What am I thinking right now?"

He grabbed her ass. "You dirty girl. We can't do that here."

"Such a man."

"I'm *your* man, and the quicker we buy a gift, the faster we can get to all those dirty things going through your mind. What will Sophie's kid need help with? She was pretty smart, right? Is Brett smart? Creative?"

"He's wicked smart, and as far as his creativity goes, all I know is that Sophie is always *satisfied* and never bored." She ran her finger down the center of his chest and said, "So maybe we need to get her baby something to keep it occupied for more than a few minutes at a time so she can enjoy Brett's *creativity*."

"I like how you think." He waved at the display. "We'll scour the shelves until we find a box that says the toy will occupy the baby for hours so Mommy and Daddy can enjoy their own playtime."

They left the store with two bags full of gifts, still laughing about how creative and smart Sophie's baby would be and how she and Reed missed out by not being given expensive toys that promised to make them brilliant.

"With these time-consuming, brain-sharpening gifts"—he lifted the bags—"Sophie will be on baby number two before you know it."

While he put the bags behind the front seat of the truck, Grace took the gift she'd secretly purchased while he was busy talking to a salesperson out of her purse. "I got you a little something. I want all your dreams to come true, too." She handed him the toy piano. "Now you can learn to be as musical as Mozart."

He drew her into his arms with an awestruck expression. His lips brushed over hers like the wind, time and time again, until she was barely breathing in anticipation of the real thing.

"Thank you," he said softly.

His hand was warm on her neck as he caressed her lips with his own, teasing and tantalizing masterfully. He knew just how to make her body crave him and her mind surrender to him. He backed her up against the side of the truck, taunting her with whispered promises against her lips. Her heart pounded erratically. She was *this close* to begging for a real kiss when his mouth *finally* covered hers, demanding and possessive. Desire seared through her as she shoved her hands into his back pockets, keeping his powerful body against hers as she gave herself over to their passion. Her knees went weak, and he eased his efforts.

"Love you, Gracie," he said tenderly, and trailed kisses along her cheek. He glanced down at the piano still in his hand and said, "You're going to make a great mom someday."

Someday...

A flicker of worry breezed through her. Their lives really were hundreds of miles apart. This time together was a gift. Sure, she was growing tired of dealing with arrogant actors and the headaches of producing, and she wanted more time to write, but she wasn't ready to put it all aside. She knew Reed well enough to realize he wanted kids one day. He had so much love to give. He always had. How would that work if they were commuting back and forth?

She was getting way ahead of herself, and when he brushed a loose strand of hair from where it had fallen over her eyes and flashed a boyish grin, she pushed those worries aside, vowing again not to let future worries steal a second of the time they had left.

"Do you want kids, Gracie? Or is your life too full for them?"

"Someday," she answered honestly.

"Someday," he whispered. Then louder, "Someday sounds good to me."

Chapter Seventeen

REED FOUND WHAT he was looking for in the attic Sunday morning and took a moment to gaze out the window at Grace's car in the driveway. Their lives had fallen seamlessly into sync. They'd played Frisbee at the park last night, and then they'd walked into town, where they'd run into Sable and Amber, who were on their way into the pizzeria, and they'd joined them for dinner. Grace had laughed so much with her sisters, she seemed like a different person from the woman he'd seen standing with them at the party that first night. After coming home, they'd thrown a blanket down in the backyard and stargazed, kissing and talking until they were both too tired to think, and then they'd finally gone upstairs to bed. His house had felt like something was missing for all these months, and now he knew exactly what it was. *Grace.* They'd loved this house all those years ago, and just like he'd never forgotten her, he'd only buried those memories. They were as much a part of him as the blood that ran through his veins.

He went to the window on the opposite side of the room and looked out at the creek, thinking about the walk they'd taken earlier that morning, reminiscing about the past and dreaming about the future. They'd come home and showered together, and then they'd gone out to the veranda, where he'd worked on his plans for the theater and Grace had taken notes on scripts. He went there now and stood in the doorway, watching her. She looked relaxed in her cutoffs and T-shirt, writing in a notebook. It was the perfect start to a beautiful, sunny day, and Reed wanted more. More sexy nights and loving mornings, more of Grace relaxing and coming into her own. More days to hold her hand and more nights to fall even more madly, passionately in love.

Hiding his surprise behind his back, he joined her on the couch and tucked her beneath his arm. She tipped her face up with a sweet smile and set her notebook in her lap.

"I *love* writing here." She dug her hand into a bag of M&M's and popped a few into her mouth.

"Did you find a good script?"

"No. I stopped looking a while ago. When we were at the park playing Frisbee last night, I had an idea for a story. I thought I'd take some notes so I didn't forget it, and look how much I've written." She turned her notebook toward him and began flipping pages.

"That's one benefit of playing Frisbee over going jogging."

"I had more fun last night than I've had in a long time. It's inspirational. This story has already taken on a life of its own, which proves that I really do need to get outside more often. Clearly, sunshine and *Reed* equals inspiration." She sat up and snuggled closer.

"We spent so much time outdoors when we were younger, I can't imagine you living your life any other way. I think that's why the gym comment seemed strange to me. And I've got just the thing to help you get inspired to go outside when you're in the city. Give me your shirt."

She laughed. "You think sex will help me remember to go outside more?"

He shook his head as he lifted the hem of her shirt. "Close your eyes, and keep them closed."

He took off her shirt, slipped his high school football jersey over her head, and guided her hands into the sleeves. "Okay, babe. Open your eyes."

She glanced down and squealed. "Your jersey!" She threw her arms around him. "I'm wearing this today, and I don't care what we do or where we go. In fact, this might just have to be my Sunday outfit from now on. Can I keep it?"

"Of course, babe. It's yours."

"I can't believe it's *mine* after all these years."

"Just like me." His lips descended slowly upon hers, and he felt her smiling into the kiss.

"I have a great idea!"

"You're going to put on your cheerleading outfit and let me go for a touchdown?"

She laughed and straddled his lap. "That wasn't my idea, but…I bet my mom has that outfit in a box somewhere."

"Have I told you lately how great your mother is?" He kissed her smiling lips.

"If we're going to do the long-distance relationship thing, then let's agree not to work on Sundays like my parents do. They've never worked on Sundays. I mean, they take care of the animals, but they don't do any real work. It's always been a family day for us."

"I love that idea, but I thought you had to work some weekends with your productions."

"I do, but that's usually just at the beginning. Once the production is underway, I'm on to the next for selection and prep, but Sundays aren't mandatory. That's just been how my life has evolved, I guess." She ran her finger along his jaw and said, "I've never had a reason not to work on Sundays, but now I do, and I don't want to miss out on days like this."

"That sounds perfect to me. There's not a property in the world that I'd rather work on than spend time with you."

"Speaking of properties, do you think we can see the inside of the theater before I go back? I can't stop thinking about it."

"Sure. I want to show it to you. I'll make arrangements with Meggie Tipster, my real estate agent."

"You're working with Megaphone Meggie?" Her smile got even brighter. "I cheered with her. She could cheer louder than anyone on the team. I haven't seen her in so long. Is she still as tiny as a waif?"

He shook his head. "I wouldn't call her tiny. I mean, she's got a nice figure, but she's not waiflike, and she's still as loud as a megaphone. She's been great, really on top of things."

The sound of car doors caught their attention.

"Expecting company?" Grace asked as they pushed to their feet.

"No," he said as they went inside and headed downstairs. He pulled open the front door as Nana, Hellie, Janie, and Janie's guide dog stepped from the car. A second later, two younger girls climbed out of the backseat. Nana wore a pair of big, dark sunglasses. She squared her shoulders and looked at the others, as if she were the leader of the pack. Hellie smoothed her dark tunic over her hips. Her colorful skirt swept around her legs as she and Nana led the others determinedly toward the porch.

"What the heck are they doing here?" Grace descended the porch steps while simultaneously tying the hem of his jersey into a knot at her hip.

"There you are," Nana said, and glanced at Hellie. "I told you they were busy making out."

Reed chuckled.

"We were *not* making out," Grace said sharply. "How did you even know where I was?"

She looked so damn cute in his jersey, he wanted to… *Why not?* He pulled his phone from his pocket and snapped a picture of her.

"After movie night at the Majestic?" Nana waved her hand dismissively. "As if you'd be anywhere else?" She ducked into the car again.

One of the younger girls, a redhead, said, "Sorry to interrupt. We tried to call."

"It's okay," Grace said. "Reed, this is Lauryn."

The girl smiled sheepishly.

"And this is Phoenix." Grace motioned to the other young girl, who waved.

"Nice to meet you both."

"If Grace had answered her phone, we wouldn't have had to interrupt your lovefest." Nana handed Reed a bag. "We brought breakfast since everyone knows you don't have a functioning kitchen."

"How does *everyone* know that?"

"Never mind how," Nana said with a sigh. "Just say thank you."

"Thank you." He peeked into the bag at the Tupperware containers. "Did you *cook* us breakfast?"

"We baked as we worked," Lauryn said. "Nana and Hellie taught me and Phoenix how to make corn bread and cinnamon rolls."

"Kids these days are so busy with phones and Facebook, they don't learn the basic skills of life," Hellie said.

"The reason we're here is that we're just *so* excited, we couldn't wait to tell Grace our news," Janie explained.

"News?" Grace turned to Reed and said, "Sorry."

Amused by the whole scene, he said, "It's all good. And now we have breakfast."

"We finished our script!" Phoenix blurted out.

Hellie handed Grace a folder. "It turned out even better than we hoped."

Grace opened the folder and scanned the contents. "You finished the *entire* script? You must have worked all day and through the night."

"Yes, ma'am. We practically had ourselves a slumber party. Worked right up until midnight and started at the crack of dawn again this morning. Now we're here, and we're going to make our masterpiece into a play." Nana lifted her chin and said, "And *you're* going to produce it."

Grace smiled, studying the script. Without taking her eyes from the papers, she said, "Uh-huh. Sure. This is *really* good, you guys."

"I tried not to sex it up too much," Janie said, "*despite* Nana's prompting."

Nana threw her hands up in the air. "What is it with you kids and your hang-ups about your bodies? Sex is as much a part of love as compromise and that squirrelly feeling in the pit of your stomach. It all goes hand in hand. And, Janie, I saw you and Boyd smooching at the ice cream shop the other night. You can't tell me you don't love to touch that man."

Lauryn giggled.

"Yes, but I wouldn't want to be up onstage doing it," Janie

said.

Nana mumbled something Reed couldn't hear, and then she said, "Let's get down to business. Grace, can you produce this for us?"

Grace's brows knitted. "Well, I'm leaving in less than two weeks, but that gives us time to go through the script and tweak it. Maybe we can think about doing it as a community play when I come back over the holidays. Do you have friends in mind for the cast? And what about a venue? Do you want to do it in one of your backyards or something? We'll need sets and props, and—"

"The *holidays*?" Nana shook her head. "Oh no, that will not do. We're ready to do it now, and this is not a play for a *yard*."

"This story is worthy of a bigger venue. A huge audience," Hellie said. "And it's not a winter play. It's a summer story. It really *must* take place in the summer, regardless of where we do it."

"What about next summer? Will the Majestic be done by then?" Grace asked Reed.

"It's a huge project," he said. "A year might be enough, but it's hard to say until we're inside."

"But that's such a long time. We don't want to wait a year," Phoenix said. "Can't we do it before you leave, Grace?"

Grace's expression softened, and she closed the folder. "I wish we could, but productions take time. Even elementary schoolers have several weeks to prepare. The cast has to be chosen, and they have to memorize their lines. You know that can't happen overnight. And if you want to try to hold it someplace…" Her eyes lit up. "Like the Jerichos' barn?" Her voice escalated with excitement. "Or maybe the No Limitz community center? I could ask Haylie. They have a great auditorium. Or the high school auditorium? Brindle might be able to pull some strings."

"The community center!" Lauryn clapped her hands. "That's a great idea. They have lots of room."

"I like the barn," Janie said. "The story revolves around a small town. What's more small town than a barn?"

"I like the barn, too. But, Lauryn, if you're set on the community center, we can consider that," Hellie said.

"No. I think Janie's right. The barn is even better," Lauryn said.

"That's set, then," Nana said. "I'll talk to Nancy Jericho, and my granddaughter Lindsay can throw together a party in a heartbeat!"

"A party? You're getting way ahead of yourselves," Grace said. "There's costumes, seating…" Her brows knitted again. "Morgyn might be able to help with costumes."

"And my knitting club gals can pitch in." Hellie withdrew a phone from the pocket of her skirt and began typing a text.

"The high school drama club would probably help with sets." Lauryn whipped out her phone and began texting, too.

Grace paced. "This is exciting on so many levels! You guys are from very different generations, and you were able to come together and create something wonderful. Or at least it seems like it will be wonderful. I haven't had time to read all of it, obviously. I think the community would be excited to see this play, but we still can't pull it together that quickly. There are things we *can* do to get started. We can come up with a list of what we need to accomplish, and when I come back in a few weeks, we'll see where we are."

"A few *weeks?*" Nana's gaze moved between Grace and Reed. "Do not tell me that you're going to go a few weeks before seeing Reed again. Oh no, missy. That won't do any more than waiting a few weeks to do the play will."

"I still need to *read* the script, Nana. I'm sure it's good, and I want to give life to your play because you have all worked so hard on it, but some things can't be rushed. Why don't we have breakfast and work through a timeline?" Grace suggested. "Once we have a breakdown of who's doing what for the prep, we'll have a better idea of how long it will take to reach out to the right people. Productions cost money, so we might need to reach out to local businesses about sponsoring the event, or putting ads in the program, like they do in the schools for fundraising. I think Brindle would be willing to help with that, too. And my mom spent years on the PTA. I bet she'd love to pitch in."

Reed could practically see the gears turning in Grace's mind as she mentally ticked off ideas. He loved seeing her so enthusiastic.

"We need music," Phoenix said. "Do you think there's any chance Sable would be willing to help out?"

"I'll call her." Grace pulled her phone from her pocket, and then, as if a breeze had swept the wind from her sails, she lowered her phone and turned her back toward the others, speaking quietly to Reed. "I just realized we agreed not to work on Sundays, and here I am...*working*. Sable's right," she said just above a whisper. "I don't know how to draw a line between relaxing and working. I'll tell them we'll do it tomorrow."

He took her face between his hands and said, "Baby, are you having fun thinking about this project? Because you sure seem excited."

"Well, yes, but we just said we'd take Sundays off, and I'm leaving in two weeks."

Reed was aware of the others listening to their every word despite Grace's hushed tone. But it wasn't just the girls waiting with bated breath. *His* girl was waiting, too, looking at him like she was ready to walk away from the dance she'd waited a lifetime to attend.

"I don't want you to think I'm a workaholic." Her brows wrinkled, and then she added, "But I'm pretty sure Sable's right. I have some of those traits."

"*Some?*" Nana said. "Your mama says you work twenty-four-seven."

There was a collective, "Shh," from the others, and Grace's expression became even more strained.

Reed wanted to kiss that worry away, but since that wasn't an option at the moment, he said, "When you fall for a passionate woman, you have to know her passion touches all aspects of her life." He felt the tension around her begin to dissipate. "It's not work if we're doing it together, and I'm sure you'll need someone to help pull together sets." He felt himself grinning. "I have tools, and some people think I'm pretty talented with my hands."

"Really? You won't mind?"

"Absolutely. Let's do this, Gracie. It'll be fun to see you in action."

Cheers rang out, and in the next second, the ladies were hugging one another—and Reed—and making plans as they headed inside the house.

As he led Janie and her pup into the dining room, she said, "Thank you for sharing Grace with us today. I promise we won't always barge in like this."

He took in Grace's smile as she opened her laptop, chatting excitedly about casting and production calendars. This was something else his house—*their house*—had been missing from the day he'd bought it. He could create beauty, but insurmountable love and friendships could only come from the heart.

Their house was becoming a *home*.

"You're welcome anytime, Janie. It's not barging in when our door is always open."

Chapter Eighteen

AFTER ONLY A few days of staying with Reed, Grace felt like she had never lived anywhere else. Monday morning they'd picked up the rest of her things from her parents' house, including Greedy Boy. The giant bear now sat on a beautiful, tufted velvet antique chair that Reed claimed he'd brought home because they'd *needed* it, but Grace had a feeling he'd bought it for the bear. His ever-present nostalgia was just one more thing she loved about him. Nothing beat waking up in his arms and creating new memories and future dreams with the man who knew her best, except maybe *finally* being able to openly spend time with their families. They'd taken Roy and Ella to the Stardust Café for dinner last night. It was wonderful to see how protective Reed was of his aunt and uncle and how loving they were toward him. They'd extended that warmth to Grace as if she'd always been part of their family. This morning she and Reed had jogged into town as the sun rose over the mountains and talked about all the things Reed could do with the Majestic. They'd even arrived at her parents' house early enough to have breakfast with them before Reed started painting the porch.

Now it was midafternoon, and Grace was in the gazebo

working through emails about her next production, while also stealing glances at Reed painting the gingerbread around the porch. He was shirtless, his jeans riding low on his hips as he stood on the ladder, steadying himself with one hand on the edge of the roof as he painted. Reed had worked with her group Sunday morning straight through the afternoon. Grace had since had time to read the whole script, and while it needed a few adjustments, it was a beautiful mix of generations, with themes of old-fashioned family values and modern youth all wrapped up with more than a hint of rebellion and an overwhelming amount of humor. She and the girls continued meeting in Amber's bookstore, as Grace had promised to teach the class in order to help her sister gain customers. That's why they'd decided to make flyers asking for volunteers for the play, and distribute them at local shops and at the high school. Anyone who was interested could meet them at their class. Nana and the girls had taken charge of that endeavor yesterday, and Grace hoped they'd get at least a few willing participants. The girls were so excited, she didn't want them to be let down.

Reed looked over, his cheeks lifting with that sexy, crooked smile that always sent shivers of awareness through her. God, she loved him so intensely. She hadn't known what she was missing.

She blew him a kiss just as her phone rang, and her stomach sank when Satchel's name appeared on the screen.

"Don't kill the messenger," Satchel said before she could say a word.

She sighed heavily. "What's Keagen doing now?" She listened to a litany of complaints, from his bitching about the talent of the supporting actors to his unprofessional behavior onset. Another call beeped through, and she glanced at the screen. *Amber.* "Hold on, Satchel. I have another call."

She switched over. "Hey, Amber."

"Grace, you've *got* to get over here."

"Why? We don't have class today."

"My phone has been ringing off the hook," Amber said in a hushed and hurried tone. "You didn't tell me you put flyers out. My store is *packed.*"

"I don't think the girls put them out yet, but that's good news. Do you need help with the register? I can be there in fifteen minutes." The perfect excuse to end her call with Satchel.

"Just get here. I need more than register help."

After ending the call, she told Satchel to deal with the issues and reminded him that she was supposed to be taking time off. Then she went and filled Reed in on where she was headed.

He wrapped his arms around her. His skin was warm from the sun, and when he touched his lips to hers, she wished she could stay right there in his embrace forever.

His phone vibrated, and he pulled it out of his pocket, quickly scanning a text. "It's Roy."

"You can get back to him. I have to run to the bookstore."

He tightened his grip as he slid his phone into his pocket. "I'll call *him* later and kiss you *now.*"

Twenty-five minutes later, which was totally Reed's fault for kissing her until she almost forgot Amber was expecting her, she walked into the bookstore. Or rather, she *squeezed* in. There was barely room to inch into the store, as people filled every aisle.

"Grace!" Amber waved from behind the counter, looking a bit frazzled.

"Grace?" someone called out from the back of the store. "I can help with makeup!"

Suddenly people began calling out to her as the crowd

pushed forward like concertgoers trying to get backstage. Energy radiated through the shop, as real as the encroaching crowd. Grace mouthed, *What's going on?* to Amber as she pushed through a gaggle of girls hanging around the checkout area.

Amber held up a flyer, and Grace quickly read it. WANT TO BE A STAR? COME TO THE STORY TIME BOOKSTORE! WE NEED ACTORS AND VOLUNTEERS FOR...It went on to describe the play and list all the areas in which they needed help. Grace was overwhelmed with the realization that all these people had come out to help.

She stepped behind the counter, and Amber said, "It's been like this for more than an hour."

"I'm so sorry. They must have forgotten to add the class times to the flyers." Grace held her hands up and turned to the crowd in an effort to gain some semblance of control. "Hey, guys, can I have your attention, please?"

As the din of the crowd quieted, Grace took in a host of familiar faces—women and men she'd gone to school with, her friends' parents, and a slew of teenagers. Among them, Nat stood quietly, a smile on her pretty face.

"Thank you all for coming out. First, I want to be sure you understand these are not paid positions, but voluntary."

"Of course," a woman said from somewhere off to the left.

Grace was shocked. She'd expected a number of people to leave when they heard that. "Okay. I never expected this many volunteers."

"Why not?" a teenage boy asked from the back of the crowd.

She glanced at Amber, whose eyes held the same silent question, and when she answered, the truth came easily. "Because I've been entrenched in a cutthroat world for too long." *And I've*

213

forgotten how amazing and supportive this community is.

Unexpected emotions bubbled up inside her.

Amber must have seen something in her expression, because she took Grace's hand and said quietly, "*We've* got this."

Grace cleared her throat, struggling to push past her racing heart and find her voice. "We'll find places for everyone who's interested," she said loudly. "It's going to take me a few minutes to get things organized. While I'm getting ready, why don't you show Amber some love and see if you can find a book to buy for yourself, or as a gift for someone else."

"Good idea!" someone said loudly.

The crowd shifted, moving toward the shelves and talking among themselves as Grace dug in her messenger bag for the outline of the play.

"I can't believe this," Grace whispered as she pulled out her notebook. "I need to call Nana and the girls and text Reed and tell him it looks like I'll be running later than I thought. This could take hours."

"First, that was brilliant. Thank you," Amber said. "And second, you've been gone a long time, but don't you remember? This is what it's always been like. When someone needs help, there are more people than you could ever dream of who are willing to pitch in. Remember when Mom had her hysterectomy and so many people brought dinners over that we had to give most of them away? And when the tree fell on the Jerichos' barn, nearly the whole town turned out to help repair it?"

"It was the dead of winter. I remember," Grace said. "I froze my butt off."

"But you were there, Grace. Just like these people are here for you. That's why I couldn't ever figure out why you wanted to move away so badly."

"I wanted more than this," she said reflexively, but the words left her lips dulled and unenthusiastic.

"And you got it. The question is, is *more* always better? Because this…" Amber gazed out at the crowd, and her hand covered her heart as she said, "This is everything I could ever hope for in a community."

Grace asked herself if she'd wanted more than this *community*, or more than what the area had to offer her in terms of a career. She was no longer able to decipher the answer.

REED CLIMBED FROM his truck Tuesday evening as his phone vibrated in his pocket. He pulled it out, and as he read his uncle's message, he realized he hadn't returned his earlier text in which Roy had also asked him to call. He rubbed an ache in his shoulder and gazed up at the house, missing Grace after only a few hours. He'd wanted to see if she had time for a quick dinner and had driven by the bookstore before coming home, but even from the road he'd seen a swarm of people inside.

He texted his uncle, *Just got home. Will call after I shower. We're confirmed for tomorrow at 7pm to get inside the theater.* He wanted to show his relatives and Grace the interior of the theater. He grabbed his tools from his truck and noticed a beat-up old white car crawling past. The trunk was rusted, and one of the back windows was blocked with a piece of cardboard. The hair on the back of Reed's neck stood on end, his built-in *trouble radar.* He set his tools down and strode toward the street. There was nothing beyond his house other than Sophie's family's properties, and he'd be damned if he let trouble find them.

The car pulled over and parked by the curb. Reed folded his arms over his chest, watching a disheveled-looking man climb from the car. He walked with a limp as he opened the trunk and withdrew a shoe box.

"Can I help you with something?" Reed asked.

The man closed the trunk and turned squinty eyes on Reed. He had thick brows, a slightly bulbous nose, and yellowish skin. His pants and shirt hung on him like a boy wearing his father's clothes, only this wasn't a boy. It was a weary, sad-looking man with hair the color of pennies and dimes and a beard that was white on the sides and brownish around the goatee area. He took a few uneven steps, and a smile lifted his thin lips, making his eyes look even smaller. A pang of pity rang through Reed.

"Reed," he said with more than a hint of familiarity.

A spear of recognition shot through Reed as he studied the man's aged face, trying to pull the image of his father from memories of their visit when Reed had been only four years old, but it was like tugging a fishing line that was hooked on the bottom of a lake, refusing to break free. Could he be wrong? He swallowed hard, breathing harder, and forced his voice from his lungs.

"Yes?"

The man's gaze dropped, a pinched expression forming on his face as he limped closer. Reed unfolded his arms, feeling the man's presence like an enemy approaching the gates. Gates that had been erected to protect Reed. Gates he had no interest in unlocking after more than twenty years of absence. A violent storm raged within him as the man stopped arm's distance away, meeting—and holding—Reed's steady gaze.

"It's been a long time," the man said.

His voice was a gravelly remnant of the cloudy memories Reed held. The man wiped his brow, and Reed's gaze caught on the mangled skin on the back of his left hand and forearm, a map of angry scars. Reed's stomach pitched at the hauntingly familiar sight of the burn. His phone rang, but he was laser focused on putting the fragmented pieces of his memories into place. They felt dark and ugly, causing ice to form around his heart.

"It's me, Reed. Frank." His pleading eyes begged for recognition. "Your father."

Reed's jaw clenched tight, his hands curled into fists. Anger roared up like a wild animal, and he was powerless to stop hurtful words from flying out through gritted teeth. "Roy Cross is my father."

Frank looked at the box in his hands, and then his eyes shifted to the house. Reed didn't want this man anywhere near his home or his *life*. He didn't want to feel the pity and longing battling against his anger, his burning *hatred*, for the man who had given him away like an old dog. Reed stepped closer to the curb, drawing Frank's attention away from the house.

"I came a long way," Frank said. "I thought we could talk."

"You *came a long way?*" Reed scoffed and crossed his arms again, steeling himself against the hurt child trying to claw his way up from the depths of hell. He lifted his chin toward Frank's car and said, "I suggest you turn around and head back the way you came."

A painful expression climbed across Frank's face. "I deserve that." He held the shoe box in a shaky hand toward Reed. "I thought you might want a few of your mother's things."

Reed stared at the box, wanting desperately to have a connection to the mother he'd never known but felt that accepting the box might somehow let Frank in. He kept his arms crossed and said nothing.

Frank set the box on the sidewalk, like an uncapped grenade that might blow if handled incorrectly, and said, "I'm staying at the Marriott Courtyard at the edge of town until Monday. Room 433, in case you change your mind."

Reed stood stock-still, shoulders back, head held high as Frank limped to his car and drove away. Only after the sound of the car was long out of earshot did the air rush from Reed's lungs, leaving him panting as his knees gave out, and he sank down to a squat, his mind too numb to think, his eyes locked on the box Frank left behind.

Chapter Nineteen

ON HER WAY home Tuesday night, Grace passed Roy's truck as he drove away from the house. The house was dark, save for a light in the kitchen, where she found an old shoe box on the table. It was taped shut, and she wondered if Roy had brought something over. She set her messenger bag down.

"Reed?" she called out as she headed upstairs. Morgyn had finished the gifts she'd asked her to make, and she couldn't wait to give Reed his.

As she walked through the master bedroom, she paused by the foot of the mattress, remembering the adoration in Reed's eyes as they'd made love that morning. His sweet words—*How will I make it through a single night without you in my arms?*— had plagued her all day, making her warm with emotions and sad about their impending separation in equal measure. Once again, she braced herself for that reality, telling herself to treasure each day rather than ruing the end of them.

She headed out to the veranda, but there was no sign of Reed anywhere other than his truck in the driveway. Gazing out over the backyard, she caught his silhouette down by the creek. *How romantic.* She tugged off her high-heeled boots, skirt, and blouse, pulled on a pair of shorts and a hoodie, and put his gift in her pocket. She slipped her feet into a pair of flip-flops, feeling light as air after the amazing day she'd had. Nana and the others had come in to help her organize groups of volunteers and create callback lists so they could coordinate auditions and teams to work on different aspects of the play. There was no way they'd be able to pull it off before she left, even with a big group of volunteers, but it was coming together, and that was exciting as hell.

She hurried down the stairs and flew out the kitchen door and off the deck, humming the song "Stupid" by Levi Hummon. She wanted to be *stupid* with Reed and do crazy-in-love silly things together without thinking about the ramifications. She sang a few words as she neared Reed. He was gazing out at the water, his knees pulled up, the crook of his elbows hooked around his knees, hands clasped. She put a hand on his shoulder, feeling his muscles tense beneath her fingers.

"Hey, handsome," she said softly, and pressed a kiss to his cheek as she sat beside him in the grass. "I brought you something."

He turned, and her heart sank at the tortured look in his eyes, the firm set of his jaw. His gift forgotten, she asked, "What's wrong?"

"Nothing, babe." He wrapped his arms around her and held her tight, one hand on the back of her head, keeping her close. "I'm glad you're home."

"Sorry I was so late." She wondered if that was the problem. It was nearly eight o'clock.

He pressed his lips to her cheek and said, "How did it go? I drove by, but there were so many people there, I didn't come in."

"It was amazing. We have volunteers for everything—set

building, the cast, we even have the place worked out. The Jerichos were happy to let us use their barn, and there are a group of high schoolers who are apparently really great artists, who volunteered to put together posters and flyers. Morgyn came by, and she's going to help with costumes, along with a group of Hellie's friends and some high school girls. Lindsay came with Nana, and I swear those two are a powerhouse. You know how Nana loves to celebrate anything and everything. Lindsay is putting together a whole rebellious-Cinderella theme with decorations and food. It's going to be amazing."

One side of Reed's lips tipped up, but it was a half-hearted smile. "Good, babe. I can't wait to see it all come together."

"Me too. Are you sure you're okay? I'm sorry I was late, if that's what's bugging you."

His hands slid to the nape of her neck, and he touched his forehead to hers. "No, babe," he said softly. "I'm not sure I'm okay, and it has nothing to do with you or the time. I don't mind that you worked late."

"Then what is it? Did something happen? I saw Roy driving away. Are he and Ella okay?"

"They're fine." He pressed his lips to hers and sat back, gazing out at the water again. His hands curled into fists, and even in the moonlight she could see the muscles in his jaw bunching. "My...*Frank* showed up here earlier."

"Frank...?"

He looked at her out of the corner of his eyes, and the darkness of his stare brought understanding. Her mind reeled with a crazy mix of anxiety and hope. Reed had carried so much anger toward his father, it was no wonder he was acting strange.

"Frank, as in your *father*?"

He gave one curt nod.

"Here? At the house? Did you guys talk? How was it?"

"No, we didn't *talk*," he said sharply. "That man has no business anywhere near my life." He pushed to his feet and paced. "Roy tried to warn me, but I was too tied up all day to call him back, and then Frank was *here*."

She went to him, but he took a step back, holding up his hand to warn her off.

"I'm sorry, babe, but I'm too tightly wound. I don't want to take it out on you."

She'd never seen Reed like this, but she didn't want to be shut out, and she *really* didn't want him to think he was stuck dealing with this alone. She put her finger into his belt loop and pulled herself forward, until they were standing thigh to thigh. His lips curved up, though his eyes remained tortured, and he lifted his gaze toward the moon.

"Gracie, please don't."

"Don't what? Love you?" she said. "Because for me to stay back while you're hurting, or conflicted, or angry at your father, that's what would have to happen."

"I'm so angry," he said through gritted teeth. "*Too* angry. I don't want you to take the brunt of it."

She wound her arms around his waist and pressed her cheek to his chest, feeling his heart beating fast and hard. "I know. You won't let me. I'm not worried."

"Who does he think he is, showing up like that?"

She knew he wasn't looking for an answer.

"What right does he have to interrupt my life? What makes him think I'd *want* to see him?"

She eased her grip enough to look up at him. Worry lines deepened along his brows and beneath his eyes. His mouth twisted angrily. And yet somehow the weight of sadness overshadowed all that rage, making her ache even more for him.

"Did he say anything? Explain why he came after all these years? Did Roy offer any clarity?" she asked.

He shook his head and finally put his arms around her, letting out a long sigh before responding. "Roy said Frank had stopped by his place asking where he could find me. Roy asked the same questions you did, but I don't have the answers. I sent Frank away. In my head, he's like an infectious disease I don't want to risk being around. I'm sure that makes no sense. There was a time I would have given anything to have a relationship with him. But that's gone, Gracie. Maybe it makes me a terrible human being, but I don't want it. Frank Gilbert does not exist to me. As far as I'm concerned, I'm Roy Cross's son. I don't want or need to hear excuses about why Frank's been absent from my life for all this time. He abandoned me once, and it took forever for me to move past it. Hell, babe. I'm still not past it. He's not a part of my life. He never was."

She had so many questions, so many things she wanted to say, but none of them mattered, because she wasn't Reed. She hadn't been the child asking Santa for his father's love or the preteen harboring resentment, curiosity, and hope, all of which went unanswered. And she wasn't the boy who had to find his way to manhood with all the unanswered questions Reed carried on his shoulders. She was only the woman who had loved him long enough to try to keep those thoughts and questions to herself in an effort to help him heal.

Chapter Twenty

IN A SPAN of forty-eight hours a man could reunite and fall in love with his high school sweetheart, he could finish renovating a Victorian porch, and, Reed discovered, his house could become a home. What he didn't expect was that just as quickly that home could become the place where his demons came back to haunt him. Reed stood in the kitchen, staring at the shoe box and wondering if it held the answers he'd always wanted or decades of hurt. Twice he'd driven by that damned hotel at the edge of town where Frank was staying. And twice he'd cursed a blue streak and driven away.

He still wasn't ready to play that game of Russian roulette.

"I'm ready," Grace said as she rushed down the stairs. They were meeting Meggie, Roy, and Ella at the Majestic to take a tour of the inside. "Sorry we ran late with the auditions today. I can't believe how many people want a part in this play. I changed as quickly as I could."

He closed his eyes for a moment to regain control of his emotions and felt her arms circle his waist. Her cheek pressed warm and loving against his back, and he reached behind him, keeping her close. She'd been careful not to push him toward seeing Frank, but he knew in his heart she thought he should.

He also knew she didn't need any more angst in her life. She had enough on her plate with running around town to coordinate the play, dealing with the director about her next production, which seemed to take hours of emails, texts, and phone calls, and handling the asshole actor who was causing problems on her current production. Reed wanted to head to the city and shake the shit out of him, tell him to grow up and do his fucking job. It was probably a good thing Grace was more levelheaded, because his unresolved anger and hurt toward Frank made him less than rational. He tried to concentrate on Grace and happier things, like the fact that he finished the porch two days early, celebrating this coming Friday night with their families at the barbecue, and buying the Majestic. He needed the distraction of that project now more than ever, as Grace's—and Frank's—departure loomed.

Grace spread her hands over his stomach and said, "How about if we move the box out of sight until you're ready to deal with it?"

He turned and embraced her, telling himself to man up and look in the damn thing already. She smiled up at him, and it sliced right through the heartache to his very soul. Grace was what mattered, not his past. He'd never be able to bring his mother back, and no matter what Frank had to say, it wouldn't repair the damage he'd done. It was time to close that door for good, and putting the box away was a start.

He pressed his lips to hers and then said, "I'll put it away after we get back. Everyone's probably waiting for us."

They arrived at the same time as Roy and Ella and greeted them outside the theater.

"Grace, we're excited to see your family Friday night." Ella embraced Grace. "It was awfully nice of your mother to invite us."

"Everyone is looking forward to it. Amber is even planning to close her bookstore early so she can be there." Grace looked lovingly at Reed and said, "Reed did such an amazing job on the porch, Mom and Dad want to break it in properly. I think the words my father used were 'timeless perfection.'"

"This get-together is a long time coming," Reed said.

As Grace and Ella talked about the barbecue, Roy ran an assessing eye over Reed and slung an arm over his shoulder. "How are you holding up?"

When Roy had shown up at their house minutes after Reed had sent Frank away, he'd listened to Reed bitch for a long time. Roy had always been good at knowing when to listen and when to push. The thing was, the few words he'd said were still battering Reed's head. *That man's your blood, and where you take it from here is your decision. But keep in mind, your mama loved him, and she was no pushover.*

He stood up a little taller for the man who had raised him and said, "You know that feeling when you're working on an old foundation and you pull out a brick only to find that what lay behind it was never solid?"

Roy rubbed a hand over his jaw and lifted his brows. "So, you find a bit of decay, some crumbled mortar. Son, how many times has a poorly built foundation ever gotten the best of you? You're a Cross. You find the best parts of everything, and you breathe life into them. It's who you are at your very core. Nothing behind those bricks is strong enough to change that. The question is, are you strong enough to face it? I believe you are."

Grace's fingers slid into Reed's, offering silent support. Reed thought about how they'd hidden their relationship and how much potential angst they'd saved by doing so. They could have challenged those old rivalries and they could have spent their senior year of high school arguing with their friends. His answer didn't come easily, but it came just the same. "Sometimes just because you can do something doesn't mean you should. Come on. I assume Meggie's already inside? Let's go check out our next project."

Inside the lobby, Reed was as awestruck as the others, just as he'd been when he'd first seen the multicolored inlaid marble floors and intricate woodwork around the refreshment counter.

"Just like I remember," Ella said as she wrapped her hand around Roy's arm and snuggled closer. "It was right here at this counter that your uncle proposed to me."

"At the *popcorn* counter?" Reed laughed. "Real romantic, Roy."

"It was more romantic than roses and diamonds," Ella said. "He pointed to the soda fountain, which was right there at the time, and asked me what I wanted to drink. I told him it didn't matter. I'd share whatever he was having."

"And I said, 'How about you share the rest of my life with me?'" Roy leaned down and kissed Ella. "If I were able to do it all over again, I'd probably do it just the same way. I caught you off guard and got you to agree to marry me before you had time to think about it. I'd say that's the biggest *win* of my life."

"Oh, Roy." Ella wrinkled her nose.

"I think it's perfectly romantic." Grace squeezed Reed's hand. "It was on this property that Reed first told me he loved me."

The look in her eyes told Reed she was remembering that night as clearly as he was. He'd told her he loved her behind the theater, as they lay kissing, naked as the day they were born, beneath a blanket of stars, only moments before they'd made love for the very first time. Afterward, as they lay in each other's arms, basking in the aftermath, he'd gazed into her eyes and said, *I'm going to marry you one day.* And he'd meant it.

The heels of Meggie's boots tapped out a hurried rhythm as she raced out of the auditorium in a red paisley dress belted around her thick waist, with a short jean jacket over it. Her blond hair was gathered on one side in a thick braid, a few long, wispy bangs framing her rosy cheeks and bright brown eyes.

"Hey, y'all! I'm so glad you made it out. Isn't this place just to *die* for! Can you believe the shape it's in?" Her arms moved animatedly as she spoke. "Gracie Montgomery, get on in here and give me a hug, girl!"

The amusement in Grace's eyes was priceless as she embraced her old friend.

"Hi, Meg. It's been a long time," Grace said. "It's nice to see you. You look gorgeous."

"It's *Meggie*." She patted her hair and set one hand on her rounded hip. "Yes, I do look mighty fine, don't I? After all those years of being thin as a twig, I finally got my groove on. Country livin' will keep a girl in shape." She dragged her gaze down Grace's body, taking in her blousy blue top, skinny jeans, and high-heeled boots. "Looks like the city's gotten its trendy claws into you." She waved her hand and lowered her voice to a conspiratorial whisper. "Don't you worry yourself none. I'm sure Ella can plump up those hips, give Reed something to hang on to. You must not have time to eat with your crazy schedule, Miss Big-Time Producer." She gave a little *whoop* and headed back toward the theater, motioning for them to follow. "Wait until you see the auditorium. Reed sure got a steal on this baby…"

Grace looked down at her body as they walked in, and Reed pulled her close and whispered, "You're perfect, baby. Thin, fat, in the middle, makes no difference. It's what's inside that counts."

"My heart?" Grace said softly.

"Well, I was talking about what's beneath those clothes, but your heart works, too." He chuckled, dodging her hand as she swatted at him.

A look of awe came over Grace as she took in the auditorium's domed ceiling, elaborate chandeliers, and balconies. "This is gorgeous, and it's in amazing shape. I can't believe it."

"It sure is," Meggie said.

As Meggie ran through the details of the property at breakneck speed, Grace whispered ideas to Reed. "There's so much you can do here—presentations, weddings, outdoor movies. But you have to crunch the numbers. It's easy to get carried away and excited, but it takes money to keep a theater afloat. And in a place like Oak Falls, you need to have a niche."

The more ideas Grace had, the more infectious her enthusiasm became, and by the time they'd toured the whole facility, everyone was tossing out ideas.

"You could have Tweet seats," Grace suggested.

"I hear they do that in the bigger cities, give away seats so people can tweet during the show and drum up buzz," Meggie said. "I bet you'd have customers from all the neighboring areas."

"And a mailer," Ella offered. "We used to do them for Roy's company when things got slow. People love to get mail."

"Yes, but these days email works better, and it's more cost-effective," Grace said. "I read about one stage company that put a call out for original material, and they received more than four *hundred* submissions."

"That sounds like a job in and of itself, to weed through them." Reed inhaled deeply.

"Yes, but it also gave the company an identity, a niche," Grace explained. "They're now known for producing original plays, and they have an audience of more than thirty thousand loyal followers from all over the world, not just their small town."

Reed was blown away. "I know very little about running a theater, but you guys are way ahead of me. I still have to do all the work, remember? That's going to take a long time. I've got meetings scheduled next week with subcontractors to discuss the project, and my buddy Graham Braden, a structural engineer, will come down and help me out when I'm ready. But hiring is a long way off, and while I thought I'd hire people to run it, you're talking about really specific experience. I'm not sure we have that around here."

"Sure we do." Ella looked adoringly at Grace. "She's just living someplace else. But Grace could teach someone."

"Oh, Ella, I don't know about that," Grace said. "But if you start small, I'm sure you can find someone with enough experience to get it off the ground."

"I know just the person!" Meggie exclaimed. "I had a client, Mr. Mosby, who's niece was in theater in Chicago. Mr. Mosby said she was talking about moving back to Wishing Creek to be near her mama, who's been living overseas for the past few years. Her mama had married a rich French man and, well, I guess he found a younger model. Mr. Mosby said she was over the moon about the reunion. Can you imagine? After all those years? Why, I think I'd cry a river if I went that long without seeing my mama…"

She continued talking, but Reed's mind had taken a detour, and now he was thinking about Frank again. Tension puddled in his gut, seeping through his veins, until his jaw was so tight he stepped away from the group to keep them from noticing.

Meggie followed him and said, "Anyway, if you go that direction, I'd be happy to reach out to Mr. Mosby and connect you two, if you'd like."

Reed gritted his teeth, trying to temper his frustration. Why the hell couldn't he put Frank out of his head? "Thanks, Meggie. I'll keep that in mind. I think we've seen enough. I appreciate you coming out."

"Okeydokey. I'll see you at settlement. You just give me a holler if you need me between now and then." She winked at Grace and said, "But I'd imagine you'll be a little busy as long as Grace is in town."

They headed outside, and after Meggie drove way, Grace said, "Are you okay?"

His gut reaction was to say yes, to shrug off his angst and move on, but the concern in Grace's eyes deserved the truth. "Just trying to shake off some history of my own."

"Frank?" she asked. "Maybe you just need to talk to him. Hear what he has to say. He is your father, Reed."

Reed shook his head and pointed to Roy. "That man is, and always will be, my father."

"Son, I love you—you know that—but you are one stubborn son of a gun." Roy held his gaze as he closed the distance between them.

"You want me to talk to that guy?" Reed tried to temper his anger, but it bubbled out in his rising voice. "The guy who turned his back on me? Who tossed me in your laps with no regard for what life plans you had?"

"Hey," Ella said sharply. "Don't you go there, sweetheart. The minute you were born, you took hold of our hearts and you've never let go."

"I'm sorry, Ella. I know that," he conceded. "I didn't mean it like that. I meant—"

"We *know* what you meant," Roy said. "And we know how difficult this is for you, because we're just as tormented by his reappearing in our lives. But he's your fathe—"

"No," Reed hollered. "*You're* my father. You will always be my father. As far as I'm concerned, he's just the man who supplied the sperm. No more important than an anonymous donor."

Sadness washed over Roy as he placed his hands on Reed's shoulders and spoke solemnly. "No, son. I'm the lucky man who got to raise you. But he'll always be your father. You can't deny blood any more than you can deny that a part of your mother lives on in your love of history."

"Goddamn it." Reed tried to twist out of his uncle's grip, but Roy held him too tight. "I'm finally *happy* and *whole*, and you want me to put it all on the line for a guy who couldn't give his own son the time of day?"

"No," Roy said, hands tightening on Reed's shoulders. "I want you to *think* about this long and hard before you run from it."

"I've never run from a thing," Reed seethed.

Roy's gaze darted to Grace for only a fraction of a second, but that was long enough for Reed to connect the dots back to when he'd left town after high school.

Roy lowered his hands and said, "You feel whole right now because you think you're in control and because you have us and Grace and a project to bury your thoughts in. But that anger you're carrying around will eat away at you worse than anything Frank could ever say. All I'm asking is that you think about talking to him and deal with the anger before it deals with you."

"I have nothing to say to him," Reed said tightly.

"You don't have to convince me, son," Roy said. "Just ask yourself one question. When you have children of your own, what will you tell them about your father? That he came to talk to you and you turned him away? Are you going to spread your anger to your children? Have them hate the man for what he did to you? Because I sure as hell hope we raised you better than that."

Ella stepped tentatively toward Reed. "We love you, honey, and we'll support whatever you decide."

"Will you?" Reed kept his eyes trained on Roy, who nodded curtly, then headed for his truck.

Chapter Twenty-One

TENSION ROLLED OFF Reed like gusts of wind as he climbed rigidly into the driver's seat, his jaw working overtime. He started the truck and gripped the steering wheel so tight his knuckles blanched. Grace knew of only one way to tame that type of emotional turmoil—complete and utter sidetracking.

"Do you still have the blankets in the truck?"

He nodded curtly, just as his uncle had.

"Great. Two stops. Pastry Palace and Dempsey's Overpass."

Dempsey's Overpass was a dilapidated covered bridge they'd come across when they were teenagers looking for a private place to park and fool around. The bridge was located down an old country road that hadn't been in use since the new overpass was built a few miles farther downstream. Below the bridge was a service road, also out of use and blocked with a concrete barrier. They used to drive around that barrier and park down by the water. It was the one place they gravitated toward whenever one of them was in a bad mood.

He pulled swiftly out of the lot, and Grace put her hand on his rock-hard thigh. If she'd been with any other man who was strung this tight, she might worry he'd snap and lash out at her, but not Reed. She didn't say another word as he drove to

Wishing Creek, and by the time they arrived, he was breathing a little easier. He put his hand over hers, locking them together. She leaned against him, glad to feel some of his tension falling away.

When they reached Pastry Palace, she said, "Just pull up out front and I'll run in."

He parked by the curb, but he didn't release her hand, staring out the front window for a long, silent moment before finally lifting her hand and pressing a kiss to her palm. He placed her palm to his cheek and leaned into it, closing his eyes. Grace put her arms around him, and he returned the embrace, holding her so tight, she could feel how deeply he was hurting.

"Sorry, Gracie. I feel like a runaway train when I think of Frank, and I don't know how to put on the brakes."

"I know, and I understand. Wait until you see me when a production goes wrong. I'm like the Tasmanian devil, only louder. I get it."

He kissed her neck, her cheek, and then his mouth found hers, tenderly at first, then frantic and rough, as if he could escape the pain of the unknown through their love. And oh, how she wished he could. She took as eagerly as she gave, wanting to erase his pain. She didn't care that they were parked on the main drag or that anyone walking by could see them making out. All that mattered was that Reed was her world, and he needed her.

"Why are we here?" he asked heatedly, his fingers tangling in her hair.

She grinned and said, "There's only one remedy for this type of angst."

Confusion riddled his brow, and she kissed those worry lines. Then she crawled over him, squeezing in between the steering wheel and his broad chest.

"I like where this is headed." He flashed a cocky grin.

She gave him a sweet kiss, opened his door, and climbed off his lap and out of the truck. "Try to hold on to those thoughts while I grab provisions."

A few minutes later, Grace was back in the truck, her hand on his thigh, her fingers tucked between his legs as he drove toward their destination. His body heat burned through the thick denim. She cuddled closer, feeling a lot like she had all those years ago, completely head over heels with a man who was as easy to read as he was to love. She pressed her lips to his shoulder, breathing him in. When he laced their fingers together, she squeezed his leg, inching her fingertips to the juncture of his thighs.

"Grace," he said in warning.

He placed his hand on hers, moving it to his erection, and her entire body wanted to open up for him. Her heart hammered foolishly, like they were teenagers sneaking out to console each other. As kids Reed had been the salve to her worries, her secret treasure at the end of her days. Now he was her everything. She unhooked her seat belt and went up on her knees as he drove around the roadblock and headed down the old service road toward the river. She hadn't been down this road for so many years, she didn't expect recognition to hit her as they ambled along the steep hill. Adrenaline and desire sped through her as she kissed his neck, stroking him through his jeans, earning one sinful, greedy noise after another. His big hand still covered hers, squeezing her fingers tight against his erection.

He parked by the riverbank and kissed her slow and deep. His masculine scent coalesced with the pungent smell of damp earth, and memories gathered around them like old friends.

"I'm crazy about you, baby," he said in a gravelly voice. "I remember the first time we came here. We were both upset about having to hide our relationship."

"We said we'd tell everyone the next day."

"But the next day was homecoming, and we both thought we should wait."

They were breathing hard from the emotional evening and the heat between them, and surely from the memories knocking on their door. Grace took in the old covered bridge standing sentinel against the gray night sky, its weathered wooden boards missing in places, hanging cockeyed in others. The long grass on the hill shifted in the May breeze, bringing a memory, clear as the love between them, of sometime before they'd broken up. A week, a month, she couldn't be sure, but she remembered confiding in Reed her biggest secret. As much as she'd wanted to go to New York, she'd been terrified of leaving everything she knew and loved behind, despite the fact that Sophie would be going with her and attending the same school. He'd looked into her eyes with the most earnest expression, those dark blue eyes of his giving her courage before he'd even spoken a word. But then his words had given her even more fortitude: *You're the bravest, strongest girl I know. There's nothing you can't do, Gracie, and I'll be cheering you on every step of the way.* She'd clung to those words so often, she was sure they had been the shovels that had dug the holes for her roots to begin sprouting in the concrete jungle.

"It was always me and you," she said as he climbed from the truck.

Reed put his arms around her, pulling her to the edge of the seat and wedging himself between her legs. He buried his face in her chest, holding her tight.

Seconds later he was studying her face. "Why is your heart beating so hard?"

"I just realized how selfish I was when we broke up."

"Don't you *ever* think that, Grace. We both thought I would never leave here, and we both knew you had to."

"But I was watching out for *me*," she said with an apologetic gaze. "It was selfish."

"All kids are selfish at that age. Hell, I was *supremely* selfish. I'm the one who said I'd never leave, remember? A better boyfriend would have said he'd follow you anywhere."

He brushed her hair over her shoulders, the anger and tension she'd seen replaced with that serious, loving look that made her insides dip and flip.

"In the long run, you did what was best for both of us. If I'd stayed here I never would have made enough money to buy the theater. Let it go, babe. We both made mistakes, but you ending our relationship when you went to college wasn't one of them."

She nodded, afraid if she opened her mouth, she might ask him why he was so willing to forgive her but not willing to even speak to his father. But she knew the answer. Their decision had been mutual, but Frank's was one-sided, and what reason could be valid enough to warrant walking away from his own child? Maybe some wounds really were too deep to ever heal.

She grabbed the bakery bag while Reed collected the blanket and spread it on the grass. As she watched him, she wondered how he fought his curiosity. She wanted to know Frank's reasons—for closure for Reed as much as to find out the answers herself. And she couldn't stop thinking about what his uncle had asked him about his future children. That was something she hadn't thought about, but Roy was right. How did a parent handle such a touchy situation? Was there a right way to do it? She knew Reed wasn't ready to talk about any of that yet, so she tried to move past it for now.

She tugged off her boots, pointed to the blanket, and said, "Sit."

The heated look in Reed's eyes made her all kinds of glad she'd tabled the heavier topic. He sank down to his butt, and she pulled off his boots, aware of his watching her every move.

"The night we broke up..." She straddled his hips and reached for the bakery bag. "I went to Pastry Palace and bought every éclair they had. All seven of them. Then I drove out here, but when I got to the top of the hill, I saw your truck by the water. I sat for the longest time watching you. You were pacing, and then you sat, your knees pulled up, arms crossed over them, head down. A few minutes later you paced again. I cried a river that night and ate every single one of the pastries. And when I got home, you texted me and said you could feel me all around you."

"You were here...? All that time?"

She took a pastry from the bag. "Yes, but I knew if I came down, we'd end up in each other's arms, and that would have been even harder. I don't know what you're thinking about Frank, or Roy, or any of it, and I don't need to know until you're ready to talk about it. But this"—she broke the éclair in half and set half on the bag—"will certainly help."

She dipped her finger into the creamy center. His gaze blazed through her as he grabbed her wrist and sucked her finger into his mouth, swirling his tongue around it. She made a seductive show of licking more cream from the pastry.

"Mm. Try..." She held the éclair by his lips.

He chomped off a hunk, and in the next second he had her

pinned to the blanket, devouring her with chocolate, creamy kisses. He pushed roughly at her shirt, thrusting it up over her breasts and taking her bra with it. He moaned appreciatively as he lowered his mouth over one breast, sucking so hard she felt herself go damp. She clung to his hair, arching against his mouth. The graze of his teeth had her clawing at his back, pushing at the waist of his jeans, whimpering and begging—*begging!*—for more.

"Fuck the sweets. You're all I ever need," he rasped against her breast as he drove her out of her blessed mind.

THEIR SHIRTS FLEW through the air. Grace's bra went next. She sat on the blanket and wiggled out of her jeans as Reed stepped from his and kicked them to the side. She reached for him, her naked body bathed in moonlight. He took her hand and sank down to his knees, riveted by the love in her eyes.

He lowered himself down slowly, drinking in her smooth warmth as their thighs touched, and the feel of her wetness against the head of his cock. Her fingers trailed lightly along his back as their chests melded together. She didn't close her eyes or look away. She held his gaze, just as she had the very first night they'd made love, looking a little nervous and truly, utterly, *captivatingly* beautiful. He cradled her within his arms, his fingers curling around her shoulders, and brushed his lips over hers.

"I want to tell you everything." He kissed her softly. "After…"

Their mouths and bodies came together heavy and urgent

and somehow also weightless and easy. She glanced down at their connected bodies, her eyes hazy with desire.

"Go *really* slow," she whispered.

They weren't good at slow, but she was well aware of how every kiss made them crave each other even more. Driving him wild used to be her favorite game. How could he have forgotten the way she used to love to beg him to go painfully slow, so they both felt every inch of his cock, the heat and tightness of her sex, followed by the slow drag of cold air as he withdrew, then the rush of heat that consumed them as her body swallowed all of him again.

She pressed into his flesh, pushing him deeper as she lifted her hips, silently telling him to drive even deeper—past the point where he felt he could go no further. He thrust slowly and continuously, until her arousal drenched his balls, and it was physically impossible to bury himself any deeper.

"*Oh!*" Her voice was high-pitched, *needy*. "Stay right there."

Using his toes for leverage and grasping her shoulders so he could hold her still at the same time, he rocked his hips.

"*Oh...Yes!*"

Her nails cut into his skin as her hips moved up and down in a quick, dizzying pattern.

"*Staystillstaystillstaystill*," she pleaded.

Like he'd change a thing? Not a chance. Her inner muscles squeezed him so tight, he fought against the urge to drive into her fast and frantic and pull them both over the edge. Her eyes slammed closed, her neck arched, and in the next breath, she was writhing, clawing at his skin, her body spasming around his shaft. Her face contorted with pleasure as a string of indiscernible sounds flew from her lips. Heat shot down his spine, pooling at the base like a pulsing bomb ready to blow. He fought against the pressure, wanting to stay in this blissful moment, to sear their bodies together, so they'd never be apart again. Her noises turned sweet, slipping soft and alluring from her lungs. Her eyelids fluttered, and tremors vibrated through her, teasing his cock with deathly precision.

"Gotta move—"

His words were both demanding and apologetic as his body took over. He pulled her legs around his thighs. Her heels dug into them as he pushed his hands beneath her ass, lifting and tilting, hitting the spot he knew would send her flying again. He captured her mouth, electricity arcing and peaking inside him, between them, around them, turbulent and erotic. *Hypnotizing.* Every inch of him—from his scalp to his abs and back, all the way down to the tips of his toes—ignited as she moaned into their kisses, her body shuddering with ecstasy, shattering his last thread of restraint. Hot tides of passion raged through him as he struggled to remain coherent enough to try to pleasure her even more relentlessly. But he was lost in a whirl of sensations, unable to hold on to a single thought, and surrendered to the magnificent force of their love.

Long after their breathing calmed, they lay on their sides, braided together beneath the starry sky.

"Maybe I should have come down to the river that night after all," she said with the sated voice of a satisfied lover. "That was *so* much better than éclairs."

He kissed her flushed cheeks. "I'm madly in love with your distraction techniques."

"Oh yeah?" She glanced at the river and squirmed free from his arms.

"Grace…?"

With a mischievous look in her eyes, she pushed to her feet

and sprinted into the water. Reed ran after her, catching her around the waist. She shrieked and clung to him, kissing and smiling.

"How was I ever stupid enough to let you go, Gracie?"

"You weren't stupid. We both needed to get out there and find ourselves. Now I know exactly where I belong."

Then stay was on the tip of his tongue. But that request would be unfair. "In my arms, babe. That's where you've always belonged."

Much later, full on éclairs and drunk on love, they made their way home.

"Do you want to put the shoe box away for now?" Grace asked.

"I don't know what I want," he said honestly, drawing her into his arms. "Other than more of you."

"I can't help but think…I spent all those years feeling hurt and deceived because I thought you left town for someone or something else. When we first saw each other again, if we hadn't taken the time to clear the air, if you hadn't pushed me to talk to you that night by the creek, we might never be where we are today. What if Frank has something to say that *you* should hear?"

He thought he'd be ready to talk about Frank by now, but apparently he wasn't, because his gut roiled at the thought of the man.

Grace reached up and caressed his cheek. "I'm not saying you should talk to him. I will support whatever you decide to do or not do. Just be sure that when Monday comes and Frank leaves, *you're* okay with your decision, whatever it is."

Chapter Twenty-Two

GRACE ROLLED ONTO Reed's side of the bed Thursday morning expecting to feel the tickle of his leg hair and his hard, muscular frame as he gathered her close. Instead, she landed on an empty mattress. Blinking the fog of sleep from her eyes, she said, "Reed?"

"Right here, babe."

She crawled to the other end of the bed. Reed sat against the wall wearing only a pair of jeans, his long legs crossed at the ankle. The shoe box lay open beside him. He met her gaze with a pained expression, and her heart pitched.

"Are you okay? How long have you been up?" She climbed off the bed, wearing one of Reed's T-shirts over her panties, and sat down beside him. His hair was damp, and the scent of soap clung to his skin. How had she slept through him showering?

He draped his arm around her and kissed her temple. "I'm okay. I've been up for a few hours, I guess." He waved a photograph he was holding. "I just started going through these."

"You should have woken me so you didn't have to face them alone." She rested her head on his shoulder, and he held her a little tighter.

He laid the picture on his thigh, and her breath caught in

her throat at the young pregnant woman in the picture. She had thick dark brows and long lashes, green eyes that seemed almost too big for her slim face, full lips, and an angular nose, like Reed's. Her hair was a few shades lighter than his, cut just past her shoulders. She was lying on a sofa wearing a red-and-white flannel shirt, which was buttoned only between her breasts and fell to the sides of her round belly. One hand rested over her chest, the other on her baby bump. She had a wondrous look in her eyes, as if she were having a secret conversation with her unborn child. She looked so young, so *alive*, it was hard to believe she had died giving birth.

"It's Lily, my mom, pregnant with me," Reed said softly. "I've seen dozens of pictures of her, but never anything like this. Look at her face. It's like she didn't know the picture was being taken, and yet whoever took it must have been right there."

A lump formed in Grace's throat. "Or she was too caught up in thoughts of you to care."

A half-happy, half-sad expression came over him. He picked up a few pictures from the box and said, "Look at her jacket in this picture. Suede collar, black fringe on yellow shoulders, and that choker..." He smiled and ran his fingers over the thin black choker circling her slender neck. A single jewel hung from the center. She was looking over her shoulder at the camera, and her hair was blowing across her face. In the sunlight her hair had a reddish tint. "She sure wasn't boring, was she?"

He set that picture down and studied another. His mother was laughing, her lips painted bright red, her eyes faintly lined. She stood with a man who could have been Reed's brother, the same toffee-brown hair, serious, thoughtful midnight-blue eyes. His mother wore a fancy black dress with a white collar, and he wore a suit. Her hair was longer, and she looked younger than in the first picture. Eighteen, nineteen maybe?

"I guess that's Frank," he said tentatively. "He looks nothing like that now."

She knew his parents had met at college and wasn't surprised when he handed her another picture of the two of them sitting on the grass with a bunch of other college-aged kids in front of an academic-looking building. His mother's expressive eyes were hauntingly carefree.

He set that picture down and picked up the last two. One of his mother with a bowl of popcorn balanced on her pregnant belly, reading a book as she leaned against a tree.

"I wish so many things right now," Reed said quietly, "and it's crazy knowing none of them can ever come true."

Grace hugged him. "I'm sorry."

Reed studied the last picture for a long time. It was a photograph of a tiny baby in a man's arms. The picture covered the man chest to belly, the only identifying marks the scars on his arm.

"Do you think that's you?" she asked.

He nodded. "I saw Frank's scars."

"What happened?"

Reed shrugged. "Who knows."

He set the picture down and picked up a faux-leather journal, his uneasy gaze shifting to her. The world seemed to still around them.

Reed inhaled deeply and opened to the first page. They both silently read the inscription.

Lils, thank you for bringing our love to life. Here's to forever and a day, Frankie.

Reed's eyes misted over, and Grace was right there with him. She cuddled closer, hugging his arm and trying not to let her emotions swamp her. She needed to be strong for Reed. She was so glad he was going through the box. She knew how much courage it took, but as much as she wanted to tell him so and praise him for his strength, she didn't want to break the spell and interrupt his search for answers.

He turned the page, and Grace looked away, wanting to give him privacy. "I'm going to shower."

Reed pulled her closer and kissed her. "Thank you," he whispered in a tortured voice, making it harder for her to walk away.

She tried to shower quickly, but as the shower rained down on her, the ache inside her bloomed, making her chest feel full and sore. She hurt for Reed and all he could discover, for the pain of never knowing a mother who clearly loved him, and that pain morphed to guilt. She had a family who adored her. A mother who wanted nothing more than to continue having her children come and go from her house at all hours. A father who cared enough to be overprotective. And she had run far and fast at eighteen years old and had rarely looked back.

Until now.

Guilt sank deep into her bones as she leaned against the tile wall, sobbing into her hands, her tears mixing with the shower spray. And then that guilt shattered into a million pieces, slicing her like shards of glass, and she was no longer crying over what she had but for what Reed never would.

After her shower, she found Reed pacing the living room, red-faced, swollen veins mapping his body, neck, and arms, and his eyes—those serious, loving eyes she fell head over heels for day after day—were dark torrents of grief. She went to him, and he stopped cold, eyes drilling through her.

"DON'T COME NEAR me, Grace," Reed warned.

"Why? What happened?"

"What happened? That's what I want to know." He flipped open the journal and read from it. "'I can't wait to meet our baby. Frankie is beside himself, talking to my belly, telling stories about when he was a boy and about how we fell in love the day we met. He's as in love with our unborn child as I am.'" He flipped angrily through a few more pages and continued reading. "'Some days I don't think I could breathe without Frankie. When my feet ache, he rubs them. When I'm sad, he dances with me. Dances! Our baby is the luckiest child in the world to have him as a father.'" Reed snapped the journal closed, gripping it tight.

"But that's all good, right?"

Grace's worry and confusion were as palpable as the fucking journal in his hand.

"Good?" He scoffed. "It's fucking wonderful. What happened to *that* guy? Where'd he go when she died? Because that man? That *Frankie*? He can't be the man who left me behind."

"W-wha…?"

"Exactly," he seethed, and took the stairs two at a time, with Grace rushing after him. He grabbed a shirt from his drawer and tugged it on. Then he jammed his bare feet into his boots and headed downstairs.

She followed him. "Where are you going?"

"To get some fucking answers."

"Give me a sec to get my shoes on."

"You're not coming, Grace." He grabbed his keys.

"You shouldn't do this alone," she pleaded. "You're too upset."

"That's exactly why I have to do it alone." He reached for the doorknob, his hand fisted around his keys, and hesitated only long enough to say, "I love you, Gracie," before storming out the door.

Chapter Twenty-Three

REED STALKED INTO the Marriott with tunnel vision, determined to get some answers, or at least to tell Frank what he thought of him for letting his late mother down. His heart hammered as he rode the elevator up to Frank's floor and even harder as he strode down the empty hallway toward room 433 with the journal in his hand. Why the hell did Frank give it to him if not to fucking torture him even more?

He stood before Frank's door, battling rage and staving off no small amount of fear for how he'd react when he faced the man who had abandoned him. He pounded on the door, then pounded again. He heard the sound of the chain sliding, bringing a pulse of anxiety. The *thunk* of the dead bolt curled his hands into fists.

Blinded by rage, the second the door opened Reed pushed his way inside, waving the journal. "You were a great husband, a great *man*. What the fuck happened?" He spun around, and his gut seized. Frank's eyes were sunken, shadowed by dark crescents, his unshaven face even more gaunt than Reed remembered. His pallor was yellowish, contrasting sharply with his wrinkled white T-shirt. His flannel pajama pants hung from his frail frame. He looked more like eighty- than fiftysomething.

Reed turned away, gasping a ragged breath. His eyes caught on pill bottles beside the bed, a half-empty glass of water, and a framed photo that nearly took him to his knees. In the photo, his mother's hair was pinned up in a bun. She was kneeling on the grass, wearing a striped shirt bunched up below her breasts, her pregnant belly too big and round for her tiny frame. A big red heart was drawn on her belly, the words *our love, our life* written above the rounded tops of the heart. His father knelt behind her, his arms around her shoulders, holding her so tight it broke Reed's heart. His father's face was tilted down, eyes closed, his lips against her cheek. His mother's eyes were also closed. She was leaning into the kiss, wearing the smile of a woman in love.

He became aware of his father moving and forced more air into his lungs.

"I lost her," his father said in a defeated voice as he lowered himself down to a chair. "We lost her."

"That's not good enough," Reed said angrily, his gaze locked on the picture, drawing strength to ignore the meaning of what was so clearly before him: the pill bottles, Frank's weakened state and pallor. He wanted to cling to his anger, to let it fuel the hurt and hatred he harbored.

"No, I suppose for most people it wouldn't be enough," his father said. "She was my world, Reed. She was the reason I breathed from the time I was barely a man."

Reed spun around, hands fisted, ire pulsing through his veins, unable to keep it from burning out in hateful words. "Then how could you let her down? How could you turn your back on her—*your*—son?"

Frank's gaze drifted to the picture on the nightstand. "Because you weren't mine to keep," he said evenly, as if he didn't have the energy to raise his voice.

"What?" Reed snapped.

Frank lifted sad eyes to Reed. "You weren't mine to keep. You aren't my son."

"I don't know what kind of game you're playing, but cut the shit. I saw pictures of you when you were young. We look alike."

"No games, Reed. I don't have time for them. When I lost my parents, I went off the deep end. Hit the bottle pretty hard. Your mother wanted no part of a drunk, and I didn't blame her one bit for kicking me out. It was almost four months before I was clean and stable enough that she'd take me back. During our separation, she got together with a musician."

Reed's entire body flexed, disbelief coursing through him.

"She broke it off with him when we got back together. At least that's what she told me. A few months later we found out she was pregnant. I thought you were mine. I had no reason to believe otherwise, and, Reed, I loved you then, and that love has never died." He tapped his fist over his heart with damp eyes.

Reed bit back the urge to call bullshit on the love part.

"Then one day your mother gets a call. The guy she'd been with died. Overdosed. She collapsed right there by the phone into a sobbing mess on the floor."

Tears welled in Frank's eyes, drawing tears from Reed—for his mother, his father, Frank, or himself, he had no idea.

"That's the day she went into labor. The day she told me the baby wasn't mine. But she swore—swore on everything she'd ever known—that she loved us both, me and the other man."

Reed sank down to the edge of the bed, dragging air into his lungs, trying to process this new, awful information.

"When she died," Frank said, "part of me thought she'd just given up. That it was the other guy she loved and it was all too much. It wasn't fair, and it wasn't right, but I was a wreck, and then I had this tiny baby, *someone else's* baby, to take care of when I couldn't even take care of myself. I had lost the woman I loved and found out the life she'd nurtured belonged to another man. I could barely function. I *tried*, Reed. I tried to do the right thing, but every time I looked at you, I saw her and another man. After two days in our apartment, the apartment where…" He swallowed hard, wiped his eyes with his palm, and said, "Where I loved her. The apartment that held her lies, it was overwhelming, like riding a train that had careened off the tracks. I hit the bottle again, woke up with you screaming in your crib, and I knew I couldn't do it."

Reed clasped his hands behind his neck, staring down at the floor, and tried to remember how to breathe.

"I never told a soul about the other man. I never knew his name, where he lived, who called that day. Nothing," Frank said. "I didn't even tell Roy or Ella. I didn't want them to think poorly of her."

After all that, you protected my mother?

Reed's eyes remained trained on the floor, which seemed to sway beneath him. "So…what? You left me and never looked back?"

"I left you with people who loved you and were capable of giving you the life I couldn't. I knew if I was in your life, I'd only screw it up. I drove out of the state and kept going, stopping only long enough to get shit-faced, sleep it off, and start all over again. I came back to see you once. You were so little and happy. You had people who loved you, whose entire *worlds* revolved around you. Lily would have wanted you to be with Ella and Roy. I thought maybe I could beat the alcohol again, but I was too broken, and seeing you only reminded me of everything I'd lost. I was too weak, and I'll always be sorry for that. I knew you were better off without me, so I hit a bar. I took off the next day. I drank, lived in my car, on the streets, got by however I could. And then I got sick."

Reed pinched the bridge of his nose, trying to stave off the sinking feeling inside him.

"Your mother came to me in a dream and told me to get to a doctor." Frank's voice was shaky. "My guardian angel, even after everything. I went to a clinic, had a bunch of tests. Been sober six months, and they say I have a year to live, give or take. Stage four liver cancer."

Reed closed his eyes, a pained noise escaping before he could stop it. His world had spiraled out of control, and he didn't know what to hold on to or how to make sense of it. His real father hadn't abandoned him after all; he'd died. Was that any better? Did his real father know his mother had been pregnant with his child? Had his mother loved the other man more than Frank? Those were questions he couldn't ask, answers he'd never know. And Frank, this man who *wasn't* his father, was *dying*? It hurt to breathe, to think…

He looked at Frank, a broken man living on a timeline, putting himself through hell for…? "Why did you come back? Why put yourself through this?"

Frank's gaze sank to his hands worrying nervously in his lap. "I was madly in love with your mother. I thought we'd have a lifetime together, and then all in one day, she shattered my beliefs, I lost her, and I had you, but you weren't really mine. Not a day has passed that I haven't thought about you and wished I were a stronger man. That's my fault. I'm not asking for forgiveness. I'm on my way out of this world, and I'll carry that guilt to my grave. But once I sobered up, I knew I had to find you. I wanted to apologize. She'd want you to know the truth about your history, and for you to have her things. She adored you from the very moment she found out she was pregnant. Her love for me might have waxed and waned, but not for you. Never for you. She sensed that you were a strong boy even before you were born. She said a girl wouldn't kick that hard." He smiled, as if he were reliving the memory. "She named you Reed the month before you were born. Said reeds were strong and had long roots that spread far and wide. She wanted you to be strong, to have roots you could count on. Roy and Ella gave you that, and I'll be forever grateful to them for doing what I couldn't."

Chapter Twenty-Four

GRACE SCRUBBED THE heck out of every surface in Reed's house. She washed the linens, made the bed, and was busy polishing Reed's boots when she heard his truck door close. She ran down the stairs and nearly bowled him over on the front porch.

She grabbed him, searching his expression. "You're back. Are you okay? How was it?"

He touched his lips to hers, a small smile settling into place as he lifted her wrist, eyeing the gloves she wore.

"I was polishing your boots."

"My boots? Grace, guys don't polish their boots." He took her hand, and they sat on the porch steps. He set his mother's journal beside him.

"You were so distraught when you left. I wanted to do something for you, but I didn't know what to do in a situation like this. So I cleaned the house top to bottom. I picked flowers down by the creek to try to make the rooms seem brighter to cheer you up. And I was going to attack the attic, but I didn't want you to think I was snooping. So I polished your boots."

He pulled her closer. "Do you know how much I love you?" He pressed his lips to her temple. "Thank you, babe, but next time you get the urge to polish something, I've got a very willing body part."

She smiled, but her worries drowned his attempt at levity. "I'll tend to that body part after I tend to this one." She put her hand over his heart.

He placed his hand over hers. "It'd be easier to deal with the other."

He went on to tell her what he'd learned from Frank, and her heart broke more with each fact as it was revealed. By the time he was done, he sounded exhausted, and she was speechless. So many things that Reed had believed weren't true. It wasn't lost on her that Frank was in the same situation. Her heart broke for Frank as much as it did for Reed.

She climbed into his lap and held him. "I'm so sorry. But I don't understand. You look just like the pictures of him. How could that be?"

"The world's full of brown-haired guys, babe. He's *not* my father. He seemed pretty damn sure of it." He touched his forehead to hers and said, "Just tell me what we have is real."

"We're real, Reed. We've always been real."

He was quiet for a long time before saying, "I went from thinking I was abandoned by my father to being an orphan. It's going to take some time for me to come to terms with this."

"But you're not really an orphan. I mean, you are in one sense, but Roy and Ella adopted you, and they love you *so* much."

"Absolutely. I didn't mean to undermine everything they've done for me. I just meant…"

"I know what you meant, and I understand how much that must hurt. Do you think you'll tell Roy and Ella the truth?"

He shook his head. "I've been trying to figure that out, but what will they gain from knowing that my mother might have loved another man who is no longer around? I'll tell them about Frank's illness and that he just couldn't handle being a father after he lost my mother. I believe that's the truth of it, anyway. I'll never know if he would have done the same thing regardless of if I was his son or not."

He sat up straighter, inhaling deeply as he rolled his shoulders back, as if he were searching for a comfortable position to carry this new weight. "I'd like to call them and see if I can stop by later today, get it out in the open before the barbecue tomorrow. I'd really like for you to come with me."

"Of course. I know you'll probably have a million unanswered questions forever, but at least it sounds like Frank loved you both more than he loved himself. He did what he thought was best for your well-being, and he kept a secret for the woman he loved, despite being heartbroken."

He looked out over the yard, and when his eyes found her again, they were softer, a little less pained. "Is it strange that I feel a connection to him? Maybe I should be angrier, but it took a hell of a lot of courage to come forward when he didn't have to. Especially given his poor health."

"I don't think it's strange. You believed he was your father your whole life, and in some ways he kind of was. He was the one taking care of your mother when she was pregnant, and in that sense, he was also taking care of you. I think you're going to feel all sorts of things, good and bad, toward him, and maybe toward your mother, too, for a long time. It might come and go, but whatever it is, whatever it becomes, we'll get through it."

"Thanks, baby," he said softly, embracing her again. He looked down at his mother's journal and said, "Do you think it's possible to love two people at once? Could my mother have loved Frank and this other man? Frank didn't know his name or anything about him other than that he was a musician."

"I don't know," she said honestly. "Maybe for some people? I've only ever been in love with one man, and nobody else has ever come close. I can't imagine it, but..." She shrugged. "In your mother's journal, she sure sounded like she loved Frank, and she thought of him as your father, didn't she?"

"Yes. That's why I asked. I can't see things very clearly right now."

"Don't take this wrong, but I don't know that it really matters. She loved one man enough to create you, and she loved another enough to make a life with him *for* you. That's a lot of love for a woman who was only on this earth a short period of time." She wound her arms around his neck and said, "I'm just glad she had you. I love you, Reed. And I'll be here for you no matter how hard this gets."

BY THE TIME Reed and Grace went to see Roy and Ella, Reed was in a little better place than he had been earlier. He was far from okay, but he and Grace had spent the day alternating between conversations about Frank, the Majestic, and sheer nonsense. Reed had been glad for the distractions, and for the serious conversations, too. Grace received a call from Satchel that had put her on edge—and she was right, she was a bit whirlwindish after the call, like the Tasmanian devil, but it had endeared her to him even more. After she'd vented, Reed had swayed the conversation toward the play she was putting together with Nana and the others, and that had put her in a better mental space, too. If Reed had learned anything over the years, it was that life didn't come without trials and tribulations. He never considered himself someone who *needed* anyone. But being with Grace, talking through his most intimate problems with someone who knew him so well, and being there for her when she was at her wit's end, had him redefining the meaning of "need."

He looked around the patio table at Roy and Grace as Ella came outside with a plate of cookies, and he realized he *needed* all three of the people he was with.

Ella set the plate on the table and glanced at Roy, who had been watching Reed like a hawk. Reed had told them the reason for his visit when he'd called earlier, and he knew they were waiting for him to say something about Frank.

"Your favorite," Ella said to Reed as she took the seat between him and Roy. "Coconut cranberry."

Grace wrinkled her nose. "I might have to rethink this relationship. What happened to chocolate chip?"

"Darlin', if that's his biggest downfall, you're doing pretty well." Roy snickered and winked at Reed.

That single wink sent Reed's gut into a tizzy. He'd never been one for keeping secrets, and now that he was looking into his relatives' eyes—blood-related relatives he could count on—Frank's secret threatened to claw its way out.

"So, you went to see Frank?" Ella said as conversationally as if she'd said he'd gone to work like any other day. "I'm proud of you, honey. That couldn't have been easy."

Reed sat back, worrying with his hands, and realized it was exactly what Frank had done. That gave him pause, and just as quickly he realized he had to stop thinking of Frank as if he were his father, and pressed his palms to his thighs. Grace put her hand on his, as if she realized he didn't know what to do with them.

"It was anything but easy," he agreed, "especially since I blasted him the second I first walked in."

Ella winced. "Oh, honey."

Roy's brows knitted, but he said nothing.

Reed told them about the contents of the shoe box, how upset he'd been when he'd arrived at the hotel, and finally, about Frank's illness. "He's not who I thought he was. Well, he *is*. He left me behind, but after talking with him, I'm conflicted, because I can see how losing my mother was too much for him."

Roy's chin fell to his chest, his eyes trained on Reed. "The apple doesn't fall far from the tree. I seem to remember you taking off after you lost the love of your life, too."

Reed glanced at Grace, the truth in Roy's words hitting him hard.

"Love's a powerful thing," Roy said. "I admit, when Frank came here looking for you the other day, my first thought was to give him hell. I was madder than a mouse in a hornet's nest about him leaving you behind and showing up just that once. But then I saw him, and he looked like all his gumption had bled out."

Reed waited for him to say more, and when he didn't, he said, "What did you do?"

"We invited him in for tea," Ella said carefully. "He's punished himself for years, and he's nearing the end of a very hard, very lonely life. What good would it have done for us to beat him down further? He knows…Instead, we gave him something to brighten the days he has left. We talked about you, Reed, and the incredible little boy you were, the inquisitive, smart young man you were, and the honorable man you've become. We talked about your mother, how much she loved him and how much she was looking forward to raising you. And then we thanked him for trusting us with his son."

For the millionth time that day, Reed struggled against emotions clogging his throat. He looked at Roy and said, "You didn't think to tell me that when you saw me after he stopped by my house?"

"Just because you can do something doesn't mean you should." Roy tossed another wink as he threw Reed's words back at him.

"We didn't want to influence the way you handled the situation," Ella explained. "It wouldn't have been fair. He gave us a chance at parenthood, but he took something bigger than that from you."

Not telling them the truth about his father felt like a betrayal to the people who had always offered him unconditional love and support. But telling them felt like a betrayal to the mother he never knew and to Frank, a man who had given him clarity, honesty, and *history* he would probably never have learned otherwise.

He took a moment to simply breathe, which wasn't something he felt like he'd done enough of since Frank had shown up at his house. He was adrift in a sea of emotions and truths he hadn't been prepared for, and it seemed there were lifelines everywhere if he looked hard enough. All Frank had wanted was to tell Reed the truth before he died. But maybe Reed needed more of a relationship with him, even if Frank wasn't his real father. He had a feeling Frank wouldn't fight that and might even welcome it. Roy and Ella would stand by him no matter what. Even if he kept this secret, he knew they'd forgive him for it, because that's what parents did.

Roy watched him expectantly, the ever-present father who would worry about him until the day he was no longer able. Ella had lost her sister and gained a son, and she was an incredible mother. He'd hurt for a long time over choices other people had made, and he didn't want to hurt either of them. He was damn sick of hurting. For the first time ever, he no longer wondered why his father had given him up. It was time to start healing. What *healing* actually meant, he wasn't sure, but he knew that he couldn't—that Roy and Ella couldn't—even begin to heal if he opened a new wound.

He felt the pull of Grace's loving gaze. *The brightest lifeline of all.* His sweet Gracie offered everything the others did—unconditional love, support, honesty, history, clarity—and so much more. She was his past, his present, and hopefully his future.

He took her hand in his and said, "If Frank's visit taught me one thing, it's that life is too short to dwell on the past or on what-ifs. I don't know what will happen with Frank, or *anything*, for that matter. But I know we have tonight, the four of us, and tomorrow our families are getting together, and those are things I've waited a long damn time to enjoy."

Chapter Twenty-Five

GRACE WAS MESMERIZED by Tuck Wilder, the twenty-six-year-old guitarist in Sable's band who was auditioning for the lead role in the community play, *I Ain't No Cinderella.* She'd known Tuck since they were kids. He'd had a rough life, and it showed in his cold, dark eyes as he strutted across the auditorium of No Limitz, nailing the attitude and badass vibe for the role perfectly. They'd been holding auditions all afternoon and had already cast several of the supporting roles. If only off-Broadway plays were this easy to produce. She'd been battling with Keagen all week, and his threats to walk away from the play had the investors up in arms.

As Tuck finished his audition, Grace scribbled a few notes. He was the last audition of the day. Grace thanked him and said they'd send out email notifications for the roles as they made decisions. They had auditions booked through next Saturday evening, and she was leaving the day after that. She had a feeling they just might get the casting set by then.

"His voice inflection is perfect," Janie said. "What does he look like?"

After Tuck left the auditorium Lauryn said, "He's *beautiful*, with rich cocoa skin and soulful eyes, but he gives off a tough, edgy vibe."

"He's our bad boy," Phoenix said. "No doubt about it."

"You got that right," Hellie agreed. "The poor young man has had it hard. I think that band is about all that holds him together. I want to bring him home and start all over. Give him the parental love he never had."

Good luck with that. Tuck's parents were as gruff as could be, and there was no doubt his grit was as much a part of him as the blood that ran through his veins. The perfect male lead for the play.

"I say we cast him, but that might mean Sable's band won't be able to help with the music," Grace said. "All for it?"

Everyone chimed in with affirmations.

"Oh goodness, I have to run!" Nana said as she began gathering her notes. "I didn't realize it was so late. Poppi and I are going to the Jerichos' jam session. Tonight's the night Phoenix and Lauryn are playing their instruments. You know Poppi; he'll want to dance to every song." She sighed dreamily. "I'm a lucky lady. Grace, don't you have your family barbecue tonight? I don't want your parents getting upset with us for monopolizing you. They get so little time with you."

Grace had been to so many jam sessions at the Jerichos' barn when she was younger she wouldn't typically feel a desire to go. But now that she was getting more involved in the community, she was excited to spend time with the people who had reached out to help with the play. And knowing how Phoenix and Lauryn had supported each other to finally get up the courage to play in front of everyone, she felt a pang of disappointment about missing it. At least she didn't feel guilty about not spending time with her family as she had in the past.

"I'm sorry I'll miss your debut," Grace said to Phoenix and

Lauryn. "Maybe someone can video it for me?"

"My mom's videoing it for our family's Facebook group," Lauryn said. "I'll send it to you. I'm so nervous I'll mess up."

"That's perfect, and you'll do great. Just remember, if you mess up, nobody will know but you. Just ad-lib—that's what actors do. Pretend it's part of the song." Grace gave her a quick hug. "And, Nana, my family is probably getting sick of me by now. Reed and I had breakfast with my parents and Sable this morning. Sable's apartment is *finally* done being renovated. We helped her move back in after breakfast." She loved being part of her family's lives instead of just hearing about them. She would miss them when she returned to the city.

After the others left, Grace stopped by Haylie's office and peeked her head in. Haylie and Sin, the athletic director, were deep in conversation. "Hey, guys. Sorry to interrupt. I just wanted to say thanks again for letting us use the auditorium. We're done for the day. Sorry we stayed so late."

"No worries," Sin said. "We're closing up early so we can go to the jam session. I hear it's going to be wild tonight."

"Phoenix and Lauryn are playing. I'm sure it'll be fun." They talked for a few more minutes, and then she texted Reed to tell him she was on her way home. Her father had asked Reed to help with a repair in the barn, so they were meeting at her parents' house anyway, but she hated being late for something her mother had worked so hard to prepare for.

Grace was the last one to arrive. Add another layer to the guilt cake.

She parked on the street, and as she climbed from her car, the sounds of laughter and familiar voices filled her ears. Reed's deep voice was easy to pick out. Reba and Dolly greeted her with slobbery kisses to her bare legs. She crouched, and her messenger bag slipped from her shoulder. Why did she even have it? She wasn't going to work during dinner. *Old habits die hard.* Reba stuck her nose into Grace's bag, knocking Grace on her butt and causing papers to slip out.

"Oh, Reba," Grace said, surprisingly not at all irritated.

The pup heard it as an invitation and went paws-up on Grace's shoulders. She fell back, catching herself with her palms. Dolly licked her face, and Grace relented, lying back on the driveway as the dogs loved her up with playful kisses. She tousled their fur, laughing even as Reba stepped on her bag and more papers slipped out.

"Oh no, Gracie!" her mother cried from the top of the driveway. "Reba, Dolly, sit!" she commanded as she hurried toward them.

Grace wanted to tell her it was okay, but she knew the importance of obedience training and held her tongue. When the dogs were safely settled, she sat up, unable to stop smiling as Reed, Amber, and Reno rushed toward her.

Reno stood beside Amber, her ever-present guardian angel, as Amber collected Grace's papers and put them in her bag.

"Are you okay, babe?" Reed helped her to her feet, looking darkly handsome with clean-shaven cheeks and wearing a white button-down shirt with his jeans.

Grace wiped the dogs' slobber from her cheek and said, "Sure beats coming home to an empty loft. You look pretty fancy for a family barbecue."

"I've waited forever for this special night. Nothing's too fancy for my girl."

Reed hugged her as Brindle and Morgyn ran down the driveway, their blond hair flowing loose and wild behind them. Their blue eyes radiated mischief as they each took one of

Grace's arms and dragged her toward the house.

"Hey," Grace complained, wanting to be with Reed.

"Change of plans," Morgyn said, looking cute as ever in one of her own designs, a pink jagged-edged dress with several colorful necklaces and a bright blue and purple shirt, sleeves cuffed, hanging open in pure hippie style. "We're going to the jam session."

"But Mom's been planning this barbecue for two weeks. She won't be happy." She glanced at Reed, sure he'd be disappointed since they were both looking forward to their first real family get-together, but he shrugged and smiled, like he was cool with it.

"She's fine," Brindle said as they dragged her toward the front door. "We need to get you out of those city clothes."

"What?" Grace looked over her shoulder at Reed. "Reed!"

"I love your clothes!" he hollered as they climbed the porch steps. "But I also love you in cutoffs!"

"Since when has a Montgomery girl let a man decide what she wears?" Brindle pointed out.

"You guys, all my clothes are at Reed's."

Amber and Reno caught up to them at the front door. "Don't worry. I helped pick everything out. You're going to look *amazing*," Amber said.

"You too?" Grace complained as they dragged her into her bedroom and began stripping her down. "I can get undressed myself, and I'm *not* wearing cutoffs in public!"

"Hush up, sugar lips," Morgyn said. "You've been in control of your life way too long. Tonight you're one of us again, like it or not."

"We miss you, Gracie," Amber said. "Give us tonight. Please?"

Unexpectedly bowled over with emotions for the hundredth time lately, how could she say anything but, "Just be kind, please. No ass-baring skirts or halter tops."

"But you have the best legs in the family!" Brindle complained.

"I do *not*!"

"Best legs for sure," Morgyn said. "Best boobs goes to Brindle. Best ass is Amber—"

"Really?" Amber squealed and turned in front of the mirror, trying to see her butt.

"Hell yes," Brindle said. "Best overall figure is—"

"Sable," they all said in unison, then tumbled onto Grace's bed in a heap of laughter at the silly Best Of game they used to play.

Grace lay between Amber and Morgyn, smiling up at the ceiling. "Where is Sable?"

"She got stuck rebuilding an engine at the shop. She'll be late, but she'll meet us there." Morgyn paused for only a second before saying, "Best *hidden* figure is—"

"Pepper!" they all said at once.

"Morgyn's best lips, eyes, and hips," Amber said. "You're so lucky, Morg."

"And Axsel's got it *all* going on," Grace added. "Lucky dude!"

She felt Morgyn and Amber lace their fingers with hers and knew Brindle's and Morgyn's were also linked. How had she gone so long without this closeness? When they all lifted their hands, hers were right there with them as they all recited the silliness they had since they were kids: "Not a loser in the bunch!'"

Amber and Morgyn jumped off the bed and pulled off

Grace's heels. Brindle danced around the room singing a senseless song about country girls and sexy dresses, and Grace realized this wasn't *silliness* at all. She pulled on the dress Brindle handed her, and Amber gathered her hair to the side and zipped it up. The dress was snug around the bodice, but soft and surprisingly comfortable.

Morgyn draped several necklaces of varying lengths around Grace's neck, and Brindle pushed bangles onto Grace's wrist as if she were their personal Barbie doll.

"Wait!" Grace grabbed her skirt and dug the boyfriend-girlfriend bracelets Morgyn had made out of her pocket. "Help me put these on under the bangles."

"You haven't given him his yet?" Morgyn helped her put them on, then slid the bangles down over the beaded bracelets.

"We've had a lot going on, but tonight's the night. I can't wait to see his face when I surprise him."

Their mother appeared in the doorway, smiling the way mothers do when they're happy to see their children playing nicely with one another. Grace rolled her eyes as if to say, *I didn't have a choice*, but inside she was enjoying every second of it.

"We packed up all the food to bring with us, and the dogs are inside," her mother said. "We're ready when you are. And oh, my word. Reed is going to lose his mind."

"You think so?" Grace asked hopefully.

"Goodness, yes," their mother assured her. "Not that he needed any incentives."

"Sit down, Gracie," Morgyn urged. "I repurposed these just for you."

Morgyn slipped Grace's feet into a pair of gorgeous cowgirl boots embellished with lace, leather straps, and beaded rope.

"I've never seen anything like these. Not even in New York. Thank you, Morg!" Grace hugged her. Then she went to the mirror to admire her outfit. She could hardly believe she was looking at herself. Her legs looked a mile long in the cute sleeveless floral minidress. The bodice had ribbing down the center with tiny unmatched buttons, and the skirt flared out with three ruffles. The boots and accessories made the entire outfit look like a fashion statement.

"Morgyn, did you make this dress?" Grace asked.

"Yes. Would you believe it was ankle length, long sleeved, *and* plus sized when I got it? Check this out." Morgyn turned her by the shoulders. "Look in the mirror." She pointed to button-embellished darts she'd sewn into the back of the dress.

"Aren't they fantastic?" Brindle said.

"Yes. It's so pretty," Grace said. "You have the best vision. I'd never pick out anything with ruffles or flowers."

"We know," her sisters and mother said in unison.

"You look gorgeous, Gracie," Amber said.

Then they were hugging again, laughing as Brindle began messing with Grace's hair, and they convinced her to let them do her makeup. Their mother went outside as the girls huddled around the bathroom mirror, and Grace's heart swelled. These were the people, along with her other siblings, who made her believe she really *did* have great legs, who had encouraged and inspired her to move to New York and chase what probably had seemed to everyone like an impossible dream, despite how much they'd each miss her. And they were the ones who had unknowingly held her together all those years ago when she and Reed had broken up. Only Sable had known why her heart had shattered, but nevertheless, they'd all been there to pick up the pieces.

She wondered how many of their crises she'd missed over the years and who was there to pick up the pieces for Pepper and Axsel, who both lived so far away. She silently vowed to make a concerted effort to stay in closer touch with *all* of her siblings.

After they made her feel more beautiful than she had ever been, she was excited and nervous about seeing Reed. What if he hated her in ruffles?

With the support of her sisters, each linked arm in arm, she walked out onto the porch, which was beautiful in and of itself because of Reed's hard work.

Reed looked over and his jaw dropped. His eyes found Grace's, full of love, heat, and everything in between, and her heart tumbled anew.

"WOW, GRACIE," REED said as she stepped off the porch. "You look amazing. I mean, you always look beautiful, but you look...Aw, *hell*." He pulled her into his arms and kissed her through her smiles, dipping her over his arm as he took the kiss deeper.

Their family and friends cheered them on, making them both smile, but he continued kissing her until Brindle said, "Dude..."

Reluctantly bringing her upright, Reed said, "You look like the sexy small-town girl I fell in love with, only ten times hotter."

"Now, tell me that didn't make all your sisters' efforts worthwhile," her mother said.

"I'm not sure. Maybe I should come back out and get that kiss again," Grace teased. "Reed, Morgyn *made* this dress and embellished the boots. Aren't they cute?"

"Almost as cute as you," Reed said.

"That's my sweet-talkin' boy," Roy said, and opened his arms to Grace, drawing her into a hug. "You look beautiful, darlin'."

"Thank you," she said. "I'm so glad you both are here. We've waited a long time for a get-together like this."

"The best things in life are worth waiting for," his aunt said.

A troubled expression washed over Grace's face as she returned to Reed's side. She turned away from the others, speaking quietly. "I feel guilty that your family has known about us for all these years and my dad and sisters didn't. Would you mind if we told them? I want them to know that this was a long time coming."

"Baby, I am so done hiding, you have no idea. Let's do it." He kissed her softly. "But you know within fifteen minutes of being at the jam session everyone in town will know."

"I know. I'm kind of counting on that." Her smile reached all the way up to her eyes. "It bugs me that no one knows we have history together. I love our history."

"Are we ready to go?" her mother interrupted.

"Go ahead, baby," Reed urged.

"Actually, we have something we wanted to say." Grace drew in a deep breath, her eyes moving from her parents to her sisters. "You know that Reed and I would never purposefully hurt any of you, but we have a confession to make, and we hope you'll understand why we did what we did."

She turned a nervous expression to Reed, and he squeezed her hand encouragingly. She smiled and said, "Reed and I dated in high school."

"I don't remember that," Morgyn said. "When?"

"Our senior year," Reed explained. "We kept it a secret because Grace was a cheerleader here, and I was the quarterback for Meadowside. I didn't want her to be ostracized by her friends."

"And I didn't want his friends to give him a hard time," Grace added.

"Oh my gosh," Brindle said. "See? That's just *one* reason why the schools have made strides to eliminate that ridiculous rivalry stuff that used to go on. I am *so* glad life is not that complicated for kids anymore. Being a teenager is hard enough without worrying about whether your friends will hate you for something like who you're dating. And I have to say, I wondered if you two had hooked up before, because Grace never gets all lovey-dovey with guys. Like...*ever*."

"Well, I'm glad to hear that." Reed pulled Grace closer. "We missed out on doing a lot of things together, and I want to make up for each and every one of them."

"Well, you obviously didn't miss out on *everything*," Brindle said under her breath.

Grace glared at Brindle, and her eyes shifted to their parents, as if to remind her of their presence. "Dad, I'm sorry for lying to you. And Ella and Roy, I'm sorry we asked you to keep our secret. It wasn't a fair position to put you in."

"That's okay, honey," Ella said, exchanging a glance with Marilynn that Reed couldn't quite read. "We did the right thing."

"And I'm sorry, Cade and Marilynn," Reed said. "It wasn't our intent to be disrespectful, but we worried if Grace's siblings knew, it would be too much to ask for them to try to keep a secret."

"What?" Brindle threw her hands up. "You're blaming *us*? We're awesome secret keepers!"

Grace smirked.

"We *are*," Brindle insisted. "I never told Mom and Dad about the time me and Morgy—"

"Stop!" Morgyn slapped her hand over Brindle's mouth, causing everyone to laugh. "Whatever was going to come out of that trap of yours needs to stay locked up."

Grace went to her father and said something Reed couldn't hear. The look in Cade's eyes and the hug he gave her told him things were going to be okay.

Better than okay, he thought when Grace returned to his side.

She hugged him and said, "Thank you."

"I'd do anything for you, Gracie. I would have told the world back then if I hadn't thought it would come back on you."

They followed the others down the driveway, and Reed said, "Let's let the others leave first. That way I don't have to drive three miles an hour behind my uncle."

"You always did hate driving slow."

"Or maybe I want a reason to be alone in the car with you." He gathered her in his arms and pressed his lips to hers.

"Hurry up, lovebirds!" Brindle said as she and Morgyn ran past. "We have rumors to spread!"

Chapter Twenty-Six

REED STOPPED FOR gas on the way to the jam session, and the pump must have been slow, because it took forever. When they got on the road, he drove past the Jerichos' street.

"You missed the turn," she pointed out.

He pulled her tighter against his side. "I got a text when I was pumping gas. I need to make a quick stop, if you don't mind." He drove through town and to the high school. The parking lot was packed.

"It looks like there's something going on," she said as they climbed from the truck.

"There's a fundraising meeting tonight. I'm bidding on a job and just have to pick up the papers from the family. They're going out of town tomorrow."

"I thought your next job was the Majestic."

"Mm-hm. This is a small one. I don't close on the theater for a few weeks yet." They ascended the stairs, and he held the door open while she walked inside.

It was eerily quiet. "Where's the meeting?" she whispered.

"In the auditorium. Why are you whispering?"

"I don't know. It feels like I should."

He chuckled. "For a girl who snuck out to hang with a guy

from the wrong side of the tracks, you don't seem to have another rebellious bone in your body."

She poked his side. "Don't make fun. I used up all my rebellion on lying to my family. That was hard for me."

"I know, baby. I remember. I love that you're only a *bad* girl with me, in private." He stopped outside the auditorium and wrapped his arms around her, gazing deeply into her eyes. "Sorry we're late to the party, baby."

"I don't mind. It's not like I haven't been to a hundred jam sessions at the Jerichos' before. If Phoenix and Lauryn weren't playing instruments for the first time, and if my sisters hadn't gone to so much trouble to make me look half decent, I would say let's skip it and go lie out under the stars by the creek in your backyard."

"You look way better than half decent, and we're not missing this party. We're not missing anything ever again." His lips came coaxingly down over hers in a deep, slow, penetrating kiss. "Ready?"

"The way you kiss, I'm always ready."

"Damn, I love you, baby." He took her in another delicious kiss.

"Maybe I should wait out here?"

He shook his head, his slanted smile playing with her heart. "No way. We have only one more week before you go back to New York. I want to spend every minute with you."

He pushed open the door, and it was pitch-dark inside. She leaned into him and said, "I think we have the wrong room."

The lights came on, and Grace gasped. Balloons and streamers hung from the ceiling, along with sparkly gold stars and silver crescent moons. A banner was strung above the stage that read STARRY NIGHT PROM.

MELISSA FOSTER

"That was the name of my prom," Grace said. "I didn't go, of course, but…When's their prom?"

"This is your prom, baby. It's *our* prom." Without taking his eyes off her, he shouted, "Let 'er roll!"

The curtains went up over the stage, revealing Grace and Reed's family and friends, along with nearly everyone she'd gone to high school with, as well as what looked like half the town—including a very pregnant Sophie and her husband, Brett, the Jerichos, Nana and Hellie and their husbands, Phoenix and Lauryn, Janie and Boyd, Chet, Haylie, Sin, and dozens of other friends. Even Winona was there. Tears sprang from Grace's eyes as people poured down the steps, filling the auditorium, and Sable's band began playing "I'll Be" by Edwin McCain.

"Our song," Grace said as he swept her into his arms and began dancing. She was trembling, crying like a fool, and so in love with Reed, she couldn't even think straight. She couldn't believe what he'd done, or that so many friends were there. Girls she'd cheered with, some with pregnant bellies or toddlers on their hips, and parents of the girls she used to hang out with. Practically everyone from town she'd ever known danced around them, calling out greetings, as Reed gazed adoringly at her.

"How did you pull this off and get all these people to come? And *Sophie*! She wasn't supposed to be here until tomorrow. I don't know what to say." She wiped at her eyes, trying not to smear the makeup that her sisters had worked so hard on. "Nobody's ever done anything like this for me before. Thank you."

"Baby, I told you I want to make all your dreams come true, and we have a lot of time to make up for." His eyes skimmed over the crowd. "I made the most out of the time you spent working on the play, and I had some help from the prom fairies. I asked Sable and Lindsay if they could reach out to your friends. Once word got out, we were barraged with volunteers."

She looked around them, smiling and waving at everyone as they danced. Volunteers? For her?

"That's what friends do, Gracie," Reed said. "And this is what *I* do. The man who adores you."

He took her hand and dropped to one knee. A sound of disbelief rushed from her lungs as the lights dimmed and a spotlight shone on the two of them. Rivers of tears slid down her cheeks, and she was vaguely aware of Sable's band playing a slower, softer song, but she was riveted by the man who held her heart in his hands, kneeling before her.

"My beautiful, sweet Gracie. I went too many years wishing you were in my arms, regretting what I never said or did. If these last couple days have taught me anything, it's that we never know how much time we have left. I'm done waiting, baby. I don't want to regret a single thing. I know our lives are complicated. You're living in New York, and I'm here, but I don't care. We'll find a way to make it work. I will never ask you to give up anything, and I will support your every dream. You are the light of my life, baby, my best friend, my lover…"

Her throat swelled to near closing, and she was sure it was because her swollen heart had invaded every other part of her body.

Roy appeared by Reed's side and handed him a velvet box. Roy winked at Grace before stepping back, but Grace was too stunned to even acknowledge him as Reed rose to his feet and opened the box. He placed his hand on Grace's cheek and wiped her tears with his thumb, smiling when fresh tears slid in its wake.

"Gracie," he said in a voice so loving she cried harder. "You have owned my heart since you were just a breathtakingly pretty cheerleader who challenged my very existence, and you will own it long past the time I take my last breath."

He slid the most gorgeous ring on her finger. A ring she'd seen before. Memories climbed from the recesses of her mind. *What type of ring do you want?* he'd asked when they were teenagers, walking along the main drag in Wishing Creek. *You know I'm going to marry you one day, Gracie. You might as well show me what you want.* It had taken her only a second to show him, because she'd seen the display in the jeweler's window every time they'd walked by on their stolen nights together, and she'd fantasized about one day…

Now that cushion-cut diamond with the pink sapphire halo was on her finger, and Reed was gazing into her eyes, his boyish grin and loving heart already a part of her.

"It was hell trying to describe this ring to the jeweler who took over the shop after his father retired," Reed said with a smile, "but he got it right, don't you think?"

You remembered. The words lodged in her throat. It was all she could do to nod.

"This is *our* script, baby. We'll revise it however many times we need to until it's perfect. You're my leading lady, and I'll always be your man. Will you marry me, Gracie? Be my wife? My forever?"

"Yes!" came out on a sob. She launched herself into his arms, and the crowd *whoop*ed and cheered as they kissed through salty tears. "Yes, yes, yes," she said between kisses.

They were passed from one embrace to the next, congratulated, kissed, and danced with. Brindle and Morgyn had Axsel and Pepper on FaceTime during the proposal so they were able to watch the whole thing. Grace was so overwhelmed when she finally landed back in Reed's arms, her head was spinning.

They danced and kissed as Sable belted out "Kiss Me" by Sixpence None the Richer. Grace hadn't even known Reed knew how to dance, but the man had serious moves.

When the song changed to a slow song, Reed gazed into her eyes and said, "I told you I'd marry you one day, Gracie."

"You did, and I'm so glad. I love you, Reed, and I can't imagine a day without you. We live so far apart," Grace said anxiously.

"You'll never be without me. I'm with you always, baby. Distance between us or not, I'm with you. We'll make this work. I'll come up every weekend. I can't go without seeing you for too long, so I'm thinking we might put FaceTime to a test, too."

Her heart hurt just thinking about leaving, but she had commitments, an apartment, a life in the city. And now she had a life here, too.

"Cutting in to dance with my girl," Sophie said as she pried Reed's arms from around Grace and hugged her. Sophie's royal-blue dress clung to her burgeoning belly. "Congratulations again! And happy prom!"

"I can't believe you kept this a secret! And, oh my gosh, you look too sexy for a pregnant woman!"

"She does, doesn't she?" Brett said. "My wife is hot as *fuuuuck*."

Sophie laughed. "That's my man, always dirty talking."

"Hey, babe," Brett said with a raise of his brows. "I'll be happy to act that out if you'd like."

Sophie batted her handsome husband away. "I love you, but

take Reed and go do guy things. I want to chat with Grace for a minute."

Reed pulled Grace into a quick kiss. "Have fun. Tonight's your night, baby. Enjoy."

"Holy cow, Grace. I never thought I'd see you with a dreamy look in your eyes," Sophie teased.

Grace sighed. "Look around us, Soph. He went to so much trouble. Who would know how much this would mean to me besides Reed? All the people we grew up with are here. And you came home *early*." Her eyes welled with tears again. Her breathing hitched, and she gulped for air.

"Oh boy, come here." Sophie pulled her into another hug.

"My baby girl is completely overwhelmed tonight," her mother said as she joined them, and put her arms around both of them.

"It's not just tonight. It's *everything*. It's Reed and how much I love him, and Pepper and Axsel being included, and…I practically ran from this town as fast as I could after high school, and nobody hates me for it." Grace wiped her tears, but when she looked at Reed, then at Sophie, the faucet began again. "And now I'm engaged to the man I have always loved, and Sophie's having a baby and staying here for the next few months. I'll be in New York all alone. How can I leave Reed? And you guys? Mom…?"

Her mother hugged her again, *tight*. She brushed Grace's hair away from her face as she used to when Grace was just a girl. "Reed made sure our entire family could be here tonight, honey. He was very specific in not wanting Axsel or Pepper to miss out. We'll have a chance to Skype with them tomorrow morning at breakfast, which, by the way, Reed arranged so you would have a chance to celebrate with just the family. You won't ever be alone, Gracie," her mother said. "No matter where you are, a piece of us is always with you."

Grace looked across the dance floor at Reed, bursting with love for him. She was pretty sure she left *loveprints* everywhere she went, like footprints in the sand. Reed was talking with her father, Brett, and Sophie's parents, and she knew her mother was right. Even when she and Reed had been apart, he'd remained in her heart. That's what had kept her from feeling anything for another man.

"We need to change the subject or I'll cry all night," Grace pleaded.

They talked about Sophie's baby shower, which was taking place Sunday at her parents' house, and were interrupted umpteen times as friends congratulated Grace. Nana and Hellie came over, and Nana went on about how hard it had been to keep the secret of tonight's event.

"I'm shocked you were able to," Grace said honestly.

Nana's eyes twinkled with mischief. "We're mighty good at keeping secrets when it's in the best interest of those we care about."

"*Years* of secrets," Hellie said with a wink, before they disappeared into the crowd, giggling among themselves.

"Why do I have a feeling Reed and I weren't quite the secret we thought we were?" Grace said to her mother and Sophie.

"Oh, honey," her mother said casually. "I told you mothers know things. Nana is a mother too."

A little while later, as Phoenix and Lauryn played their instruments with Sable's band and Grace chatted with Sophie and her mother, Grace's mother motioned toward Brett, who was dancing with Nana, and Grace's father, dancing with Amber, while Reno stood watch.

"Your man did good, baby, and so did you," her mother said. "Amber is beside herself over how much you're doing for the community."

"This all started as a way to help Amber with the bookstore. It just grew to something bigger."

"Yes, and you did help her," her mother said. "But you know Amber. She loves this town and the people in it as if they were family, and you've never shown much interest in them. It means the world to her that now you are, and how much you've helped everyone here. Thank you."

Grace noticed Reed walking toward them, his eyes trained on her. "I think I should be the one thanking Amber."

"If we're being blatantly honest," Sophie said, "it means the world to me that you're doing more with the community, too."

Sophie had always loved their small town, even though she'd gone to New York in a blaze of glory alongside Grace. She was happiest here, among the people who had known her all her life. The people whom Grace was finally starting to appreciate as they deserved to be appreciated.

"Oh, girls." Her mother draped an arm around each of them. "It's like I told Gracie the other day. Just because you have what you thought you always wanted doesn't mean you always have to want those same things. I'm elated that you and Reed have finally given in to what your hearts have wanted all along." She lowered her voice as Reed joined them. "Your beau can't stay away for very long. I like that in a man."

"Sorry, ladies, but if you don't mind," Reed said, "I'd like to dance with my fiancée." He swept Grace into his arms and swayed to the music. "How's my girl?"

"Still in shock, and so very happy I can barely see straight. How are you holding up? Did my dad give you a hard time about our secret?"

"No, baby. But he did say that he knew about us. I think his exact words were, 'Do you really think a father of seven would let something like monthly orchids go without knowing exactly who was wooing his daughter or son? One call to the Meadowside florist and I learned everything I needed to know. But I wasn't going to worry Grace's mother over it, because any boy that would work at a florist before school every Monday just so he could earn enough money to buy my daughter flowers was a boy I knew I could trust.'"

Grace didn't think it was possible for her heart to get fuller than it was, but between the news of Reed working in exchange for those monthly flowers and knowing her father had approved of them back then, she was teary-eyed again. "You did that for me?"

"I've always said I'd do anything for you. And I meant it."

She fell deeper into love right that very second. "And my father knew all this time?"

"Crazy, right? We're meant to be together, Gracie. I knew it from the moment I saw those mossy-green eyes of yours." He pressed his lips to hers and said, "Take it all in, baby. Our families and friends are all here."

His gaze moved over the crowd, and the shine in his eyes dimmed just enough for her to notice. She knew in her heart what was eating at him. Even though Frank wasn't his real father, they'd had a breakthrough of sorts, and she felt Frank's absence in Reed's life tonight even more than she had when they were kids.

"Are they all here?" she asked carefully.

"You know me so well. You feel it too, don't you?"

She nodded.

"There's so much love in this room, and Frank's just down the street, probably sitting alone. I think I'm kind of all he has, and I wonder if I should have invited him."

She placed her hand over his heart and said, "That special body part is sure getting a workout lately. Frank's visit taught you that life is short, but didn't he also teach us—didn't *we* prove to the world—that it's never too late to make things right? You can still invite him. I think we're going to be here for a while."

His breath whispered over her lips. "You don't mind?"

"Not at all, but first I have something for you."

He waggled his brows.

"That'll come later." She leaned closer and whispered, "Hopefully *many* times." That earned a luscious kiss that made her entire body wish *later* was *now*. "This isn't as glamorous as diamonds, and it's kind of silly, but…"

She lifted her bangles, revealing the girlfriend-boyfriend beaded bracelets with their names on them that Morgyn had made. Reed's infectious grin told her it wasn't silly at all.

"I didn't know you could still get these," he said as he took the one that had her name on it off her wrist. "I love that you got these, and I'll wear mine everywhere."

"I asked Morgyn to make them for us." She helped him put it on his wrist. "You don't think they're ridiculous?"

He pushed his hands beneath her hair and brushed his soft, warm lips over her cheek. "I happen to have an affinity for history—and our history is anything but ridiculous." As he lowered his lips to hers, he said, "And we've only just begun."

Chapter Twenty-Seven

"I NEVER WOULD have guessed Gracie was *the bad girl*," Axsel said over a joint Skype call with Pepper and the rest of the family Saturday morning at Grace's parents' house. He raked a hand through his dark hair and yawned. It was only seven o'clock in Los Angeles, and he'd gotten up just for their call.

"She might have been sort of bad," Brindle said, "but I hold the bad-girl title, and I'm proud of it."

"That's my girl," their father said sarcastically, giving Brindle's shoulder a loving squeeze.

Brindle blinked innocently up at him from her perch on a chair at the kitchen table. "I love you, Daddy."

He kissed the top of her head. "I love you, too, pumpkin. I have you to thank for most of my gray hair."

"Good thing you're such a silver fox," their mother said, and the girls all agreed.

"Y'all are going to make my head swell," Cade said, leaning down to kiss Marilynn.

Reed realized he'd been staring at Grace as she chatted with her sisters, and when he shook his head to break the spell, he noticed Pepper watching him.

Cade must have noticed because he said, "What is it, princess?"

"I was just thinking how rare of a breed Reed is," Pepper said.

"He's not a horse," Morgyn said.

"He might be hung like one," Sable said under her breath, earning a harsh glare from her father.

Brindle choked on her juice.

Grace turned flushed cheeks toward Reed. Her confirming smile was not missed by her sisters, who went wide-eyed seconds before falling into hysterics. Reed stifled a chuckle.

Pepper rolled her eyes. "I meant that he treated Grace like a diamond before he even had a penny, with flowers and protecting her reputation."

"Aw, isn't that the sweetest and truest thing anyone could say?" Marilynn put her hand over her heart. "I wish you were here so I could hug you, honey."

"Me too," Grace said. "I miss you, Pep, and you, Axsel."

As Reed took in Grace's family, he was glad he'd made the call and invited Frank last night. Even though Frank had already settled in for the night and wasn't able to make it, Reed had heard deep appreciation in his voice. Reed wanted Grace to meet him and had invited Frank to come over to his house at eleven thirty, after they visited with Grace's family. Reed still wasn't sure where Frank should fit into his life or of his own emotions toward him. But as he listened to Grace and her family discussing ideas for their wedding, Cade came to Reed's side and said, "Welcome to my estrogen-filled family, son," and he realized he could never have too many people who cared for them.

"Thanks, Cade. Maybe someday Grace and I will give you a few grandsons to even things out."

"Did I hear something about grandbabies?" Marilynn's smile lit up her whole face. "Sophie's baby shower is tomorrow. I bet Lindsay and Nana would be happy to make it a double!"

"What?" Grace spun around with a confused, though delighted, expression. "Babies?"

"Now you've done it," Cade said for Reed's ears only.

"*Someday*, baby." Reed reached for Grace and drew her into his arms. "I said someday."

"Someday," slid off her tongue in a whisper with a hefty amount of relief. "We can't live in separate states when we have kids."

Worry washed over her beautiful face, bringing Reed's lips to hers in a tender kiss. "We'll figure everything out. There's no rush. First we build the foundation and get married, and then I'm taking you on an amazing honeymoon. *Then* we'll figure out the rest."

"You make it sound so easy and doable," she said with a sweet smile.

"Loving you is easy, baby. That makes anything doable."

"Sorry, sis, but I seriously think I just fell in love with your fiancé," Amber said.

"No shit," Sable said. "And I don't *do* love."

"Yeah, put me on that love list," Axsel teased. "Damn, bro. You really know how to make 'em fall."

"Oh, heck no." Grace threw her arms around Reed. "First of all, Axsel, he's *straight*. And the rest of you? Keep your paws off my man, or you *will* see me turn wild."

Reed buried his face in her neck as her family went wide-eyed in shock. "Damn, baby, that was the sexiest thing I've ever seen."

Grace's phone rang. "That's probably Sophie. I promised to

come by after we meet Frank to help decorate for the shower." She dug her phone from her pocket and glanced at the screen. All the joy drained from her face. She turned the phone toward Reed, and he saw Satchel's name.

"Tell Soph to come over," Morgyn called after Grace, who was walking into the living room to take the call.

Brindle waved a croissant and said, "And tell her to bring that hot husband of hers!"

"It's not Sophie," Reed said. "It's work." His gut twisted in irritation over the casting director not handling his own responsibilities and Grace being drawn into what seemed like every little thing these last few days. Not that he minded Grace doing her job, and apparently hand-holding *was* part of her job. He was proud of her for her dedication to the production, even when she was supposed to have time off. But she'd claimed to have *little* downtime, and he was beginning to wonder if even that was an understatement.

GRACE WAS NOT a crier, despite the tears she'd shed over the past few days, when it seemed years of emotions had come bubbling up. But as she ended the call with Satchel after agreeing to return to the city as soon as she could pack her bags, she was powerless to stop tears from falling. She sank down to the arm of the couch, trying to regain control as she thought of leaving Reed and her family, missing out on meeting Frank, and missing Sophie's baby shower. But the unfairness of it all was too much, and she could do little more than bury her face in her hands and weep.

"Baby? What happened?" Reed pulled her into his arms.

"I have to—" Sobs stole her voice as he caressed her back, telling her that whatever was going on, it would be okay. *No! It won't!* She heard the words in her head, but every time she opened her mouth, more sobs came. And then suddenly everyone was in the living room witnessing her meltdown, including Axsel and Pepper because her father had carried the laptop with him.

Great. Just freaking perfect.

"What's going on?" Sable asked, glaring at Reed. "Who needs to get their ass kicked?"

Embarrassment set in for her loss of control, and that quickly morphed to anger, because Grace Montgomery did *not* lose control.

She straightened her spine and swiped at her tears. "Nobody's," Grace seethed, fire and ice filling her up like a well. "I'm going to do it myself."

"What happened?" Reed asked.

"Keagen, the lead in the play, threatened to walk off because of some bullshit." She eyed her parents. "Sorry, but…"

"It's okay, honey," her mother said. "But why are you crying?"

"Because I have to go back." Tears burned her eyes again. *Damn it.* She blinked them away and said, "I have to leave now and get him to continue in the role and placate the investors, who are going to pull funding if we lose him. We have a meeting at eight o'clock tonight."

"You're leaving *now?*" several of them said at once, but it was Reed's voice that clawed at her heart.

It was all she could do to nod as her family all converged on her at once, hugging, saying goodbye, and telling her they understood. Their support made her as thankful as it did sad, and the whole situation made her angry.

After so many hugs she felt depleted, her family walked them out to the truck.

Her father took her by the shoulders and said, "Chin up, Gracie Jean. I know you're sad and angry, but they called you because you're the head honcho, and we're all very proud of you."

He kissed her forehead and stepped back, allowing her mother to hug her one last time. She smiled the encouraging smile Grace remembered from the day they'd said goodbye when she went away to college. Why was this suddenly so hard? She'd come and gone dozens of times, usually anxiously awaiting her departure and the madness of her life in the city.

"We'll be right here when you come back, honey," her mother said.

"Will you video Sophie's shower?" Grace pleaded. "I want to see everything. All the decorations, every gift, her face as she opens each one…"

"Of course, honey," her mother said. "Now go, before you're late. And remember, you're not leaving us behind. We're always with you."

Chapter Twenty-Eight

GRACE THREW HER clothes into her suitcase, not bothering to fold them. She was shaking too much to even try. "I can't believe this!" She threw a pair of jeans so hard the suitcase jiggled. "We were supposed to have another week!" She gunned a shirt at the suitcase. "Stupid!" *Throw.* "Self-absorbed." *Throw.* "Actors!"

She went to the closet and yanked her dresses off the hangers. Once she arrived in the city she'd have to go straight to the meeting, so she stripped off her jeans and put on her expensive black slacks and silk blouse. As she shoved her feet into her heels, she heard her sisters' voices telling her she wore *city clothes* and Phoenix saying no one would ever think Grace was from Oak Falls.

Great. Now she was pissed about having to dress for a meeting in the city. She bit back a stream of curses, thinking of all the loose ends she was leaving behind.

"Please tell Frank I really wanted to meet him. I have to call Nana and the girls and let them know they're on their own for the rest of the auditions, and I promised Nat I'd go over her final draft one last time. I'll call her and do it over Skype. And Sophie. Oh God. I have to call Sophie. She's going to be so upset."

Tears filled her eyes again. She picked up a pair of high-heeled boots and threw them toward the suitcase. They bounced off the bed, landing on the floor with a *clunk*.

"I've got them." Reed bent to retrieve the boots, and she plopped down onto the edge of the bed.

"I'm sorry. I just hate this."

"It's going to be okay, Grace." He put her boots in the suitcase. "I'll call Frank and tell him I can't make it. I'll go with you."

"No! That poor man is leaving Monday. He came all this way from…wherever he lives. He needs you more than I do."

Reed sat down and lifted her onto his lap. "We'll get through this. Don't worry."

He was so calm and understanding, it made her angrier. "Why aren't you mad? This ruins everything. We were supposed to have more time together. And I wanted to meet Frank and go to Sophie's shower and spend more time with my family…"

For once in her life, she didn't want everyone to understand or tell her it was okay. She wanted to *stay*, and for someone else to handle the issues and investors. That was the attitude of a weak person, not a professional producer, and that upset her even more. Was she not allowed to *feel* what a normal person would feel? She was so confused, had kept her life and feelings in check for so long, she didn't even know what was right anymore. But she knew one thing for sure. Pissing and moaning wouldn't handle the situation any faster. And she needed to handle it quickly—for the sake of the play, and to return home to Reed and spend whatever time they had left of next week together.

She forced herself to sit up a little taller and pull her shit together, but one look at Reed, and that weak girl inside her crumbled again.

"Come here." He embraced her again and said, "Why aren't I angrier? Because this is your job, and I'm not a kid who doesn't get it. We both have lives, roots, commitments. This is a bump in the road, babe. Yeah, it fucking sucks, but you know what?" He lifted her left hand and kissed her fingers. "You're going to be my wife, and I'm going to be your husband, and there's nothing we can't get through."

He pushed his hands into her hair the way she loved and held her gaze. Oh, how her heart softened and her sadness eased with his touch.

"We're going to be fine," he said confidently. "I promise."

He lowered his lips to hers, filling her with love and pushing away those other awful feelings. He took the kiss deeper, made it sweeter, then rough and demanding, and then easing once again, claiming all of her attention.

Their lips parted with a series of tender kisses. She felt a hundred times lighter, wishing she could stay within the warm safety of his embrace, lost in him, instead of giving in to the clock ticking away in her head.

"Okay?" he asked softly.

She nodded, hating the way thoughts of her long drive ahead pressed in on her. Any traffic would make her late to the meeting, and she still had to figure out the best way to handle the situation with Keagen.

Reed's lips tipped up in a sexy smile. "I see the gears of your brain churning. I'll pack your stuff, since you clearly want to break something in the process," he said teasingly. "You can get started on that list of yours."

They finished packing, and Grace called Nana, who promised to call the girls. She decided to call Sophie from the road, since she'd need her comfort anyway.

They packed her car, and she stood beside it clinging to Reed, their hearts pounding furiously against each other.

She buried her face in his chest and said, "I want to be five years old again just for ten minutes."

He tipped her face up, his sad eyes cutting straight to her heart. "Why?"

"Because then I could throw a tantrum and get my way so I can stay."

"Aw, baby." He crushed her to him. "I love you, and we'll see each other soon. Don't worry about us. We're solid, babe. We'll always be together. You just concentrate on handling the things you need to."

"Tell Frank I'm sorry?" Her entire body ached with sadness.

"Of course."

She pushed up on her toes, and he met her halfway in another soul-drenching kiss. She clung to his back, soaking in his strength as their union turned fierce and hungry.

"Wish I could stay," she said between frantic kisses.

"Me too. Love you." *Kiss, kiss, nip, kiss.* "Call me the second you get there." *Kiss, kiss, grope, kiss.* "And at any rest stops." *Kissssssss.*

By the time they finally parted, she felt flushed.

"Better go," she managed. "I can't be late."

He opened her car door, and she sank down to the seat, then popped back up, tugging him down by his shirt for another passionate kiss. Frustratingly aware of the minutes ticking by and the urgency of her trip, she reluctantly pressed her hand to his chest, the dreadful weight of their separation looming between them.

Neither of them spoke as she settled in behind the wheel. He hooked her seat belt, gazing into her eyes, his big body taking up the space between her and the steering wheel.

He pressed his lips to hers one more time and whispered, "Go get 'em, Gracie."

Fighting against tears as he climbed from the car and closed the door, she started the engine and feigned a smile. *Don't cry. Don't cry. Don't cry.*

He blew her a kiss, and she pretended to catch it and press it to her lips.

She watched him in the rearview mirror as she drove away. He followed her into the street, his hands in his pockets, broad shoulders rounded in sadness. Frank was due there in ten minutes. She hoped her leaving wouldn't affect their visit. With one last glance in the rearview, she turned the corner as tears slid down her cheeks.

REED STOOD IN the middle of the road feeling like he had years ago, when he'd told Grace she was doing the right thing by going away to college but he'd wanted to beg her to stay. He wasn't that fucking kid anymore. Why the hell was his mind doing this to him? He had commitments, had to work out the subcontractors for the Majestic, order supplies so they'd arrive right after settlement, and most importantly, he had only a couple days to spend with Frank. It wasn't like he could up and leave.

Frank was leaving Monday. Maybe Reed could postpone his

other meetings and drive up then. Monday felt a lifetime away.

Frank's car ambled down the street, and Reed stepped to the curb. Frank had enough on his plate; he didn't need to see Reed's distress. Forcing a smile and a wave, Reed vowed not to make the man's life any more difficult than it already was.

"How's it going?" Reed asked as Frank stepped from the car, looking a little less disheveled than he had the last time he'd seen him. He had about a day's worth of scruff and his clothes were wrinkled, but there was a renewed spark in his eyes.

"Not as well as it is for you." He reached into the car and grabbed a bouquet of orchids and handed them to Reed. "Congratulations again. These are for you and Grace."

Another pang of longing stroked through him with the sight of the orchids. Reed didn't quite have it in him to tell Frank she wouldn't be joining them. Instead, he said, "Thank you. These are her favorites."

"They were your mother's, too." Frank said as they headed for the house.

Reed's legs stopped working. "They were?"

Frank nodded. "That's how she chose our apartment. There were orchids in the rental office, and she took it as a sign."

If Reed hadn't believed in signs before, he sure did now. It was as if his mother was thanking him for sticking around to see Frank. "Want to go inside?"

"Actually, I spend a lot of time indoors. Would you mind if we sat on the steps for a bit?" Frank glanced at the house. "You are definitely your mother's son. She would have loved a house like this."

As they sat down, Reed caught sight of Frank's scars. In an effort to distract himself from thoughts of Grace, he asked, "If you don't mind me asking, how did you get those scars?"

Frank ran his fingers over his mangled skin, and a small smile lifted his lips. "Protecting your mother. She loved children. One summer she volunteered at the refreshment stand at a local pool on the weekends. I went with her because, well, I didn't want to miss out on the time with her."

He tossed Reed a knowing smile, and hell if Reed's mind didn't sprint back to Grace, looking like a million bucks in her fancy clothes. How had she remained single for all these years? Were the men in New York blind and deaf? She was the most fascinating woman he'd ever known. And now his gut twisted with longing again.

"Your mother and I were behind the counter," Frank explained, bringing Reed's mind back to their conversation. "I was cooking burgers and hot dogs and she was handing out candy and chips. Somebody tossed a plastic ball over the counter, and she leaned back so it wouldn't hit her face and lost her footing. She was going to fall right on the hot grill. I put my arm out"— he extended his arm to the side—"and caught her before she hit it."

A chill ran through Reed, imagining Frank's arm on a hot grill, his skin burning.

"I didn't even feel it at first," Frank said. "She'd fallen into my arms, and neither of us realized what had happened. I was too swept up in Lily's smile. That woman mesmerized me."

"But the pain." Reed winced. "That must have been awful."

"It was pretty horrible. But your mother learned to look after the burns. She took good care of me. And if I had to do it a hundred times over, I would to save her the pain. Even now, knowing about that other man, I'd still do anything for her. That's what love is, but you know that." Frank glanced at the house. "Where's Grace? Did she change her mind about meeting me?" Sadness rose in his eyes. "It's okay if she did. I understand."

"No. She didn't change her mind. She had to go back to New York to take care of a few things."

"Back? She doesn't live here?"

"It's a bit complicated. She lives in New York City." Reed explained their living situation to him.

"Lord knows I have no business advising anyone in the ways of love, but why are you still here?"

He'd asked himself that a hundred times over the last fifteen minutes, but he was afraid the truth might make Frank feel guilty, so he said, "I have commitments."

"Commitments." Frank shook his head. "Whatever commitments you have, and whoever they're to, are they more important than the woman you love?"

"Hell no," Reed said angrily, even though he knew his anger was misdirected, and the truth came out despite his efforts to hold it back. "And because I've only just found you and I want to get to know you. I don't even know where you're living. From what you've said, you don't have anyone else, and..." *You don't have much time left.* "I think it's important to be here for you."

"I truly appreciate that, Reed. It's very honorable," Frank said. "I live in New Jersey, and there's not much else to tell. But you've given me what I needed, which was to make sure you knew the truth before I left this earth. But what you need is on her way to New York. Don't let our past hinder your future."

Reed's pulse ratcheted up. "But you're only here until Monday."

Frank shrugged. "And then I'll be in Jersey, a few hours away. I don't claim to know much about you, but if that pinched expression and those fisted hands are any indication, you'll likely kill someone before Monday if you let your gal get away." He picked up the bouquet from between them and handed it to Reed. "Go, before she gets too far."

Adrenaline sent Reed to his feet. "You don't mind?"

"Hell no. *Go.*" Frank rose beside him, a wide smile in place.

They stood awkwardly looking at each other, and Reed could tell that like him, Frank wasn't sure if they should shake hands or hug. They both leaned in, then pulled back. Reed thrust out his hand, and when Frank accepted it, Reed pulled him into an embrace.

"Thank you, Frank. Thank you for coming back to tell me the truth and for kicking my ass out of here." As he ran to his truck, he hollered, "Leave your number for me at the hotel. I'll be in touch."

Reed sped out of the driveway, determined to be with his girl.

GRACE UNHOOKED THE gas pump and stuck it in the tank, cradling her phone against her shoulder. She and Sophie cursed blue streaks about her having to leave town early and miss Sophie's baby shower. Realizing she was nearly out of gas had sent Grace into another hateful rant.

"I swear, Soph, I'm going to wring Keagen's neck. He'll never want to work on one of my productions again, and I don't care. *I* don't want to work on another production again!"

"You don't mean that," Sophie said. "You were having so much fun with the community play, and you'll fix this thing up like you always do. Your investors will be happy, Keagen will obey your commands but always be a prick, and then you'll come back to Reed."

"And then what? Then I go back to the city again, and he's here? And what if we want babies? What if we miss each other too much and…" She struggled to keep herself from crying again.

"Grace, you'll figure it out."

"What is it about everyone thinking we'll figure things out? That doesn't just happen. It takes planning, and you know plans never go well. What if I miss the birth of your baby? Brindle's going to Paris in a few weeks, and I won't be there to say goodbye." Tears sprang from her eyes again. How had she left all those years ago? It felt like leaving the most important pieces of herself behind. She yanked the gas pump from the tank and spilled gasoline all over her clothes. "Goddamn it! I gotta go. I just…*Ugh!* Love you, Soph. I'm a mess. I'll call you later."

She ended the call and ran into the gas station to try to wash the stench from her clothes. In the bathroom, she scrubbed at the stains. "I should show up in cutoffs and boots." She scrubbed harder, but the paper towels left residue on her shirt. She lifted the wet fabric to her nose and sniffed. She smelled awful.

"Fuck it."

She stormed out to her car and threw it into drive. As she waited for cars to pass so she could pull out onto the road, she thought of Reed and her family. *You've been in control of your life way too long. Tonight you're one of us again, like it or not. We miss you, Gracie. Give us tonight. Please?* Her sisters' voices drew more tears. She gripped the steering wheel tighter, thinking about Nana and the girls and their excitement about the play. Her mind traveled to Reed and the night they'd watched the movie at the Majestic. *This would never happen in the city.*

She looked at her gorgeous ring, the exact design she'd fallen in love with years ago, and her heart felt full to near bursting. She thought of the prom and Reed's perfectly romantic proposal, how the community welcomed her, and she knew what she wanted—what she *had*—to do.

"*That* would never happen in the city," she said as she distractedly pulled out of the parking lot. She heard the sound of screeching brakes and screamed as a truck barreled toward the side of her car. She went for the gas, but hit the brake, and her body jerked forward against the steering wheel. She slammed her foot on the gas as the truck fishtailed, the back end nearly smacking into the rear of her car just as she sped across the road. She swerved onto the curb and slammed on the brakes, gripping the steering wheel so tight she wasn't sure she could let go. Then her door opened and Reed was there, pulling her into his arms, fear blazing in his eyes as he ran his hands all over her, checking to make sure she was whole.

"Baby. Are you okay?"

"Yes," she said, nearly frozen in shock. "*No.* I'm not okay. I can't do this," flew from her lungs. "Ten years was a long time. I don't want to do it anymore. I don't want to be apart. I'll move back. I need to be with you."

He clutched her to him as if he would never let her go. "No, Gracie. I'll back out of the Majestic deal and go to New York. I can work anywhere, but you have a life there."

"No! Keep the Majestic! I'll invest in it. We can both put our talents to work and bring it back to life together. My life is *here*, Reed, with you and my family and Sophie and the girls

and…" She gasped a breath. "Cowboy boots and 'y'alls'—"
Sobs burst from her lungs as she crumpled against him, and
Reed was right there holding her up, her strength, her love, her
forever.

She gazed into his midnight-blue eyes as tears slid down her
cheeks, and she said, "So much for easy and doable."

A crooked smile lifted his lips. "We've never been easy, but
we've always been doable."

Chapter Twenty-Nine

GRACE AWOKE WITH a start and bolted upright. She clung to the blanket, listening intently for whatever had woken her. She thought she knew every sound her and Reed's house made. She'd moved back for good two weeks ago, after handling the issues with her *last* off-Broadway production, which thankfully went smoother than she'd thought. She heard the creak of the stairs, and her heart seized.

"Reed!" she whispered urgently, shaking him by the shoulder. "Reed! Get up! Someone's in the house!"

He rolled over, and his arm circled her waist. "It's the wind, baby. Go back to sleep."

The stairs creaked again, and she grabbed his arm so hard her nails dug into his skin. "Reed! That's *not* the wind!"

Whispers came from the hall, and Grace's pulse raced. She snagged her phone from beside the bed. "I'm calling nine-one-one!" The bedroom door flew open and she shrieked, dropping the phone to the mattress.

All her siblings barreled into the room, laughing hysterically. Reno hugged Amber's side. "*Woof!*"

Grace's hand flew over her racing heart. "Oh my God! What are you doing here? How did you get in?" She looked at

Reed, who was lying beside her grinning like a fool. "*Ugh!* You *let* them do this?"

"Who am I to stand in the way of tradition?" He blew her a kiss, and she rolled her eyes.

"Hoodie?" Sable said in Reed's direction.

Reed pointed to the closet. Grace glowered at him, and he chuckled.

"Nat's play is tomorrow," Morgyn said, pulling Grace's arm and dragging her from the bed. "And then there's the community play."

Nat had done a fabulous job on the rewrites, and Nana and the girls had done a spectacular job of casting—and expediting—*I Ain't No Cinderella* in Grace's absence. She was excited to see the results of everyone's hard work.

"And your wedding is right after that," Amber reminded her.

As if she could ever forget the most anticipated day of *her* life? Neither she nor Reed wanted to wait to get married, especially since Frank wasn't doing so well and they wanted him to be at the wedding. They still had a ways to go before all the awkward moments were gone, but Grace was beyond thankful that Frank and Reed would have at least some time to get to know each other.

"And I leave for Paris the next day," Brindle chimed in. "We *have* to go tonight."

Pepper stood by the door in a pair of jeans and cowgirl boots, arms crossed, her golden-brown hair piled up on her head in a messy bun. She'd gotten into town last week, and the girls had dragged Grace's ass out of bed then, too. *We have to! It's Pep's first night back!*

Pepper lifted her foot to show Grace her boot. "I gave in.

There's no stopping these fools."

"Grace will probably get pregnant on her honeymoon anyway," Brindle said. "And then she'll be locked down tight like Sophie and have to miss our nighttime prowls."

Grace smiled thinking of having little Reeds running around. She wasn't ready for that *quite* yet, but she could love up Sophie and Brett's precious baby girl. She hadn't missed her birth after all. Sweet Brenna was born three nights ago, and Grace and Reed were right there waiting to greet her.

Axsel put an arm around Pepper's shoulder and said, "At last y'all included me this time." He looked at Reed, who was pulling on a pair of jeans, and said, "I swear, it's like a vagina club with these chicks."

Sable came out of the closet and ran her eyes down Grace's tank top and boy shorts. She tossed her a hoodie and said, "Cute boy shorts, Grace! Put that on." She turned her attention to Axsel. "If it were a vagina club, you wouldn't be here. Vagina clubs do their nails and hair and shit. You want to see the firemen's two a.m. calendar photo shoot as much as the rest of us."

"Damn right I do," Axsel said with a big-ass smile.

Grace laughed as she pulled on the hoodie, but she had a feeling no one wanted to see the calendar shoot as much as Sable wanted to get an eyeful of Chet Hudson.

"Maybe I can stay here since my man is ready, willing, and able, *and* perfectly willing to climb back into our beautiful new bed." Grace smiled flirtatiously at Reed. "I'm sure Reed won't want me checking out firefighters anyway."

"Go, baby. I'm secure in my manhood." He leaned across the bed and hauled her down, kissing her so hard her entire body flamed. "Besides, I'm meeting you there. There's a bonfire after the shoot. You. Me. Making out beneath the stars. Be ready." He swatted her butt and lifted his chin toward Brindle, who was holding up Grace's cutoffs and the embellished cowgirl boots Morgyn had made for her. "Best get going, pretty girl. You don't want to miss the Montgomery ruckus."

Amber offered Grace a hand and pulled her to her feet. "We'll have fun, Gracie. This is the last time you'll see the calendar shoot as a single woman."

"Only in Oak Falls would firemen come from two different towns and do a calendar shoot in the middle of the night," Pepper said.

As Grace pulled on her cutoffs, surrounded by the people she loved most, her gaze caught on Reed. His loving eyes and boyish grin sent her overjoyed heart into a tailspin as she said, "Exactly, Pep. Only in Oak Falls. And I wouldn't change it for the world."

Ready for more Bradens & Montgomerys?

Fall in love with Beau and Charlotte in ANYTHING FOR LOVE.

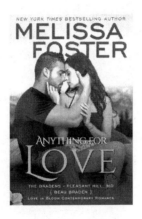

Two Love in Bloom Worlds Become One!

I am thrilled to share some exciting news with you! The Bradens at Pleasant Hill and the Montgomerys are becoming one magnificent series! In book three, *Trails of Love*, the Montgomerys and the Bradens are going to be deeply intertwined. For that reason, I am combining the series to make it easier for readers to keep track of characters, weddings, babies, etc. What this means is that after the first two books (*Embracing Her Heart* and *Anything for Love*) you will see both worlds in most of the books. Some stories might weigh more heavily in one location than the other, but they are all going to cross over. You've met the Montgomerys, now meet the Bradens in *Anything for Love*, the second book in the Bradens & Montgomerys series.

In Anything for Love...

After Charlotte Sterling loses the last of her family members, she moves to the Colorado Mountains and lives a solitary life. That is, if you only count *living, breathing* people. As an erotic romance writer, her days are filled with passion and intrigue. She loves her busy, solo life, and she learned early on that real men can't live up to the fictional heroes she creates—until Beau Braden arrives to do some work at the inn, and for the first time in forever, she's intrigued by a *real* man. But Beau lost his first love years ago, and he's never let go of his guilt over her death. Neither one is looking for an attachment or for a fling. They've never fully healed on their own, but together maybe anything is possible.

Buy **ANYTHING FOR LOVE**

New to the Love in Bloom series?

I hope you have enjoyed getting to know the Montgomerys as much as I've loved writing about them. If this is your first Love in Bloom book, you have many more love stories featuring loyal, sassy, and sexy heroes and heroines waiting for you.

The Bradens & Montgomerys (Pleasant Hill – Oak Falls) is just one of the series in the Love in Bloom big-family romance collection. Each Love in Bloom book is written to be enjoyed as a stand-alone novel or as part of the larger series. There are no cliffhangers and no unresolved issues. Characters from each series make appearances in future books, so you never miss an engagement, wedding, or birth. You might enjoy my other series within the Love in Bloom big-family romance collection. You can start at the very beginning of the Love in Bloom series absolutely FREE with **SISTERS IN LOVE** or begin with another fun and deeply emotional series like the Remingtons, which begins with **GAME OF LOVE**, also free.

Below is a link where you can download SEVERAL first-in-series novels absolutely FREE.

www.MelissaFoster.com/LIBFree

More Books By Melissa

LOVE IN BLOOM SERIES

SNOW SISTERS
Sisters in Love
Sisters in Bloom
Sisters in White

THE BRADENS at Weston
Lovers at Heart
Destined for Love
Friendship on Fire
Sea of Love
Bursting with Love
Hearts at Play

THE BRADENS at Trusty
Taken by Love
Fated for Love
Romancing My Love
Flirting with Love
Dreaming of Love
Crashing into Love

THE BRADENS at Peaceful Harbor
Healed by Love
Surrender My Love
River of Love
Crushing on Love
Whisper of Love
Thrill of Love

THE BRADENS & MONTGOMERYS at Pleasant Hill – Oak Falls
Embracing Her Heart
Anything For Love
Trails of Love

THE BRADEN NOVELLAS
Promise My Love
Our New Love
Daring Her Love
Story of Love
Love at Last

THE REMINGTONS
Game of Love
Stroke of Love
Flames of Love
Slope of Love
Read, Write, Love
Touched by Love

SEASIDE SUMMERS
Seaside Dreams
Seaside Hearts
Seaside Sunsets
Seaside Secrets
Seaside Nights
Seaside Embrace
Seaside Lovers
Seaside Whispers

BAYSIDE SUMMERS
Bayside Desires
Bayside Passions
Bayside Heat
Bayside Escape

THE RYDERS
Seized by Love
Claimed by Love
Chased by Love
Rescued by Love

SEXY STANDALONE ROMANCE
Tru Blue
Truly, Madly, Whiskey
Driving Whiskey Wild
Wicked Whiskey Love

BILLIONAIRES AFTER DARK SERIES

WILD BOYS AFTER DARK
Logan
Heath
Jackson
Cooper

BAD BOYS AFTER DARK
Mick
Dylan
Carson
Brett

HARBORSIDE NIGHTS SERIES
Includes characters from the Love in Bloom series
Catching Cassidy
Discovering Delilah
Tempting Tristan

More Books by Melissa
Chasing Amanda (mystery/suspense)
Come Back to Me (mystery/suspense)
Have No Shame (historical fiction/romance)
Love, Lies & Mystery (3-book bundle)
Megan's Way (literary fiction)
Traces of Kara (psychological thriller)
Where Petals Fall (suspense)

Acknowledgments

I hope you enjoyed Grace and Reed's story and are looking forward to reading about the rest of the Montgomerys and the Bradens, who you will meet in book two, *Anything for Love*.

If you haven't yet joined my fan club on Facebook, please do. We have a great time chatting about our hunky heroes and sassy heroines. You never know when you'll inspire a story or a character and end up in one of my books, as several fan club members have already discovered.
facebook.com/groups/MelissaFosterFans

Remember to like and follow my Facebook fan page to stay abreast of what's going on in our fictional boyfriends' worlds.
facebook.com/MelissaFosterAuthor

Sign up for my newsletter to keep up to date with new releases and special promotions and events and to receive an exclusive short story featuring Jack Remington and Savannah Braden.
www.MelissaFoster.com/Newsletter

And don't forget to download your free reader goodies! For free family trees, publication schedules, series checklists, and more, please visit the special Reader Goodies page that I've set up for you!
www.MelissaFoster.com/Reader-Goodies

As always, loads of gratitude to my amazing team of editors and proofreaders: Kristen Weber, Penina Lopez, Elaini Caruso, Juliette Hill, Marlene Engel, Lynn Mullan, and Justinn Harrison. And, of course, I am forever grateful to my husband, Les, and the rest of my family, who allow me to talk about my fictional worlds as if we live in them.

~Meet Melissa~

www.MelissaFoster.com

Melissa Foster is a *New York Times* and *USA Today* bestselling and award-winning author. Her books have been recommended by *USA Today's* book blog, *Hagerstown* magazine, *The Patriot*, and several other print venues. Melissa has painted and donated several murals to the Hospital for Sick Children in Washington, DC.

Visit Melissa on her website or chat with her on social media. Melissa enjoys discussing her books with book clubs and reader groups and welcomes an invitation to your event. Melissa's books are available through most online retailers in paperback, digital, and audio formats.

74597126R00197

Made in the USA
San Bernardino, CA
18 April 2018